The MASTER of EDAUN

BLOOD OF BROTHERS

The MASTER of EDAUN

Blood Of Brothers

D. E. HENDLEY JR.

authorHOUSE®

AuthorHouse™
1663 Liberty Drive
Bloomington, IN 47403
www.authorhouse.com
Phone: 1-800-839-8640

Published by AuthorHouse   09/07/2012

ISBN: 978-1-4772-6394-5 (sc)
ISBN: 978-1-4772-6393-8 (e)

Library of Congress Control Number: 2012915830

Any people depicted in stock imagery provided by Thinkstock are models, and such images are being used for illustrative purposes only.
Certain stock imagery © Thinkstock.

This book is printed on acid-free paper.

Because of the dynamic nature of the Internet, any web addresses or links contained in this book may have changed since publication and may no longer be valid. The views expressed in this work are solely those of the author and do not necessarily reflect the views of the publisher, and the publisher hereby disclaims any responsibility for them.

Dedicated to Debbie and Angel,

*Thank you for putting up with me and supporting me in the
creation of this book and it's story.*

Human kind has not woven the web of life.
We are but one thread within it.
Whatever we do to the web, we do to ourselves.
All things are bound together.
All things connect . . . .

-Chief Seattle-
-of the West coast Tribes-
-The Duwamish Suquamish People-

"My death shall be avenged, the seed shall spread doom throughout the land of evil. The three giants will strike fear in the wicked hearts and death to all that oppose the righteous people."

words of Thorn;
The Master of Edaun

Contents

Prelude

The Fall of the Sword

As the sun of the solstice was slowly melting away in the western sky, long shadows were overrunning the field of battle. Standing patiently in the southern port of call, a large leather clad figure, looks out on the cheering crowd. The crowd seated in the stands of the arena cheer their heroes on, and are ruthless toward their enemies.

Soft, warm breezes caress the multi-colored banners, inciting them to dance above the roaring on lookers. A large figure stands in a dark sally port. The shadowed giant calmly looks to the field of battle, as a pair of kilt wearing swordsmen circle one another.

The larger of the two, displays a frightful windmill spin of his broadsword. Shouting challenging jeers to his foe. His chest length beard, tied low with the leather cord, wiggles as he roars his taunts at his adversary. A shining glimpse of sun reflects off a golden circle hanging from the cord.

The second warrior just a few inches shorter than his six foot seven inch, bearded foe, cautiously circles the twirling blade before him. The smaller man, yet just as broad, stands firm. He tosses his head back as he roars. Reaching up with his left hand, he quickly removes his leather head piece exposing a top knot of hair; his long flowing mane, flares as he spins.

He quickly throws the leather helmet at the bearded man and screams his battle cry, causing his long mustache hanging below his throat to dance. As the helmet strikes his enemy, the warrior quickly assaults his foe. The bearded warrior casually taps each blow safely away with ease.

The larger man blocks the last quick jab, brushing the blade to the right. The smaller man loses his weapon. The bearded warrior grabs the shorter man with his left hand, a quick flip sends the man across the field of death. Showing extreme quickness and agility the big man leaps toward the tumbling man and lands straddling his dazed enemy. Gently he lays his large blade to the fallen man's throat, a roaring laughter replaces his cries of war.

The fallen warrior raises his hands, palms up to his captor, a bitter sweet admission of defeat.

The crowd comes to life with cheers. Some throw flowers to the field. The bearded warrior slowly turns with his sword raised high to face his fans. The crowds stand in praise of their champion.

He stops his circle to face the leather clad figure standing in the shadows. A nasty grin fills his face as he lowers the large blade to point challengingly at the dark figure.

The dark giant flexes his massive torso. A calm giggling voice breaks the silence. "He do be the blade master to beat, Hunter."

Looking down to the old squire to his right, the leather warrior grins, "He is the best as of now, but he's never faced me." Hunter grins, "Now has he?"

"Hunter, look sharp now me boyo, stand ready." A toothless grin seemed to split the old man's face.

Trumpets sound. They both look to the empty field. "No sir, he not of yet to face Ol' Jed's giant swordsman," the old man says as he pats the massive back of the warrior. "No matter you best be ready."

Tadd Hunter looks back down from his six foot five height to the grinning old man. "Jed, I'm glad you're still at my side after all these years. You've been a good friend."

Stretching as high as the little man could reach Jed perks up the two eagle feathers in the big warriors fan tail hair do, "Hunter it be me duty and pleasure to serve you." Still grinning the old man pats the warrior on the back again.

"Thanks Jed," Hunter reaches over and pats the old man on top of his head.

"You know me boyo, I learn as much from you, as I teach you lad," another grin split the old man's face. "Do me proud this day!"

Their look goes back to the field as the crowd roars again. A monstrous black stallion charges into the arena. On its back sits an armored rider. The knight glitters of emerald and gold colors. He waves defiantly at the crowd as the large war-horse stops in the middle of the field pawing the ground and tossing its large head. The rider roars his taunts to the crowd. The cheers of the crowd now become hostile to the emerald knight. The giant steed rears, and then bolts in a thunder of hooves. The whole arena seemed to shake from each hoof slamming fiercely into the soft earth. Long fetlocks dance at its ankles as they churn up the soil.

Gold streamers flow from the rider's helmet, they circle the field as if they were in a parade. The large beast slides to a halt back in its starting position. The rider stands in his stirrups and continues to shout more bold taunts to the audience.

As if from nowhere his squire appears. He stands at the giant beast's side, holding a long shiny black lance. In a fluid motion, the large knight swings to retrieve the deadly weapon. As he resets in the high pummeled saddle, he looks to the port of call, he looks to the warrior in the shadows.

Slowly the lance turns, and the knight barks a rough laugh. The lance stops to point challenging at Hunter.

The leather warrior twitches his fine tuned muscles and grabs his sword's hilt. Like a coiled spring, he was ready to bound into action.

"Easy laddy, be not your time," growled Jed. "The fool just be vexing you. Need not let 'em break your concentration." Hunter reluctantly eased his tensed muscles slightly. He nods but unconsciously strokes the hilt of the large sword hinging behind his broad back.

Trumpets sound again, the crowd is hushed. Another huge war-horse races on the field a giant stallion, white with black painted hooves.

The beast rears. It's front legs kick high in the air. Before they touch back down, the giant beast leaps. As it lands ten feet away, it's hind legs rip through the air. The explosive kick would have killed several men in one sweep. As the massive legs slam home the beast launches into motion. The ground seams a blur as rider and horse race across the arena. As suddenly as it started, the war-horse slides to a stop, facing the menacing challenge at the other end of the field.

Horse and rider stare challenging at their opponents. Before the knight receives his silver weapon he stands in his stirrups and looks to Hunter. He raises his right fist, thumb side to his heart. Hunter salutes with his fist to his heart in return. Without returning to his seat, the rider swings just as gracefully as the previous knight, to arm himself.

The arena comes alive again, with cheers and waves.

Each rider looks toward the royal box. The crowd is hushed. Suddenly the banners above fall limp. A silky lavender handkerchief takes flight from the royal box. It floats in the air, as if it were a large butterfly. Closer and closer it falls, until it lands slowly and gently to the ground.

Suddenly both war-horses snort as they rear then leap as one! The thunder charge is on! They appear as a blur; their colors closing in on itself. One side filled with black, emerald and gold. The other flowed white, crimson and silver. The arch of colors appeared to be melting into the center of the field. Closer they charge with each pounding hoof!

The smell of fear was absent from the air. Each rider lowers their long points of death. The giant war-horses race toward one another.

Closer! Closer! With each drop of thundering hooves, they race more rapidly. The earth cries out from the slamming of each massive hoof.

CRASH!!!

The two collide, the crimson knight reels but stays astride. The emerald warrior releases a hearty battle cry. No one hit the churned earth. As they reach the other side of the field and spin in the others starting point, each steed quickly turns as one. As fast as they first began, they bolted toward one another again. A second blur of charging death.

Again the gap closes quickly, weapons are set. The emerald knight tries to steal a glance of the port of call where a solid Hunter stands in wait. When he looks back, it's too late. The crash of the steel sends the emerald rider, from his massive charger.

Quick as a flash the large form in the port of call leaps to the field. His sword flashes as it comes to life in his hand.

Ol' Jed's voice springs just as quick. "You up now lad! Make haste with him!" The huge leather body was already in motion. The knight rose quickly, pulling his sword to face the new challenge racing his way. He was barely prepared as Hunter ended his last stride.

In a motion as if Hunter were chopping wood, his twirling blade slices down! The knight blocks the whistling steel and retaliates with his own blade.

Hunter easily fends it off. The dance of death had begun! The two cautiously circle one another, driving each other into a natural defensive mode.

Moving with the agility of a big cat, Hunter circles looking for weakness in his quarry. He strikes!

His prey blocks and then counter strikes! Hunter side steps as the knight lunges forward and answers the man with a big elbow to the back of the head. Jed cheers his swordsman on.

The emerald shape stumbles but keeps his footing. He quickly squares off to face Hunter. As the emerald knight tries to catch him off guard, Hunter spins with his sword quickly rising, and instinctively blocks the deadly blow.

The crowd is on their feet! Ol' Jed is stabbing the air with a quick leap.

Hunter circles his prey and the emerald knight growls and strikes back. He easily knocks the double edge sword aside.

They lock into a corrugated dance. Circling and jabbing. Blocking and parrying. In the dance of death, facing another man with a blade puts you in close quarters. One bad move, one flaw, and death ensues.

The knight begins a vicious attack! Hunter blocks and dodges with quick reflexes! The emerald knight stays persistent in his attack, forcing the leather warrior back with each strike. He shouts and laughs.

Hunter stumbles in the large divot where the emerald knight's metal encasement first landed. The knight barks another laugh as he jumps forward to end the folly.

Without thought, Hunter spins his large body. His sword is maneuvered over his head and the blades crash!

Blocking and spinning, spinning and attacking, Hunter fights just to stand on his feet again. The knight tries his best to stop him from rising, to no avail. Hunter regains his full height, a foot taller than the knight.

"Nice moves!" growls the emerald knight "Too bad 'cause movement will end for you soon!" He laughs as another flurry of his slashing blade tries to drive the large man in leather back.

Hunter's blade flows in the air, as he blocks each attack. Steel slamming into steel! Blow after each deadly blow, they stand flawlessly to drive the other into submission.

Hunter draws the knight in close and grabs the sword with his big left hand! Quick as a wink, a wicked right smashes into the knight's head piece! The emerald knight fights to free his sword hand as Hunter swings him to the right, causing him to stumble.

The knight recovers quickly from his half spin. As he turns to face the man in leather again, he quickly ducks. The deadly blade slices through the air clipping the ribbons from his headpiece.

A wicked grin fills Hunter's face. He releases a loud war cry, then sets into a violent assault toward the knight.

The crowd jumps with each crash of steel! The knight is dazed as he staggers drunkenly backwards. Hunter intensifies the attacks. His sword is a flash of silver around his opponent.

The sad sounds of bag pipers pervade the tense air. Their droning melody adds to the battle's sounds. Hunter roars, "Listen to your death march."

From the stands, the flash of Hunter's blade resemble a wind mill blowing daises in a field. The knight is driven back with each blow! To no avail, the emerald knight fights to regain the upper hand. "Whoa, easy!" He barks, as he barely blocks the advancing blade. Hunter's nasty grin is the man's answer. He spins, slices the air, and stops with a loud crash of steel.

The knight's sword takes flight and escapes from his hand. Hunter throws a fast left elbow into the right side of knight's head piece. The emerald knight stumbles as his body follows the direction the heavy blow sent him. He hits the ground hard.

As Hunter leaps toward his fallen opponent, the knight rolls to his back as he sees the large curved blade twirls, slicing rings in the air. The nimble warrior lands seconds before the sword is driven toward the knight's head piece.

The arena is in an uproar as the battle field begins to fill with more shouts of praise! Flowers and kerchiefs fly causing the ground to gain color. The stands come alive as the people connect to the energy from the field is driven by the sounds of bag pipes. Hunter raises his sword to them all as he pivots slowly.

At the end of his turn he looks down to the unmoving knight. Placing his sword in his left hand he kneels slowly beside. Hunter smiles to himself then taps on the helmet. "Tunk! Dude, you ok in there?"

"Shhh. Can't talk now bro, I'm dead remember?" The beaten knight's hearty laughter blended into the cheers.

Hunter laughs as he jumps back to his feet. He raises his sword high in his left hand, looks to the end of the field, and sees the crimson knight standing in his stirrups. His right fist is raised thumb side to his heart and his left hand, holding his sword, is raised high over his head. Hunter copies the stance. Turning, he sees the emerald knight behind him with the same salute to the crimson knight.

Looking to the northern port of call, Hunter sees the kilted warriors with their swords high and their right fist to their hearts. He turns to them and slowly bows his head.

The larger Scot has a big grin on his face and he lowers his woolly head to acknowledge Hunter's victory. The smaller man's long mustache dances as he throws his head back, his cry of battle proclaiming it all.

Hunter drives his weapon into its scabbard and turns to the emerald warrior. He reaches to the shorter man's helmet and taps again. "Tunk, you sure you're ok in there!"

Tunk laughs while he removes his helmet and rakes his left hand over a three inch Mohawk. "You know it Hunt! I'm cool! Always cool bro!"

"Cool bro! You know it's time for a cold one!" Hunter pulls up the emerald warrior.

"You bet Hunter, good match." Patting Hunter on his shoulder, Tunk laughs. "You know seeing how I'm dead, you buying right?"

"You got it! I say that was the best match yet Tunk."

"Best yet, bro!"

Chapter 1

Back to Reality

Tadd Hunter folds his leathers into his gear bag sitting on the bench beside him. The small dressing room was plain with no windows and one full size mirror. He laces his calf high moccasins after tucking in his gray cotton trouser legs. Standing, he watches his reflection in the mirror and slowly tucks his brown, cotton, collarless shirt into his pants. As he wraps his wide leather belt around his narrow waist, he speaks to the other large man in the room. "Tunk, you know that's the first time I bested the emerald knight and remained untouched."

"You're right, good match bro. Flawless!" Tunk was trying to see himself in the narrow mirror while straightening his clothes. "You done yet? The mirror ain't big enough for the both of us!"

"Hold a sec." Hunter picks out his flaring five inch peacock tail, then straightens his braid and flips it over his shoulder. He rubs his shaved head and nods, then he ties two Eagle feathers at the top of the braid. "You know I remember as a child living on the reservation, the other kids ribbed me about my size." Looking at Tunk's reflection looking back at him. "I've said it before Tunk. How many Native Americans grow this big?" Looking back to his six foot seven inch, two hundred ninety five pound, muscular body staring back at him. "I almost flipped when I met you and Jinx at jump school." Watching his own head shake, "I still think of how strange that feeling was. Two more abnormal red men."

Just then the door bursts open. "Yeah sounds pretty crazy to me too bro! I say you are the strangest looking Cherokee I have ever laid an eye on." The third man crammed in by Hunter to

1

gaze into the mirror. Tunk grunted his disapproval and sat back down.

"Now just look at Ol' Jinx here." Jinx winked at his own six foot five inch, two hundred fifty pound, chiseled body. "Jinxy, you are the best looking of the lot." He then checked the tuft of hair on the back of his shaved head, pulling his mid back length braid to his front. Checking the leather wrap holding two hawk feathers in the middle of his braid, he smiles at Tunk's reflection. Tossing the braid over his shoulder, the tip brushed Tunk's left cheek as he tried to reclaim his place at the mirror.

Jinx spins to face Tunk. "Hey Tunk! Gotcha! I am one bad brave huh?"

"Bite me fool!" Tunk pushed them both from the mirror, picked his Mohawk and striated the fan of hair covering his shoulder. Arranging his earth tone clothes, his hands stopped to check his bowie knife on his left side and a tomahawk on the right. He looked at the reflection of the other two, behind his own six foot four inch reflection. Smiling at Jinx, "No sir this two hundred sixty five pound hunk of man says I'm the better looking here!" Tunk turned and grabbed his belongings. "Who's buying?" I can't, still dead remember?" He laughed as he left the room.

Jinx looked at Hunter, "I heard some of what you said. I remember the kids too. The Catawba are usually shorter than that," he pointed at his reflection. "No matter. We three big odd balls found each other. Now let one of those clowns act up on us now. Who'll laugh then?"

Jinx gathered his own belongings and headed to the door. Without stopping he spoke to Hunter, "Guess it's time to go." Hunter followed Jinx out the door.

At the horse trailer, Tunk was finishing with the loading of his gear, his giant black stallion was pawing the trailer floor. Tunk came out of the hauler. "Jinx, I see you already loaded your stuff, you in a hurry?"

"Oh man! Messing around with you two I almost forgot!" Jinx turned around without another word and runs away.

Hunter looks at Tunk and shrugs. While their friend was gone, they talked of the past and old times together. Hunter laughed, "Remember the look we got from the others at jump school?"

"Yeah! We said we were living proof that big foot was alive."

"What was that Jinx would say? 'we were proof our grandfathers raped buffaloes."

"Yeah he does come up with stupid junk doesn't he?"

"Hunter, I still try to figure out why huge Native Americans like us learn all this white man stuff?"

"Our fathers all had warped sense of humors I guess." They both laughed. "But the funniest thing is we all like doing it."

Tunk got quiet. "You're right bro, we do like it. Swords and all."

After all the gear was loaded, Tunk looked at his long time friend. "Hunter after you got out of school, did you ever think . . . ." His words were stopped by strange noises. Someone was singing off key and sounded as if he had had too much hard liquor in him. Both of them turned in unison looking in the direction where Jinx had run off and laughed when Jinx rounded the building leading a pair of young quarter horses.

"Make room for these two babies! Just got'em!" Jinx laughed as he tossed his head toward the pair of horses. "Real cheap too!" The other two met him half way coming to the horse trailer. Jinx stopped and they immediately began to inspect the horses.

Hunter shook his head while looking at Jinx, "I knew having a vet around would have its advantages."

"Well, I would have been a vet and a good one too! But, no, you two talked me into that digging mess." Jinx laughed, "Hell Hunter, I didn't even know what an archaeologist was. An Indian archaeologist at that! Damn I couldn't even spell it!"

"Whatever, fool! You're still crazy," grunted Hunter. "What did you tell their old owner?" said Tunk while looking at the horses "What's wrong with'em?"

Jinx laughed, "I said they were sterile."

"How'd you know that?" Tunk raised a surprised look at Jinx. "They look healthy to me."

"Don't know if they are." Jinx shrugged, as he laughed again. "Said it as a joke, he believed me, and now they're ours. I tried to convince him that I was joking but you know how some people are. He still thinks I was serious."

"Cool!" Hunter looked at Tunk and shook his head, "they do look to be good pack animals."

Jinx petted the mares. "I thought so too. They would be handy scouting new sites and hauling our gear." He shrugged his broad shoulders. "Breeders too, maybe?" Jinx laughed.

"Yeah? If you say so, you are the vet." Tunk laughed as he rubbed the front leg of both animals. "They do look healthy and strong. I thought you would have gone into people medicine after you did all that training in the military."

"Naw, all I did that medic stuff for was to make sure we'd survive the gulf war and we did. I patched up Hunter and brought him back home didn't I?

Hunter laughed.

"Thieving again, Jinxy?" The three turned to see the bearded warrior stalking up behind them. A mustached swordsman in tow.

Jinx laughed, "don't you know it O'Cey!"

O'Conner McNure grabbed his brother, Omallay by the neck. The two roared a hardy rough laugh together. "See Mac! I likes this man more and more, every time we be around him!" He then slammed a big hand to Jinx's back. Jinx stumbled forward bringing another roar from the strange pair.

"He do seem to be of our people too brother!" The long mustache jiggled as Mac's head rolled back in another roaring laugh.

"You mean Jinx is Scottish too?" Jinx shot a glare at him. Tunk joined in the laughter while shrugging.

O'Cey still laughing, "Don't you know it Tunker? We all be liars, traders and thieves."

Hunter reached out for the big hand of O'Cey. "How's Dilman doing? Haven't seen him around with you in awhile." O'Cey grabbed his wrist, they shook.

"The lad be fine Hunter, no one understand him 'cept me and ol' brother Mac here." Still holding Hunter's wrist in a iron grip. "That sword hand you got do be lookin' fine. When you want to face me laddy?"

Hunter laughed as he clinched O'Cey's thick wrist. "Maybe next time brother."

O'Cey winked. "Me sword waits a good match. Ol' Mac be getting too fat and slow." O'Cey nods. "Maybe I needs to put him in the pasture, huh?"

Mac hit O'Cey on the back with a thick forearm, "I let you win, old man!" Prying his brother's hand away from Hunter's wrist and replacing it with his own. "Dil don't be fine Hunter! Tell that ol' Bill fellow', the wee one driving me crazy with all that book o' magic. He thinks he be some kind of a wizard or something.?" Hunter switched puzzled looks between Tunk and Jinx, then shrugs. "Never mind I'll deal with that Bill another time."

O'Cey slapped his brother's back, "you jus' be scared the wizard will one day make you a toad little brother!"

Mac laughed, "yeah and he said he'd turn you into a wart on a toad's butt cheek when all the spells be cast." Hunter shrugs again at his laughing friends.

"Any way we got to fix up that place we bought." O'Cey grabs Hunter's wrist again then Jinx's and Tunk's.

Mac also shook with them. "Come see us. Bill knows how to find us. He told us 'bout the land we bought. Anyway friends, you take care." Jinx cocked his head questioning Hunter again.

"Take care of you." Tunk grinned. "And tell the great wizard we said hello. And you take care as well my friends."

"We'll meet soon, be good. Look out for the wizard, Mac!" added Jinx.

"Aye! Always Jinxy!" growled O'Cey, "Until the morrow."

As the brothers walked off, Hunter shook his head laughing. "Good men, but sure are strange." Jinx shook his head.

Tunk laughed, "I think they sound strange sometimes, then I remember they are strange all the time."

Jinx laughed again. "Yeah, Mac told me once his father would take them aside and teach them of his Scottish people. Then other times their mom would try to teach them not to be like their father."

"They both talked of the fights their parents had over how each other don't know how to raise children." Hunter looked down the dark walk where O'Cey and Mac had disappeared. "But they are good people to know though." Jinx and Tunk nodded.

After loading all their gear and two hours of darkness had caught up with them, they climbed in Hunter's big crew cab truck. Tunk stretched out on the back seat. Jinx rode shot gun. Hunter started the engine and they hit the road. The truck headed out for the long ride to their campers.

A little ways down the road, Hunter looked to his right. "Jinx, Ghost sure pranced around today. He looked sharp"

"Yeah he did but Tunk's Nightmare tried to steal the show!" Jinx laughed as he cut his eyes to look in the back. "Hunter, I noticed you brought Sequoia. When you gonna joust with us?"

Hunter laughed, "I'll practice with you but that's all bro. Sequoia, ain't a jouster."

Tunk quickly sat up and leaned over the front seat. "I've seen him in action, man! Dude he's an awesome horse!" He looked at Hunter in the mirror and raised his eyebrows.

"Don't know, maybe one day." Hunter shrugged. Tunk fell back in the back seat.

Jinx laughed again "If you're scared, say so!" They all laughed. After a short ride they were heading back toward the dig site.

A serious look came over Hunter's face as he looked at Jinx. "Had that silly day dream, vision or whatever again?"

"The war council?" Jinx looked to his left to face Hunter. "It's a vision. I've said it before and I say it again bro, bad medicine! How is it they come only to you? Now, if it came to us all then I say, bad medicine. Now let's cut loose and get out of all this mess, bro."

Tunk sat up and leaned forward again. "He's right Hunter bad medicine. I said it before too. Let's cut our losses and be rid of that fool Jansen!"

"My thoughts too bro. I'm with Tunk on that." Jinx agreed. "But no matter what you decide, you know we'll be with you. Besides you are the boss."

"I'm the boss! Whatever? We're in this together." Hunter looks in the mirror, then to the passenger still leaning up behind him. "Tunk, you know what you asked, earlier?" Tunk looked back studying Hunter's expression. "My father loved these games as yours and Jinx's did too. But I still wonder why he had me learn fencing, martial arts, even rodeo. I learned the same stuff, just like you and Jinx, but I still can't figure why."

"It is strange. Just think how much we all were raised alike." Jinx laughed. "It's like we had the same fathers." They rode in silence.

Hours passed, Jinx was showing signs of his restlessness. "Hey Hunt pull over at that greasy spoon up there." He yawned as he pointed. "We still got what fourteen hours to go?"

Hunter nodded. "Wake up sleeping beauty. We are almost home." The trio went into the little diner to fill up for their long ride back to home.

After a somewhat good meal, the three travelers loaded into Hunter's truck ready for their long journey home to Montana. Hunter watched the hills roll by, glancing back in the mirror at Tunk then to Jinx. "You've both been good friends. Thanks." Each man nods their response, then all goes quiet as each thinks of old memories. Good times and bad. Times of the forgotten past. Memories.

Tunk nods as he stares out his window. His mind slips into the life he once knew. He smiled as he looked out of the eyes of a lanky eleven years old boy again. *"Father why do I have to sword fight? Wasn't this part of the white man's past?"*

His father smiled, "our past is a wonderful thing my son. I see that you've learned our ways. Are you not learning the rituals, the healing and the old ways of our warriors?" Tunk nodded his head along with the head nod of his boy hood. His father continued. *"But this white man past you speak of will help you to understand the vicious ways of their past and I think it will help you to understand them as well."*

Hunter laughed bringing Tunk out of his daze. "Tunk my father said the same to me." Jinx repeated the same words.

Tunk looked shocked "Was I talking out loud?"

Jinx looked back at Tunk "You ramble a lot when you zone out like that, bro." Jinx and Hunter shared a laugh.

"It's ok. You ain't crazy bro. We've all said it before. We lived the same life and are mirror images of each other. Funny thing is, we all know it." Jinx shook his head. "So maybe we all are crazy."

After a good laugh they rode in silence.

Chapter 2

The Door

As the black crew cab rolls down the road, Hunter's mind drifted back to another forgotten time. Two uniformed Army officers walked across a grassy field. "Lieutenant Hunter, you'll bunk with two other Native Americans. Both are Sergeants and about as big as you." The two soldiers stop in front of an old barrack. "Hawkens and Wolfe are their names. Any questions?"

"No sir, Captain Robins." As they entered the quarters, two large forms stood to attention. They were huge men who stood ridged with solid salutes. The captain returned the motion while he looked at each of the three men "Good! The three of you get acquainted. Jump school starts early." With more salutes the captain leaves the barracks.

"You must be the new Lieutenant? I'm Jinx. That's Tunk. Glad to meet you!" With a long drawn out, "Siiirrrr!" After he finished, his intro, Jinx took his seat, and slowly reopened the book he was reading. He kept a careful eye on the new big man.

"Cool!" Hunter stowed his gear then looked at his roommates. "Jinx, you're Catawba right?" Jinx nodded. "And you're Sioux, Tunk?" Tunk nodded.

Tunk mused, "Eastern Cherokee?" Jinx looked up from his newly opened book as Hunter nodded. Jinx closed the book again.

Hunter looked at the book Jinx set aside. "You're into becoming a vet?" Jinx nodded.

They talked for hours and the conversation eventually led to their childhood. "You know my dad was into that strange white man's stuff too," laughed Hunter.

"Yeah, sword fighting and jousting ain't exactly the past of our people, now is it?" All three laughed. Tunk shook his head. "Hunter you said your dad *was*. Does that mean he's past on?

Hunter nodded. "Five years now and no explained reason for his death."

"Mine too, about five years," said Jinx in a soft voice.

Tunk looked a little surprised. "Strange. Mine as well." They all looked at each other until Tunk shook his head laughing "How strange is all this? It's like we share the same life." The other two laughed and nodded with him.

The hours pass swiftly. "I was thinking, when I get out of this man's army, I'm thinking about getting into archeology. Digging into Native American past could be pretty interesting." Hunter looked at the clock. "Well, it's getting late. Almost midnight."

Tunk nodded, "That's cool. Gonna dig into our people's past?" Jinx looked between the two of them.

"Yeah, plan to." Hunter nodded. "Jinx, the capt. said you are a medic."

"Yeah but I only study to be able to do these missions. I plan to finish up veterinary medicine."

"That would be cool." Hunter looked up from his pillow.

Tunk stopped changing his clothes, "Hunt, you want a partner?"

"That would be cool."

"Cool, Then I'm in if you say so." Tunk laughed.

Jinx laughed "You're both crazy. Good night." Jinx lay there staring off into time. "I rather turn into a vet, not a mole, but it might be cool." He smiled and nodded. "Yeah, that does sound cool."

$$* \quad * \quad *$$

After their fourteen hour drive and several driver changes, the truck races toward it's home. The sun is setting over an old battle field as Tunk pulls the truck into their camp site. The base camp was set up down the road near the dig site. Jinx yelled out his open door, "Honey, I'm home!" The trio went straight to work, tending to the five horses. Ghost stomped and nipped at Tunk.

"Hey! Fool horse!" Tunk jumped away from the huge white stallion. "Jinx, that hay burner of yours is as crazy as you!"

"That's right! And I like my women just like 'em too; wild and crazy!"

Hunter laughed. "Don't you mean more like, big and hairy!"

Tunk slapped his sides. "I wish I'd thought of that!" Tunk laughed, "Good one, Hunt!"

Jinx looked at the others, then danced a little circle before he howled.

After the chores were done, Tunk looked at his motor home. "Hey, got some steaks. Ya'll wanta cook out?"

"Sure!" Jinx responded. "I got cold beer!"

"Cool! I've got to have some onions and potatoes in the camper," Hunter said as he listen to rumble from under his washboard stomach. "I may have salad fixins, too." They all set out for a quick feast.

The evening sun had been gone several before supper was finished. Jinx was gathering the last of the dirty plates and silverware from the table. Tunk was washing in the sink outside his camper.

Hunter was cleaning the grill. "That was some meal guys, but it's time to shower and turn in. Gotta meet Jansen tomorrow."

As Tunk stop bathing, soap bubbles flew from his pointing finger as he shook it at Hunter. The splashing bubbles landed down Jinx's leg and splattered on his feet. "I still say let's cut 'em loose."

Looking down at the suds running down his legs, Jinx frowned. "Too true bro." Hunter shrugged. Jinx looked at Tunk. "Thanks for washing my shoes."

Hunter waved as he entered his camper. Tunk finished then went inside his traveling home. Jinx checked his Jeep. Before heading home, he looked to the west toward the dig site, then back to the three so called homes. Letting out a big sigh he shook his head then walked to his, 'home'.

Before the sun began to light up the eastern sky, Hunter had a fire burning and coffee brewing. More steaks were placed over the open fire.

He looked to the west toward the dig and the air slowly went hazy. A large bonfire burned bright. Sitting around the fire was a ring of warriors all dressed in colored buck skin and their full head dress. They looked as if there were a ceremony taking place. All the warriors sat facing the flickering bright light. One of the chiefs wearing full head dress looked toward Hunter "My son, the door will open soon."

Another looked up. "You need to be ready little brother." The slamming doors made the vision fade away. Hunter stood still staring in the same direction.

Tunk tapped Jinx on the shoulder and nodded toward Hunter. Jinx shook his head.

The breakfast was half cooking on its own, when his two friends wandered up. Jinx coughed, Hunter jumped. With a startled look, he stared at them. "Bout time you two got up!"

Jinx looked back at Hunter. "See 'em, again?" Hunter nodded.

While they ate steak and eggs, Jinx looked at Hunter. "Me and Tunk are gonna check to the north of the dig site."

"Cool, I was thinking of that last week." After he finished, Hunter got up staring at the horizon. "Man, look at that sunrise."

"Yeah imagine what it looked like hundreds of years ago?" Tunk looked in awe.

Jinx laughed. "Just like it does now fool. This part of the world hadn't changed yet!" He set his empty plate down, still laughing. "You know what I mean, nobody lives within twenty miles of here."

Tunk picked up a small rock and threw it at Jinx. "It's your turn to check the horses, so get off your lazy ass, walk over to the corral and look after them, fool." Tunk got up and poured his coffee on the fire.

"You say some of the craziest stuff, Tunk." Jinx laughed, "Besides, you throw like a girl, too!"

Hunter shook his head. "Jinx, you two are a site for sore eyes and worst on the ears. You sure you two ain't married? Sure sounds like it to me." Hunter laughed. "Please don't have a family. You two would make ugly babies." Jinx and Tunk exchanged sour looks. "See you two at the site." Hunter walked toward his truck.

Jinx stopped at the paddock gate. "Hey Hunter, were you visited in your dreams last night too?" Hunter shook his head without turning. He adjusted the Bowie knife hanging over his right shoulder, then he waved to them.

The crew cab was on the highway in less than a minute heading west. Half a mile down the road it turned right onto a rutted dirt drive. The mile drive felt like a life time, as Hunter dodged large sink holes. He stopped at the site's office.

Entering the small trailer they used to oversee the operation, he opened the blinds. He made a quick look around the place, then grabbed two folding tables. Carrying the tables outside, Hunter went to his favorite spot under a large oak tree. He set both tables up while watching Jinx's Jeep coming down the drive. When the Jeep stopped, Hunter looked over the site again before walking back into the trailer.

Inside the small office Hunter rummaged through some folders and journals. After choosing the right ones he shoved the small pile under his left arm. He headed to the door grabbing some maps and a small leather bag that was hanging from the coat rack.

Hunter laid all the paper work out on the tables. Jinx and Tunk went straight to work, opening the two temporary security pens near the tables under the same big tree.

"Hey Tunk! Here's a few extra maps. I don't want you two getting lost." Tunk walked to the table and Hunter handed the papers to him.

Hunter dumped the contents from the bag on the table. "Hunt, did you get an answer on that ball and key looking thing they dug up last week?" Tunk looked over the maps, then to the things from the bag. Hunter shook his head. Satisfied Tunk rolled the maps up and set them on the table. Looking back to a blue crystal ball and a bone white cylinder shaped key, Tunk shook his head. He looked at Hunter for an answer before he turned to walk back to the Jeep for their gear.

"Not yet. Still haven't decided to show them to anyone yet." Hunter picked up the objects in question from the table where he had dumped them. Jinx shook his head as he made his way to the table. He strapped his Bowie knife upside down on the left side of his back, then put his two tomahawks in the notches on each side of his thick leather belt. Tunk returned from the Jeep tossing Jinx his pack.

Tunk pulled a ram horn from his pack and drew a deep breath. He began to blow steady on the horn. Jinx laughed at the echo of the sad bleat bouncing through the site. Tunk lost his wind before he joined in the laughter.

Jinx put on his back pack before he tested his horn. The second lonesome bleat carried across the plains chasing the first one. They all laughed at the echoes again.

Hunter shook his head, "It doesn't take much to amuse you two, does it?"

They both looked at him then continued to laugh at Hunter's question.

Hunter finally laughed. "I guess we each need to get some kind of lives, huh?" Tunk nodded. "Got your water skins, Jinx?"

"Yes honey and they are full of good water, too."

Tunk walked by Jinx. "Then are you ready sugar?"

"Yeah, I got the tools so let's head out. Later Hunt."

As the two walked away, Tunk looked back and waved. "Jinx, what do you think of those visions he's been having?" Tunk adjusted his knife on his left side and his tomahawk on the right.

"Can't say. It feels like something's fix'en to happen to us." Shaking his head, "I don't know, but it can't be good."

Tunk nodded. "I got that feeling too."

Hunter watched his two companions as they slowly faded over the hill. He turned back to check the site one more time. As he stared over the terrain, a now familiar thing occurred. The air grew foggy and images came to life. Again they formed around a large ring of fire. Another council? Warriors were sitting, some dancing, some looking into the fire. Hunter had been having the same vision ever since they began this dig two years ago. The warriors were often adorned in battle clothes or celebration attire.

The eldest turned to face Hunter, again. "Change is coming young Eagle. Coldness as you haven't seen will come soon little brother. Soon the door will open."

Another chief spoke. "You are needed. Be brave big one. Remember the old ways. Remember any day is a good day to die. All warriors must stand righteous."

Before his voice trailed off, another chief spoke. "Soon Great Eagle, you must stand ready. Trouble comes soon. Be the man as we know you." The vision vanished.

"Hey! Hunter! You hear me?"

Shaking his head, Hunter jumped. "Yeah! Jinx what is it?"

"It's me, Tunk!" Looking in the direction Hunter had been staring, then back. "Another vision?"

"Yeah. Same council and still it was different."

Jinx walked up "What'd they say?" "The same things about change will come soon or the thing 'bout that door again."

"Yeah, but this time two more spoke. One called me Great Eagle. Another one said, trouble is coming and more evil than I ever seen."

"Cool! Now I know it! I'm hanging around a crazy man that sees visions and a lunatic named Tunk!" Jinx laughed as he turned to head back out of camp. "Oh yeah! The trouble has a name, too! Jansen! A short fat white crook and we work for him!"

Grabbing the forgotten map rolled on the table, Tunk turns to leave. "If they are Sioux and come back to ya, tell 'em Ol' Tunk says, How!" He held his hand up as he walked away.

Hunter looked at Tunk, "I thought you two left, already!"

Jinx was still standing watching Tunk walk away. "I can't figure it out. Is he Lewis or Clark?" Jinx laughed, "No matter. The idiot forgot the maps!"

Jinx looked at Hunter, "I guess something will happen soon, bro. No matter what you got us and we'll be there for ya!" he said shrugging his broad shoulders, "Tunk knows more than I do about this magic stuff and reading visions."

Before Jinx could turn to leave, Tunk came back to the table. "Hunter, he's just as scared. We'll be back later."

"Yeah. Be careful and blow your ram horns if you need any help." His serious look turned into a laugh. "Even if you get lost again as usual."

Tunk poked Jinx with the rolled up maps as he passed him. "Ready fool?" Hitting Jinx with the maps again. "Who's scared, idiot! Man, you got problems."

Jinx laughed. "Just playing! Hey Chief 'Goof Ball', let's go." Jinx and Tunk topped the hill again then disappeared over the top. Hunter walked back to the table and opened the journals. After about thirty minutes, two large vans drove down the driveway. The driver of the first van got out. He was a little old man that could be confused as Mark Twain or Albert Einstein.

The man quickly walked up and said, "Hey Hunter!" The graveled voice made Hunter smile as he looked up from his reading.

"Hey Bill!"

The old man pulled a big curved pipe from his teeth. "Where'd Tweedledum and Tweedle Dee wander off to this fine morning boss?"

"They've gone up to the northern end. It's the spot you said that may look promising." Bill nodded. "If they're going to explore it some, maybe we can dig that area next spring. That is, if we get another backer." Hunter says with a smile, "Bill, do you ever light that old pipe or does it always just hang around your chin?"

"When I'm in deep thought Hunter or when things are going the way I think it ought to, I'll light it up." Bill laughed. "Thinking don't happen much anymore because of Murphy and his damned law. Too much goes wrong so I smoke even less now."

"Get the kids together and let's have a quick meeting." Bill nodded and returned to the crowd of restless young people standing near the vans. Hunter packed the clear blue ball and the white key back in the leather bag. He carried the goat skin backpack back in the office and placed it on desk. Turning to go outside, he flipped a switch and the diesel generator started. A steady hum sounded as the test equipment came to life.

Returning outside, he saw the students sitting on the ground near the table holding their journals. "First I want to say, thanks to each and every one of you. You've each done an excellent job. I've written letters of recommendation for each of you, even one for Bill."

The crew chuckled, as a red head young man sitting in the front, yelled, "Like that old fart needs anymore."

Bill nodded with a grin and in his graveled voice exclaimed, "Hunter, I've been with you since my third dig, and have enjoyed all of them, even your nit-wit cohorts." The group's laughter increased. "I do like those two. Boy does that sound like I am crazy too." More laughter.

Hunter raised his hand and the laughter trickled to a hush. "Speaking of those two, they went to the north. Hopefully exploring our next dig in this area."

He picked up one of the journals, then looked across the faces of each of the excited youths. He smiled as his thoughts drifted to his first dig and the feelings he experienced from his first find. "From what we found here, this was a major camp for a war party. The bones we found were sent the lab to be tested. Many were Native American males and the others were adult Caucasian males. They died of multiple stab and gunshot wounds.

"Do you have any speculations, Mister Hunter?" Spoke the same red head boy.

"Bill, would you like to answer this question?"

"You're doing fine boy. My scratchy voice will be muddled, so you just carry on."

Hunter nodded. "Yes sir. After testing the bones and some of the pottery we unearthed, the lab concluded that these artifacts dated around the late eighteen hundreds. Now did they play a part of the larger war-party that ended Custard's career? Can't say right now." All of the students looked at each other and nodded as if their guesses were just confirmed.

"Looking at the expressions on your faces, you had already come to that conclusion, but we do need more data. When Custard fell, they scalped all the uniformed soldiers. It is said that Custard was left unscathed because he wore buck skin and not a uniform. However, it is believed that many of his soldiers were mutilated so that they could not enter into the afterlife and would walk the earth for all eternity. Are you all bored yet?" The crowd snickered in unison then quickly simmered down as they all shook their heads together.

Looking at the map he pointed at a spot just southwest of where he stood. "There are two objects in question that were found here, and no one has any idea of where or what they came from. What's more puzzling is how they got here. According to the depth they were found, they are at least one hundred years old." The group was starting to look restless. A few yawns told Hunter to hurry up and end.

"Jinx, Tunk and myself teamed up to trace our ancestry and history that surrounded them. It's fun and interesting to uncover the past and I hope you all will continue in this and come to love it as much as we have. Even Ol' Bill there seems to like it a lot too, even though he's experience much of the past firsthand."

The group laughed. Bill grunted. Some taunted the old foreman earning themselves a sour look.

Hunter raised his hands to hush the students. "We'll need to finish documenting the unearthed artifacts." Looking around at the twenty-one young people seated before him, Hunter began, "The blue team can close out what you have stored in the fenced areas. Make sure you pack them with plenty of straw for their trip. Red team move to site number nineteen and finish closing it up. Yellow and green teams, fix your logs, they are a mess. Then finish cleaning your items. Blue team can help with the packing of those items as well."

Hunter ended with another smile. "I want to again say thank you and you have made some great discoveries. When they reach their destinations, each item will be shown with acknowledgment of each of you as finding them. The plaques will state the location, date found and all names present. So thanks again to all of you and your hard work." After a burst of cheers Hunter finished his speech. "Ok, that's all I have. If there are no questions, then it's time to go to work." Hunter nodded to the whole group. "I will be preparing for a meeting with our funding agent, Mister Jansen, so I'll be in the office most of the day. If you leave before I see you again, good luck and I hope to see all of you on another dig." Murmurs of 'Thank you' filled air.

Looking around, he saw the pleased faces of each of the students. Hunter smiled. "Ok! Any questions?" As Hunter continued to study each of their faces, his thoughts wandered to the war council. His facial expression slowly changed. The students didn't notice, but after several minutes, Bill coughed. Hunter jumped. He laughed to cover his day dream. "Sorry, I must have dozed off." He looked at Bill and laughed. "Now I know how you feel Bill." Bill grunted and a broad grin spread across his whiskered face. The students made a small ruckus again.

"Ok! Ok! No questions then? Cool!" Hunter exclaims as he closes the journal with a loud slap, "Let's wrap up this dig and everyone remember to be careful." Leaving the journals on the table, Hunter turned and headed toward the office. His thoughts raced ahead to his meeting with his financial backer, Mister Jansen. The thought of the meeting made his skin crawl.

The students were a buzz in Hunter's head as the crowd split up to perform their duties. Their excitement carried over to their work stations. Bill went through his normal tasks of overseeing the groups. His gravelly voice added to the faint buzz in Hunter's ear.

Hunter reached the steps of the office and turned to look the site over before going inside. The day started out smoothly and Hunter had hoped it would stay that way.

Several hours had quietly passed and then a loud commotion brought Hunter to his feet and out the door. He ran down the few steps quickly. His long powerful legs carried him with ease to a crowd gathered around the last of the opened site. He stopped to the right of his foreman. "Bill? What's wrong?"

The same red headed boy from the meeting jumped from the shallow hole. He quickly stepped up to Hunter and excitedly handed him a medallion. "It was buried near the same spot where the ball was found Mister Hunter!" Hunter looked at the trinket. Hunter's blood seemed to rush straight to his head then drop to his feet in a matter of seconds.

Hunter put his right hand on Bill's shoulder to steady himself. He faintly heard the same young man gibbering. "Mister Hunter, are you ok? I don't know how I missed it the other day, but . . . ." Hunter held up his left hand and the boy went silent.

Hunter turned his left hand over to study it close. A golden circle surrounding a black thorn. The thorn was laying on its side, pointing down and sticking out from circle. The loop appeared to be what the trinket hung by. The sharp point of the thorn was the color of crimson. Blood stains? It appeared as if it had stuck someone and drew blood. The young man's voice quivered as he tried to ask for forgiveness. "I don't know how we missed it, sir."

Bill growled and the boy lowered his head and fell silent. "What do you make of it sir? Doesn't appear to be any kind of tribal work I have ever seen."

Hunter quietly turned toward the office. He had to keep them from seeing the shocked look that remained on his face. No one could hear the questions echoing through his head. Could They, but maybe Bill could. Hunter looked for an answer in Bill's face. All he got was a smile.

Hunter's mind raced. Without a word he walked to the office with the amulet held tight in his hand. It took a great deal of control to not run to the confines of the office walls.

Bill smiled as he lit his pipe. "Alright kiddies! Back to work!" He rubbed the redhead boy on the head and smiled. "It is quite alright lad." The young man returned the smile. "You did good Red. You did good."

Hunter was walking as if in a daze, moving by instinct to find cover. He didn't notice the group of workers staring from the artifact pens. "Mister Hunter, all of our artifacts are logged in the books. Since we're done sir do you want the clean stuff boxed and marked?"

Bill blew a smoke ring. He smiled again as he watched Hunter give no immediate reaction to the student. A few seconds passed slowly before Hunter turned toward the voice. "What? Oh yes. Yes. That'll be fine." Without looking back he yells, "Bill! Make sure to label the boxes and lock'em up!" He was at the steps before he turned and said, "If you don't mind. I'll be in the office."

Bill looked up from his pipe smiling. "Yes sir! You're the boss!" The words flowed with the thin wisps of smoke around the pipe stem. He smiled to himself as he watched the puzzled Hunter jumped up half the steps into the office. Bill nodded and continued to smile as he stared at the closed door. After a few seconds, he turned his attention back to the students. "Ok people you heard the boss!"

Hunter had disappeared into the trailer and nervously wiped the new strange object. His eyes never left the amulet as he walked over to a mirror hanging in the office restroom. He removed his Bowie knife straps, then his shirt to expose his massive torso. Turning he looked at an image of a tattoo on his right shoulder. "The same design, but how? Why?" He pulled his shirt back on and walked to the window in front of his desk. "What does a thorn have to do with this area?" He stared out to the dig sight as if looking for an answer.

Slowly the now normal fog was settling on ground again. The site faded away from his searching eyes. Hunter jumps as he sees himself seated in the council's circle. One of the elders looked at the image of him. "You search too hard giant one. Forget reason as you know it and think only from the heart. You possess the heart of a great warrior."

A medicine man looked at the image of Hunter. "Let go of white man's logic my son. Open your eyes and look at your surroundings. Look through the eyes of a true warrior. Do not think so hard. It clouds your mind."

Another elder looked at his image. "The answer will be revealed soon. Be ready young blood."

The first elder looked from the image of Hunter to the real Hunter in the window and spoke again. "Soon mighty warrior. Soon life as you know it will change. Be ready. The door will open soon. Stand hard."

Another chief he hadn't seen before smiled at him. "It is time for change! The time does grow near and you are ready my son! My seed has grown and they have grown strong. Be ready sons of my sons!" The large muscular chief steps close to the window in one floating move. Hunter felt the power of this man. The look in his eyes said he was a great man of power and wisdom. A piercing look that did not know fear. A true and powerful warrior. "Remember, justice will be served with no mercy! The giants shall be the conquerors. Evil will run from the vengeance of the blood!" Hunter is shaken by the boom of the warrior's voice. "I am proud of you three." He was a powerful leader, but who was this man of war?

The office door opened and Bill walked in smiling as he looked at Hunter. "Boss? You ok?"

Hunter shuttered trying to come out of his daze. "Yes." His voice was broken and he coughed to cover it up. "Yeah yeah sure." His questioning look searched Bill's face for some kind of an answer. Hunter remembered his shirt was still open and turned his back to Bill while he buttoned it. "Everything is fine, Bill."

Bill remained silent until Hunter was finished and turned to look at him. "Hunter, I saw the performance this past weekend. Sure am sorry I never been to one until now." The nodding of his head made his smoking pipe jiggle. "How did you boys get into that type of warfare?" Smiling again as he pulled the pipe from between his teeth and waved the smoke aside. "It was impressive! You three could have been mighty warriors back in the day. And those Scottish brothers, they are some kind of blade masters too."

Hunter's questioning look turned into a surprised look. "Oh yeah thanks. You know the funny thing is Mac spoke of you."

Bill waved it off and carried on his conversation. "I still can't figure how you, Tunk and Jinx came into the renaissance. You once told me how you three met but I forget."

"Bill, I met Tunk and Jinx many years ago when we were in the military." Hunter was looking off into space and reminiscing.

"We were Army Rangers at jump school and after that we were tied to each other. It was as if our lives were mirror images of each other. Fencing classes, rodeo and the funniest thing was all of us were active in those medieval games for years; but we never met until we were older and in the military." Hunter had regained his composure, looked at Bill and smiled. "Each of our fathers had insisted we do those things. Funny thing, ain't it? Well after the war we stayed together. After I healed from my wounds, we all contin . . . ." As he was talking Bill interrupted Hunter.

With a surprised look, Bill cut in. "You were wounded? I don't remember you telling me that."

"Yeah I was. Well you know, it was one of those classic military text book operation." Hunter laughs. "It went wrong," looking at Bill. "Oh well, things like that teach you caution, right?"

"Yeah, it does teach people something about being too cautious or over thinking things, I don't know. Did it seem to help with your sword mastering?" Bill relit his pipe.

"I guess. During that time I wanted to give that part of my life up, but those two kept me in it." Hunter was trying not to let the thought of the medallion clog his thoughts.

Bill grinned, "I am glad to see Jinx and Tuck have grown to be family to you. I guess brothers at arms. Sometimes close bonds will make things in life better."

"You know, those two stayed by my side in the hospital." Hunter looked at Bill. "To me they are my brothers."

"Good friends are hard to come by." Bill sat on the edge of the desk. "Good friends are even willing to die for one another."

"You're right. I know I'd die defending them and I have no doubt they'll do the same for me. We've all proved that many times over. We've already helped each other through too many touchy situations too count." Hunter smiled.

"Well we decided to continue school to do what we're doing now, well Jinx didn't. But he eventually joined Tunk and me. We even joined every medieval society. You should have seen those guys when we did our first showing."

Bill chuckled, "I bet it started a little awkward."

Hunter nodded as he stared off to another time. "We've learned a great deal from each other and from the other men we've perform around the world with. We learned more from watching the McNure brothers."

"How did you three get into that sword fighting?"

Hunter laughed, "Our fathers, but can't figure out why they were so into us learning it all. It does seem odd."

"Amazing! It almost seems as if your fathers were instructed to teach each of you all to do the same things." Smiling, Bill drew on his pipe then blew a smoke ring. "Very strange."

"I'll say. How many Native Americans do what we do? The funny thing is, we still enjoy doing it." Hunter rubbed his right shoulder. "Besides, it is a lot of fun."

"I wish I were younger so I would try it with you. It does look fun."

"You know you can be a squire Bill."

"No, no not me! We don't have much time." Bill watched as Hunter turned to face him. That same shocked look was back on his face. Bill smiled. "Did you ever get to read that journal I gave you?" Hunter stared at Bill as he sat in the chair by his desk. "You know, the journal of my studies on that island?"

Hunter shook his head, as Bill came around the desk. "Oh yeah, yeah I did! Interesting. Who are they?" Opening the drawer of the file cabinet by the window and removing the journal, Hunter turned to Bill and handed the green book to him. "Here's your journal Bill and your synopsis. I did like you said and my overview of your writings is with it. Sounds like it was an interesting place." Hunter looked at him. "Who are they?"

Waving the book away. Bill crossed his legs. "I would like to read your thoughts but you keep the journal. I have the original. Through distant studies, I saw those island people to be like us, except they are smaller in stature. They are around five foot four, which appeared to be the average height." Hunter looked back out the window.

Bill cleared his throat and continued. "For the most part they do speak a form of English with only a few minor variations of some words. Their time is not measured in minutes or hours, but with emphasis of the sun's position and on the movement of shadows." Bill smiled as Hunter's reflection returned an intent look. "Day and night are the same as here, only time for each is equal all year round."

Bill took a quick draw of his pipe and blew a small ring of smoke. "Wild creatures also inhabitant this island, some strange and very dangerous. Most seem to be the same as the wildlife here except birds of prey are two to three times the size as you know them to be. Other creatures roam the wild too. They are different from what we know; quite large and very vicious. Most of these beasts are sworn enemies to the good people of those lands. The humans, however, don't exist in total harmony as they once did."

"You speak in present tense, Bill. Where is this island?" Hunter turned and walked behind the desk and took his seat.

"Oh I forget myself sometimes. When I talk of it, it is like a second home to me." Bill got up and walked over to look out the window. "Where was I? Oh yes! Yes, usually there was an occasional coup to overthrow leaders. The tribes who usually get along will turn quickly on one another but the leaders must have been strong. They had to be strong and merciless to be in total control." Bill noticed the vague expression of confusion on Hunter's face. "There were signs of one uprising, well maybe the last one. However, it was very large in comparison to the ones we previously discovered. One tribe possessed the power to control and destroy those that opposed them." Bill spoke clear as he turned. He looked deep into Hunter's dark eyes. "I believe the people of the island had hoped that someone would avenge their beloved slain ruler and set them free again." Bill shook his head. "At least that is my thought."

Hunter looked back at Bill as if seeing him for the first time. "You seem to be dodging my question, Bill. Where is this place?" Hunter rubbed his face, his words muffled. "You talk as if you've lived there, like speaking with an authority of it." Shaking his head. "Like you are an ambassador."

"Oh?" Bill had a shocked look come over his face.

Hunter leaned his seat back. "Oh yeah. O'Cey told me you had shown them some land and they bought it. I didn't know you'd met them?"

"Yes, fine men. I met them at one of the games and have been in contact several times since."

"Mac had said something of a book you gave to Dil." Hunter studied his old friend. 'He said it was some kind of a book about magic or something."

Drawing on his pipe again, Bill blew a small smoke ring toward Hunter. "Yes, it was an old book I found years ago. It was from the same island in my research. Thought he'd enjoy it. He's a fine but misunderstood young man." Bill smiled as he turned to look out the window again. The students were staring to the south. He turned to face Hunter again. "The subtropical island is to the east of the . . . ." Bill was interrupted by someone calling for Hunter.

"What now!" Hunter jumped from his chair to the door and in a flash he was outside "What is it!"

Bill close right behind Hunter but spoke before he was outside. "Look Hunter, over there!" He pointed to where the visions keep appearing. "Let's go see what happened boss!" Bill walked in front of the larger man toward the same location where the amulet was found. The same red head boy yelled. "Mister Hunter, someone blew a horn over the hill!" Hunter waved at the crew as he turned back toward office. The day is almost over Bill. We need to talk later if it is ok with you?"

"Yes sir Hunter, we will. By the way, everything is ready. I'll talk to you soon." Hunter didn't turn but waved over his shoulder.

*   *   *

"Mister Jansen, you know you are going to get caught with one of your crooked deals." The large black man carefully studied the road as he drove the long black limousine. A disgruntled snort is heard from the shadowed rear of the vehicle. "I think you need to hold up some on these three . . ." The driver was cut off in mid sentence.

"Shush I think you need to mind your place!" Barked the hidden figure. "You are nothing but my driver and I am your boss. Speak to me with the respect I deserve!" After a loud grunt, the voice continued. "I can replace you with no problem. Is that understood boy?!"

The driver rolled his dark eyes and shrugged. He released a soft sigh, "I guess if you think . . . ." He paused. "Excuse me sir, you do know what is best. I did speak out of turn. I apologize"

"That's right I do know best and don't you forget that." A devious giggle fills the limo as it speeds to its destination. "Do you hear me?!"

"Yes sir." No sincerity could be heard in the voice. The back seat of the big car was silent. The driver saw the mouth in the mirror work but he didn't hear any of the words coming from it.

* * *

Hunter had reached the office steps when he heard the van doors close. He spun to see Bill wave as he opened the driver's door. He thought to himself, "How did he meet O'Cey if he just saw us for the first time?" Hunter ran after the van yelling, "Bill, stop! Bill!"

Bill was in the driver seat and had started the van when Hunter had reached the door. "Bill, what are you not telling me? You know something."

Bill grinned as he put the van in drive. "I know some things and others I don't. You just have a need to be ready. All I can say is, great eagles take time to fly." Hunter stood in shock as the van pulled off. He waved both arms to stop the van but it continued to kick up dust as it rolled out of sight.

It seemed to be a long walk back to the table under the big tree. Hunter's mind raced. "How would he know? No way! Maybe I am letting him in this. No he can't. Damn Bill now I've got a headache."

As he got to the table Hunter, looked out over the site again and once more he saw the circle of warriors, but it was different this time. Jinx and Tunk had walked up behind Hunter. This vision was for all to see. The circle of warriors sat looking at the three men.

A single man, large in stature, stood up from the circle and walked to the front looking at all three men standing behind the table. Hunter recognized him to be the same man that spoke to him in the last vision. He looked first at Hunter studying him, then he looked to Jinx, and finally he stopped and studied Tunk. The warrior smiled. After what felt as an eternity he looked back to Hunter.

This chief was a large man and anyone could see that he was a man of war, solid and fearless. No fear would ever have been present in this man. When he spoke, you could hear the command in his voice. "Be wary sons of my blood. Your change is nearly at hand! The door opens for you so be ready! Beware of the evil that will surround you. Soon you will know who you are and what your purpose in life!" Jinx rubbed his eyes. Tunk stared with his mouth open. The warrior stood ridged with his arms crossed and his eyes focused on each of the trio at the same time. His glance pierced deep inside each man. "Show no mercy, for none will be shown to you!"

Slowly the other members of the council appeared and took their place next to the lead warrior. The war party all looked toward the limo pulling into the yard. They watched a short fat man crawl out of the back door. Jansen was yelling as he slammed the rear door. The first chief Hunter had just recently come to know spoke. "That is not the problem at hand, just look for the people that are in need. You will know them when you see them. Remember you confuse yourself with too much thought." The whole party silently laughed as they looked at Jansen and pointed. Hunter, Jinx and Tunk hadn't looked at Jansen. As their last word drifted into silence, the whole vision began to fade. The chorus of voices blended as they drifted from sight. "Stand fast! Stand strong! Stand as one!"

The three friends stood staring over the sight without looking at Jansen. "What are you three doing? Trying to ignore me?" They all looked at Jansen in unison. He was standing with the books from the table held tight to his chest as if he were protecting a prize possession. "Did you hear me?! Wipe those stupid looks off your stinking injun faces. I am going to check these books and I will prosecute any discrepancy!" Jensen stood red faced in front of the trio. He turned to look at the limo and screamed, "Get back into the limo!" Jerking his fat face to Hunter. "Did I make myself clear?" The three looked at each other then all shrugged as the driver slammed the door. The large man turns and grins at each of them, then nods his head. Jensen wheeled around. "Fool I said get back in the car!"

"Why are you still standing there with those stupid looks on your faces?" The little fat man's face was turning redder. "Are you all insane?"

Hunter shook his head as Jinx and Tunk came out of their own stupor.

Jansen continued. "I have had my fill of you three stupid injuns. I don't understand why I let that fool Bill talk me into dealing with you stealing savages." Jinx stepped forward. Jansen shrieked, "Touch me and I will sue!" Hunter stomped his right foot and Jensen squealed as he turned and half waddled, half ran to the limo. Yelling as he made his way to escape, "I have half a mind to report you attacking me!" Tunk finally realized his mouth was hanging open and chomped it closed.

One last screech from Jansen was heard as the slammed the door. "Hurry boy! Get me away from this filth hole!"

"Half a mind is right. About time that fool leaves!" growled Jinx. "One of these days I will lift his scalp!"

Hunter laughed, "You know the French taught the natives here to do that. It wasn't practiced much either."

"Why you got to give encyclopedia answers Hunter? You think too much." Tunk laughed, "besides scalping did scare the hell out of a lot of white people."

Hunter looked shocked at the words of his friend. He nodded. "But that is what we are remembered for."

Jinx danced before he spoke. "I still would like to peel skin from that little fat fool, wouldn't you Tunk?"

"Oh yeah, me too!" Tunk laughed, "I'll hold him down for you bro."

The limo spun around in a cloud of dust and barreled down the drive. Tunk excitedly walked around Jinx to face Hunter. "That was the council, huh? Man! I believed you, but that was . . . Whoo whoo man that was so cool! Is that the one you've been telling us about?" Tunk shook his head. "Man did we look totally stupid standing here."

"Yeah! Well, today was the first time I had seen the warrior who spoke today. It was right before you two showed up! Anyway, did you two understand that talk?"

Jinx walked around the table looking over the site. Tunk stood behind him and stared as if waiting for an answer. Jinx stopped and look across the table at Hunter. "Maybe." Jinx nodded with a satisfied smile on his face. "Tunk, you are the one that looked stupid; mouth all gaped open like a dunce. I was amazed, but maybe I think we know what all this talk is about."

Tunk stood still and dropped his head. With a puzzled look on his face he looked up to Jinx, "Really?"

"Think Tunk! Explain to me what we found today."

Tunk looked up. "I don't know what it is."

Jinx looked From Tunk then to Hunter. "The door?"

"Well maybe? Yeah, it could be!" Tunk nodded with a big grin, "Yeah! It does look like a door! But it goes nowhere. It's just a piece of stone really."

Hunter raised his hands in confusion. "What are you two babbling about?"

"Oh yeah, you don't know yet." Jinx reached over the table and grabbed Hunter's left arm. "Come on, need to see something we found today."

Tunk started running to where the vans had been parked by Jinx's Jeep. "Take the Jeep!" Tunk impatiently yells as he opens a map, "Come on let's move. Time's a wasting!"

Jinx walked with Hunter to the jeep. "I say it's got to be this door that is to bring about this change, right?"

Hunter nodded his head. "That last guy spoke to me as if I or we were family. He said sons of my blood or something like that. He was acting like we were bred for something." Hunter stopped Jinx. "Take a look at this." Hunter hands the medallion to Jinx. "It was found today."

Jinx stared at the object. "I don't understand it; all those stupid things that were found." Jinx looked toward his jeep. Hunter, do you think they were planted?"

Tunk was watching from the back of the Jeep. "Hey, what are you two clowns doing? Let's go!"

"Maybe, but why? And by who?" Hunter and Jinx started walking again to the jeep. "Bill did act weird. But how could he have known about our tats?"

Jinx shook his head as he jumped in the driver's seat. "Don't know bro. I don't see any reason for all of this yet." Hunter nodded. Tunk looked confused.

Rocks took flight as the jeep spun around. They raced down the drive. Jinx didn't stop at the end of the drive, instead the jeep races onto the main road. The tires squeal as Jinx locks the wheels to the right. The large wheels sling gravel as they try to cut into into the roadbed.

"Jinx, take a right into that small field just past that grove of trees." Folding the map, Tunk leaned forward and pointed. Jinx barely slows to make the turn in the field. "Whoa man! We do want to get there in one piece!"

The Jeep skids to a stop at the top of a hill As the dust catches up to them the jeep disappears. The hill overlooked a bowl shaped valley full of large trees. The trees at the bottom were as tall as the rim they were standing on. Jinx gets out of the Jeep. "I don't understand why that amulet looks like our tattoos." Hunter shrugged.

"Hunter, we lucked up on finding this thing. It's buried there in the trees." Tunk pointed down the ridge. "It's over there. What amulet?

Jinx handed the amulet to Tunk. Tunk studied it for a few seconds. "What we need to know now is, how does that thorn amulet, the sphere, and that key thing fit in with this door?"

Tunk took the lead by running down the hill. Hunter followed Tunk down into the big basin. "The first two don't have anything to do with this area or of anything I know. What I want to know is why were they put where they were found? And I don't have a clue about the amulet. Now what is this next thing?" Hunter stopped to look at each of them as they drew up to a small rise in the valley floor.

Jinx shook his head. "You know we were looking at the items as if they belonged here. We were trying to fit them in with the artifacts that were discovered. It looks like there's a bigger picture developing."

Tunk scratched his head, then laughed. "I do agree. Tell me who put this here?" pushing Hunter back into the hike. "We're almost there." After passing a clearing in the woods, they started into the next tree line.

"Right now I have to say that Bill knows more than he lets on." Hunter laughed. "Besides, one of the warriors told me I think too hard." The trees got bigger and thicker. Hunter looked up to see the full height of the trees. They were walking on an old trail. A lot of growth covered the trail but you could see it at one time was once well traveled.

Jinx shook his head then pointed ahead. "Hunter, walk through that opening over there." Hunter looked at the end of the trail and Jinx laughed. "Go on and explain what you see to us."

Hunter instinctively touched his Bowie knife as if he were walking into trouble. He stopped after he broke the tree line and stared for a few seconds. "Looks like a giant tombstone." Standing on a small flat rise, in the center of the bowl shaped valley, a large pillar of white stone faced the east. The floor surrounding the pillar was made of strange, flat, shiny gray tiles that were cut into a perfectly symmetrical design. Hunter slowly walked up the mount and his eyes scanned the tiles leading away from him to the center where the pillar stood. He looked up to a thick canopy of trees completely hiding the area. "What is this place?"

Jinx walked up to the stone pillar. "Hunter, come here." Jinx reaches out to the monument. "The stone feels cool."

Hunter walked to where Jinx was standing and touched the stone. "Yeah, and it has a wet feeling too." He studies his dry hand as he pulled it from the rock.

Tunk joined them and rubbed the stone. "Ain't no relative of mine built this! Yours maybe?" Tunk put his ear near the stone. "Hunter, listen! It sounds like a wind tunnel blowing." Tunk stood straight and looked around. "If you look, there ain't no trees moving! How is that?"

Hunter circled the rock studying it from the other angles. "It is arched like a tombstone."

Jinx stopped Hunter in his travel. "Or does it looks like . . . a door?" Hunter looked at Jinx with questioning eyes. Jinx pointed to a small divot close to the edge. "Does this look like it could be a key hole? It looks solid, but I don't know."

Tunk shook his head and laughed. "You know Jinx, I didn't even think of that when we first saw this thing." Tunk knocked on the face of the pillar. He laughed. "Well, I guess nobody's home." Jinx pushed Tunk away from the object they were studying.

Hunter walked back to the east side studying, the door. "Alright, you two have finally seen the council." Hunter looked around the tile floor. "And Bill said something before he left about being ready but what blew me away was he said great eagles take time to fly." Shifting his gaze to each of them, Hunter stood with his back to the strange marker. "Same words as one of the chiefs. So what you're telling me is it sounds like Bill knows something? I don't think he's a mind reader? Lucky guess, maybe?" Hunter looked toward the trail they came through. "What do you think? Am I making more of this than it really is?" Jinx and Tunk were looking at Hunter as he stumbled through his questioning babble.

Tunk looked back to the stone in wonder. "Hey guys! Look, something's going on here!" The three stare as the pillar began to shine. The glow fades leaving them in awe looking at their reflections. The stone surface shifted again.

Jinx grabbed his knife. "Ok, what's going on now?" Tunk had his knife out and looked frantically at his friends. Hunter's knife was drawn and ready for anything.

The center of the stone became misty. As it starting clearing, a black arrow whistled from the stone. The trio quickly ducked and rolled in separate directions. The battle trained men never took their eyes from dark images now forming on the other side.

Jinx moved closer to flank the door. "Am I as crazy as you Tunk! I see a battle and I even hear the sounds of a battle coming from in there.

Hunter jumped toward the door. "Jinx look! Someone's climbing through that thing!" Quick reflexes and battle readiness take over. The three poised for whatever may come.

Jinx rolls in front of the door. He grabs the small arm, with his left hand, as it tries to crawl out. With an easy jerk, a body appeared. Jinx tossed it to the tiled floor. Before the young teen age size body hit the ground, he was yelling. "Pull the key! Pull the key!" He twisted on the ground to face the door and continued his cry, "Pull the key! Pull it now!"

More arrows found their way through the opening as Tunk rolled to the door where a shiny brass key hung loosely in the keyhole. Tunk looked into the open hole. "Jinx something big is coming out!" Jinx readied his body for a defensive maneuver and watched Tunk as he grabbed for the key. Jinx threw the large Bowie knife from his right hand into his left, as a hideous monster charged out of the portal.

Easily Jinx blocks the creature's black blade with his large Bowie knife. Grabbing the creature with his right hand, he flips it with a hip roll. The beast hits the ground with a loud thud.

Rising quickly, the creature snapped it's large jaws displaying many rows of deadly teeth. Only four feet separated the beast from the armed man and he noticed that his foe stood only two hands taller than himself. The monster knew that it was the same man that had tossed him like an old rag. The man stood like a solid giant, ready to fight. The creature quickly jumps to its feet and turns to keep an eye on the new enemy standing in his way to get back home.

Tunk grabs the key and pulls, nothing happened. More arrows fly through the opening searching for a victim. Tunk gives the key a quick twist and it falls into his big hand. The images vanish from the other side as the doorway returns to stone. Tunk jumps up and stands to the right of the unsightly creature. "That thing is sho 'nough ugly!"

The beast jerks it's large head and snarls. It hunches as if ready to attack.

The boy quickly rolls from where he was laying, then jumps up to see who had spoken. Tunk looks down as the boy stood beside him. The stranger looked down at his own body then back to the man that dwarfed him. The beast rolls it's large ugly face toward his first threat and snaps its jaws.

The boy jumped away from Tunk, only to bump into Jinx. Jinx's big left hand grabbed the boy by the front of his shirt and sweeps him behind without looking. The boy looked around to the right of his rescuer and his mouth drops open at the sight of Hunter. The third man stood as a tower, the tallest of them all. He stares in disbelief as he steps back shifting his body to see each of the trio. The small stranger watched as each of the giant men readied for an attack from the beast.

The beast jumps at Jinx, swinging it's black blade in a downward motion. Jinx blocks the blade but, it catches his sleeve, tearing it to the elbow. Jinx gracefully side steps to the left keeping himself in front of the boy. His powerful right hand slams into the throat of the beast. The creature wobbles back. Jinx grabs its ragged clothes as he jumps around the creature. As he lands, he slings the green-black monster in the center of the three.

The beast lands hard on its back. Its deadly blade bounces lifeless onto the tiled floor. The boy stares at Jinx in awe. He has never seen anyone manhandle such a large creature.

Jinx reaches back and grabs the boy, pushing him toward Tunk. "Watch him!" Tunk grabs the boy placing him closer to the side of the portal and behind him. The creature was quick to rebound back on its feet. Staring at the boy then to Tunk.

Tunk stands guard in front of the young man. "Boy! What is that thing!" Tunk waved his blade at the creature as it looked at the boy.

The hideous goat face looking creature roars. Jinx moved far from Tunk's right while Hunter quickly moves ahead then right to complete a tighter triangle.

Cautiously the boy spoke. "It's one of the large Trolls!" Looking at the three giants, he realized his voice cracked showing fear. "The wizard Alexar created from them, an army he calls Nimenole Troll. This breed was crossed with the trolls from Neach." Maybe not full off fear but a lot of amazement.

The troll appeared to be coming out of its shock from the hard landing. It shook its oversized head throwing its long arms up, roaring another challenge. The beast pivoted quickly looking at each of the three giant men standing strong between it and freedom. On top of that they were protecting his quarry. Growling, it dove at Tunk, the smaller man. Tunk spun in a tight circle to his left. His left foot lands hard on the troll's left jaw.

The beast spins before it slams to the tile again, back in center of the giants. A nasty splat sounded as it landed on its grotesque face. As the troll rose slowly it retrieved its lost weapon. Tunk frowned at a greasy spot left on the slab where the thing kissed the flooring. The beast rose slower this time. Armed again, it looked cautiously at the three men towering over it. The snarling beast watched the only man it had not faced yet, Hunter. It's pride hurt, it wanted a kill. It needed a kill.

Hunter eased forward to challenge it. "Step back so it can move on me!"

It looked back to Tunk and the boy. "More room!" The beast jerked back to the yelling man and howled. Hunter released his own war cry, as he moved closer. The beast looked back at Tunk, then back to the giant man moving in on him. Hunter shouted at the creature. "No! It's my turn now! Charge me!"

The troll jerked it's head to the boy for a second. Turning quickly back to Hunter it snapped its powerful jaws again, as if saying it wanted to fight Tunk for the boy. Hunter raised his weapon as the troll snapped it's jaws again. It looked as if it were a trapped rabid animal. It eyed the larger man coming closer. Tunk pushed the boy back a few more steps. Jinx also backed away to allow Hunter to draw an attack. They both drew their tomahawks, ready to let it loose on the enraged creature if it tried to run. Snarling again at the massive human that was coming closer, the beast dove toward Hunter. The deadly black blade sliced through the still air.

Hunter had moved quicker than the creature could have imagined. A tomahawk had filled his empty hand too and a loud crack sounded as the it met the black blade. Hunter had decided to end this deadly game. He buried his Bowie knife deep into the monster's chest and lifted the troll high in the air. The creature took another flight. Hunter flipped it to the southern edge of the slab.

It hit the ground to rise no more. The four watched as the beast took its last gurgling breath.

The boy looked from one giant to the other with a surprised look and his voice cracked as he spoke again. "Each of you fought the troll with ease!" He walked to the center where the troll was trapped.

Jinx looked down at the boy. "Boy where do you come from."

The boy did not acknowledge the question, he simply looked at the dead troll. "We would do well if you come to help my people. Evil has taken over Rhea. When Thorn was slain, he spoke of the giants avenging him. I was sent to find the seed of Thorn." He said looking again at each man standing at least two feet taller than him. "I know the prophesies and they speak of the giants. It says they will avenge the blood of Thorn. Are you the giants I am commanded to seek?" He looked at each of them then to the portal. After a few seconds he look to each of the large trio for answers. Each of the large men watched as a worried look crept across his face. They wondered as the boy took a deep breath. Once again he spoke in a voice trembling not from fear but of urgent need. "The people of Rhea are slain every day. They cry for help!" His head turns to study each of the men and the worried look slowly turned into one of anger. "My people die for the pleasure of their cries." Finally, a weak smile grew on his face. "It looks as if I have been led to you."

Hunter looks from Tunk to Jinx and they all move as one to stand over the troll. The small stranger finished with a plea. "Will the giants return with me?"

Jinx walked over to the slain troll. "Are there many of these nimrods where you come from?" Jinx held his nose as he stood over the dead creature. "Is it me are does this thing just stink?" He pinched his nose harder to stop the smell from the strange dead monster. "It's blood even stinks too!"

Tunk laughed. "You stink too and not just 'cause it's blood is all over you, Jinx! You know O'Cey and Mac sure missed a fun little fight. They would've loved this."

The young man spoke with more confidence. "They're called Nimenole. This troll is not of Nimenole descent. And yes, there are many of each." Looking from the dead beast to the surrounding forest, the small man looked back to Jinx. "You must rid yourself of its blood and clean your weapons. You three act as if you know nothing of trolls or even Neminoles. Are there none here?"

Tunk laughed as he answered. "Naw. If I remember it right, our grandfathers help to kill the last of them many years ago."

Hunter walked back to the door studying it again. "That's enough Tunk!" He ran his big hand over the surface. After several silent minutes, he slowly turned to the helpless little man. Drumming his chin, Hunter walked around studying the small battle ground. The small figure watched in silence as Hunter walked back to the stone. Deep in thought, Hunter was silent, even his walking was without noise.

The young man looked close and leaned closer to hear nothing. After several minutes, he turns to his other rescuers. "Why is it that you make no walking sound for such a big man?"

Hunter stopped walking and looked from the boy, then to his friends. "What do you two say? Do we help him get home or not?" Hunter's cold stare returned to meet the boy's. Hunter stared deep into the young man's eye. The boy returned the stare without a blink. Hunter nodded, "Boy, what's your name?"

The young man bowed his chest. "I am no boy! And my name is Ian, I am a keeper of the keys."

Jinx laughs. "You do what?"

Ian moved to stand near the door. "I was made a keeper of the keys and the last one as I know it." Hunter walks over to stand by Ian in front of the portal. "The seers appoint those who had the fire in them, as they say anyway." Laughing in spite of himself. "I do not even know what the fire is, but they raised me as a keeper. I am to protect the key of Thorn's doorways." He reached out to rub the stone doorway. Tunk opens his big hand to study the key.

Hunter looked at the young man. "So someone sent you here?" Ian snapped his head and his brown shoulder length hair fanned through the air. Hunter laughed then looked at Jinx. "Jinx, he could pass for your little brother."

Ian glared at the trio as each laughed. He was beginning to become impatient. "The seer of Toll sent me, but not to this place!". He waved his arms around him. "But I believe you may be the giants I seek, so maybe yes I was sent here."

Tunk looked at the dead Nimenole. "These creatures roam freely in your world?"

"Yes. trolls and larger trolls wander also, but not as many now as before. Most of the smaller Nimenoles are controlled by Alexar, the others just attack people because we live." Tunk shook his head. Ian continued, "Alexar cannot manage trolls as easily as the Nimenoles. They roam over most of Rhea. Seeing their puzzled looks, Ian continues. "Alexar created the Nimenole Troll yet they do not match the trolls in size and they can be controlled to a certain extent. The Nimenoles are smarter. It is hard for me to believe none roam here?" The three looked simultaneously at the dead creature.

"You said, Rhea?" Tunk looked from the troll to Ian. "That is where you come from?"

"Yes, the place I come from is Rhea. I am from the township of Toll, but we waste time. My people die. They die now! The party I crossed the Outlands with, were in search of aid for Toll. The people there are under attack maybe even as we speak." Ian stormed in a circle. "My friends died back there!" Pointing at the stone, "We were attacked! I felt something from the door, so I opened it."

Jinx nodded. "So much for the visions and the door opening. What do you think now Hunt?"

Hunter shook his head at Jinx's question. "Maybe, but why?"

Tunk shrugged. "Giants?" Ian looked at him quizzical. "You said giants?"

Ian nodded. "Yes, I was taught the giants would avenge the blood of Thorn."

"The blood from that thing stinks. I'm changing this shirt!" Jinx stood facing Hunter. As he pulled his stained shirt, Ian saw his tattoo.

Ian's voice became excited. "See you wear the mark of Thorn!" He looked from Hunter to Tunk. "Do you also have the mark?" They both exposed theirs. "You are the seed! I was told I would know the seed by the mark of Thorn." He looked pleased, then puzzled. "I wouldn't have thought the seed and giants to be the same, but you must be." He looked at the tattoos again. "Prophecies say they will be known by the mark of Thorn."

Hunter put his hand on the boy's shoulder, pulling the amulet from his pocket. "Is this the mark of Thorn?"

Ian nodded. "So will you see now you must journey with me?"

Hunter held up his hand. "Hold on, tell us about your journey to here."

Ian pulled away and went in to hysterics. "No! We have no time! My people are being slaughtered as we speak! We must leave now!" Ian turned to the door as he felt for the key that usually hung around his neck. He spun to see if Tunk still had this item. "Rhea needs you! We must return to the Seer! we must go now!"

Hunter's huge body flexed as he snapped at Ian. "Stop that!" Ian cowered at the boom of Hunter's voice. "We have to know more about what we will face! Do you not understand? We will not charge in blind, do you understand that!" Ian's timid nod spoke loud enough.

Tunk and Jinx were at Hunter's side. Tunk put a hand on Hunter's shoulder. "Hunter, it does sounds like they need us." Tunk lifted Ian's bowed head to look into his eyes. "I say, yes. Let's go!"

Ian nodded enthusiastically. "We do need the help of Thorn's giant! Rhea has fallen to the evil! It must be stopped!"

Hunter raised his hand to silent Ian. Ian lowered his head as he pleaded one more time. "Please, come with me."

Jinx scratched his chin. "Once again, who sent you here?"

Ian looked at Jinx then back to Hunter. "No one sent me here.

We were attacked by the trolls. I think they were after the key." He said looking at Tunk, the man who pulled the key. "I was the last one and I saw everyone else die. I lost my sword and I used the key to escape." Turning to gaze at the troll. "I did not know that the answer to our problems stood here, but I did feel something on this side and here you are."

"If we weren't here how many of those beasts would have come through and killed you?" yelled Jinx. "They would have the key and then they could try to do their bidding here!"

"I only used it because I felt something calling me here."

Tunk put a firm hand on Jinx's shoulder. "Easy Jinx. Even if he stayed, they would have killed him and took the key." Tunk looked at the key in his left hand.

"Hunter!" Tunk yelled as he tossed the key.

Ian eyed the key as Hunter studied it. Looking to the door then back to the key, Hunter smiled. "It looks like the thing we found with that blue orb, doesn't it?" The small man looked surprised.

Ian reached for the key, Hunter closed his big hand. "You have the orb of Sumra too?" All three look at Ian in unison.

"If that's what it's called, but how it got here is the question?" Hunter looked at Tunk, but held on tight to the key. "It's something to do with Bill, I know it."

Jinx moved. "I'm with you on that, but the real question is, do we take him back or not?" Jinx took a stance by Tunk.

"Ok, ok! We'll get Ian back safely. We can try to help and then come back to our own lives." Hunter looked at his two friends. "You two get enough supplies to last maybe a week or so. Get our gear and I'll stay here and talk with Ian to sort out some things. Maybe I can figure out what we'll be up against."

Tunk slapped Jinx on the back and grinned. "Hunter, we'll be back in a flash! It's adventure time!"

"Cool bro, be back soon." Jinx raced Tunk down the trail.

Jinx looked at Hunter and laughed. "Hey big bird! I mean great eagle, remember, don't think so hard." He turned and ran to catch Tunk.

Ian watched as Jinx and Tunk disappeared in the thick growth of trees at the base of the hill. "Thank you. What do I call you?"

"Huh? Me? Oh yeah, call me Hunter."

"I am Ian. Are you the hunter of evil in this land?

"Slow down boy. If you want our help I need you to answer my questions first." Ian nodded reluctantly.

The starting of the large truck's engine, startled Ian. He jumped at the unknown sound. "What kind of beast is that?"

Hunter laughed as Ian squatted into a defensive stance. "That is the sound of a weasel." He laughed again at the slapping sound Ian made while grabbing at an empty sheath. Hunter bent down to pat Ian on his shoulder. "It's all right." Hunter pointed to a stone stool, opposite from the trail he, Jinx and Tunk had entered from. "Let's go sit under that tree and talk." They moved across the tiled flooring, away from the hill his two friends had just climbed.

Hunter listened as Ian talked of life in his world.

"Ian, how did you know the door would lead you here?"

"I did not know where it would lead me. The seers had always told me to go west and I would find the seed." Ian shrugged. "He gave me the key and told me to enter when there was an utmost need. I did feel something was drawing me to the door. But then the trolls attacked us."

"So you sensed our presence?" Hunter looked at the door to Ian's world.

"I cannot explain it but I felt like someone was pulling at me to go through the door."

"Did you know you would find help here?" Ian shrugged.

Hunter nodded. "So you know of the door as you call it. Who made it?"

"I know not who made it but maybe the seer will know."

"Who is this seer? You have mentioned it several times in our talk." Hunter stood up looking in the direction the other two had run. He then looked up to see the sun light was dimming. It would be dark soon so he gestured for Ian to walk. As they walked out into the forest, they picked up wood for a fire.

Their conversation carried through the task of finding a spot away from the smell of the dead troll. After a while the talks ended and Hunter sat quietly watching the dancing fire. He was deep in thought sorting out the information which he had gathered and how to use it to help Ian and his people.

Hunter came out of his trance when he heard the truck returning. Ian jumped as the sound of the truck grew closer. "How is it your people live with all these monstrous weasels roaming these lands?" Hunter placed a big right hand on Ian's shoulder easing his tension a little. Ian saw the confident look in Hunter's face and nodded. "Hunter if they are as big as they sound I believe I would rather fight an army of trolls in my homeland!"

"Well you just have to know how to deal with them. Anyways, we have a fire and they'll stay away from us. I just hope my half-wit friends can follow the fire's light to find us." Hunter stared in the fire for a brief time. He quickly snaps out of it. "Damn that's the place in Bill's journal."

Ian jumped to his feet at rustling coming from the forest. "What is that? Weasels!" Ian didn't move his eyes from the thick tree line.

Hunter laughed. "No it's just Jinx and Tunk."

"How do you know this, are you a seer also?"

Hunter's laughter increased. "No Ian. Any weasel would be frightened by my brave, large comrades. You think?"

Ian nodded "You are all big and seasoned warriors. I've seen all of you fight."

Tunk and Jinx soon pushed through the tree line. Jinx dismounted and Ian stood staring at the monstrous trio of horses. Tunk laughed at him. "They are only dangerous to their enemies." Ian gave a nervous nod.

Jinx was at Hunter's side and spoke. "Trouble Hunt, that weasel is on the prowl again." Jinx handed an extra Bowie knife and a short sword to Ian. "Here, you may need these."

Hunter looked at the other two and laughed. "You have no idea what you just added to my story of that engine noise." Hunter shook his head and laughed again. "Tunk how bout cook up something and keep Ian occupied. I'm gonna take a walk with Jinx."

Tunk nodded. Ian watched Hunter and Jinx walked off into the dark shadows beyond the tree line, then he turned to help Tunk. "I would like to thank all the giants for their help." They started preparing their food. As they waited, they positioned fed bags on the horses. The pot began to boil over the crackling fire. They hobbled the horses.

Tunk looked down at the smaller man, standing five foot three and smiled. "No sweat, Ian." The smaller man nodded as if he understood.

The light of the fire seemed to have been devoured by the darkness. Jinx stopped walking. "Hunter, when we were in town getting supplies, Jed talked to us. He said some FBI are here and asking questions."

"About what?"

"Jansen has been covering up stolen jewels or something." Jinx looked back to the dim light of the fire. "He said we're being blamed in it somehow." Hunter shook his head. "Jinx I can only say I'm sorry for hooking up with him. I only used him because of his money funding for this dig." Hunter shook his head. "You know what? Bill sent him to me, damn it."

"The more you talk of Bill and the strange goings on, the more I feel the same way you do. He knows more that he lets on too." Jinx shook his head. "We'll deal with that later. What do you think about all this? Do you think we can help this boy? Can we do any good for his people?"

"All of us had said at one time or another, if we lived back in the day, could have made a difference with what has been done to our own people. Well if we were to sit and think hard about that statement the answer is plain. We could have done nothing." Hunter released a long sigh. "We would have made no difference at all. We would have been rival tribes, each of our tribes would be too proud of their giant warriors." Looking back to see if Ian was visible. "But now, we are together, we are skilled and strong. We can make a difference for those people. I think we may be able to help."

Jinx laughed. "I guess we'll find out soon enough, right?" Hunter nodded as they headed back to the camp.

Hunter walked over to Ian and held out the amulet. He stared at the symbol of the thorn. "Wear this and you are one with the seed." Ian took the object as Hunter finished. "Wear it to show that you ride with the giants."

Tunk smiled and he pulled a leather cord from his pocket. He took the trinket from Ian and tied it with the cord around his neck. Tunk laughed, "Now we are all one with the Thorn!" Pulling his Bowie knife and turning to Hunter, "One Tribe!" Holding his blade flat on its side.

Jinx joined in forming their circle of three. "Yeah!" He pulled his Bowie knife and placed it on top of Tunk's. "One hand!" Jinx looked to Ian and grinned.

Hunter laughed while pulling his large blade. "I guess we do need a corny ceremony." He placed his large knife on top of Jinx's. "One blade!"

Ian squeezed in the crowd and placed his new blade on top. "We are the blood of brothers Thorn!"

They all laughed, Jinx shook his head. "That's a good name little man!"

Hunter nodded as he pushed his knife in its home. "I guess from now on we will be known by the blood of brothers Thorn."

Chapter 3

A New Life

"Hey O'Cey!" Dil looked up from the slow moving creek. The scrawny young man stood knee deep in the cool waters turning whirl pools with each hand. "O'Cey you hear me?" His eldest brother was standing on the gentle sloping bank staring at what appeared to be a large white tombstone. "O'Cey if you let me I could use a spell to move these big rocks! It would be easier that way you know!"

"Dil put yer back into it lad!" Mac roared as he shook his head. "How you think to grow strong as the others of your clan! You gotta work at it!" The third brother stood on the bank with a large flat stone clutched in his huge fists. "Are you daft boy?"

"Not now Mac!" Roared O'Cey rubbing his woolly head. "Dil I tell you again magic is not real. Maybe another time, maybe another place."

"Stop babying the lad O'Cey!" snapped Mac. "Dil! Magic is real only in those once upon a time stories!" Mac dropped the stone then knuckled his long mustache. "I still say you be touched!"

O'Cey stroked his eighteen inch long beard, as he looked down at the youngest brother, Dilman McNure, knee deep in the creek. O'Cey pointed over his left shoulder. "Dil, do you not think the stone pillar, would look nice when this creek bank be cleaned up?"

"I say it would, O'Cey! But Mac say I be touched." whined Dil.

"And you do be boy!" laughed Mac. "Put yer back into it and work lad! We got a lot of stones to move!"

Dil reached deep in the water and pulled up a handful of mud. He slung the sticky clay at the middle brother, O'Mallay McNure. "You are just mad cause you cannot do magic, Mac!" The soggy red clay made a splat as it hit Mac in his thick chest. The splatter covered his chin and face.

Mac wiped the mud from his face as O'Cey laughed. Mac jumped toward Dil. "I get you for that boy!" Mac hit the knee deep water hard. As he landed he lost his footing on the slick bottom of the creek bed. His large body did not have time to wobble, he just fell face first into the creek. Dil laughed as he jumped to freedom on the bank.

Mac stood up spewing water and thrashed around looking for his little brother. "Where you be Dil!"

The older brother stormed to the creek edge and roared. "Stop that you two!"

O'Cey's large body tensed as he threw his large arms in the air. "That be enough, back to work! Now!" O'Cey flapped his big tree limb size arms as he yelled. "We need to be done here! We got a house to build!"

Standing on the edge of the creek, Dil bent down and flipped a large rock from the bank into the creek. Mac jumped out of the way as the rock rolled towards him. He lost his balance again. The loud splash in the water made O'Cey laugh. Dil studied the soft mud where the rock had been resting.

"Hey, look, a key! Look O'Cey, a key!" Mac rebounded quicker this time jumping toward his younger brother. Before he could grab Dil, O'Cey grabbed Mac by the neck. Dil pulled the object from the mud.

Mac wiggled from the iron grip. "Boy'o! I say you be touched! Now Mac gonna touch you!" Turning to look at the eldest brother. O'Cey's scowl was all that was needed to silence Mac. Mac simply frowned at his response.

O'Cey took the object from Dil. "Mac! Leave the wee one be!" Mac pouted as Dil stuck out his tongue.

O'Cey studied the small bone white cylinder with a loop on one end. "It do look a little like a piece of an old skeleton key to me, Dil. But what do I know."

Mac took the thing from O'Cey. His quick study grew into a twisted smile. "If that be a key, boy, Mac'll kiss your grubby foot!" Dil made a circular motion with both his hands. Mac shook his head as he screamed. "What are you doing now, fool!"

"Turning you into a toad Mac!" shouted Dil.

O'Cey laughed. "Dil you do need to stop that no' sense." Dil turned to face his eldest brother making opposite circles with his hands.

Mac yelled. "Look at him O'Cey! What he be doing now!"

Dil made a quick motion stopping the circles and pointing at Mac. "I am turning O'Cey into a wart on a toad's butt!"

Mac roared with laughter as he handed Dil his key. "I tell you he be touched!"

"Why do you laugh brother? I know you have a fear he may be able to do it to you one day." O'Cey laughed.

"I have no fear of that! Not from that boy any how!" Mac pointed at Dil. "I know the fool is touched! That's all! Touched I say!"

"Am not!" In two leaps Dil jumped to the white stone slab standing near them. He quickly scooped up his staff, then in a fluid motion he stuck his key into a dimpled marked spot. He looked back at his brothers as he turned the key. "I show you who is the fool, Mac!" The stone shimmered then turned foggy.

"Dil get back!" shouted O'Cey as he scooped up his bush ax on his way to the new open hole in the air.

Mac jumped out of the creek and grabbed his bush ax as well. He ran over to the door and immediately started jabbing his weapon into the open portal.

"Who be touched now!" laughed Dil.

Mac was still stabbing into the void. O'Cey shouted "Mac stop that! What you think you are doing any how!" O'Cey then grabbed Dil by the scruff of his neck, causing his staff to fall back to the ground. "What have you done now boy!" Mac stopped his attack on the opening, but kept his eyes trained on it.

"Stop what you're doing before something else happens!" Mac growled.

Dil wiggled from his oldest brother's grip and reached down to retrieve his staff. Without looking back he dove into the dim opening. "I'll show you who be touched, Mac!"

Mac's stood opened mouth staring after Dil disappeared. O'Cey screamed at him. "Don't stand there toad go after the wee one!" Grabbing Mac by the right arm they both jumped through the opening. They tucked their large bodies in unison and rolled to a rough stop on the other side of the pillar. Together both men jumped up as one and assumed their battle stances. Ready to lash an attack while their eyes quickly scanned the landscape for their lost brother.

O'Cey couldn't see the youngest as he quickly scanned the thin woods. "Where'd he go Mac!" A sound of panic was in O'Cey voice. Dil's safety was his main thought. He had taken on raising him after their parent's death twenty years ago. If the boy had been hurt, he would find it hard to face another day.

"Don't know brother but he can't be far!" Mac tried to help the situation, but he too was showing panic. Dil was in their care and now they have failed. Mac's sporadic movements had displace the battle prowess he normally held.

As the two thrashed about in their frantic search, Dil came up behind them. "I say it be a key, but no, Mac does no listen! Do you listen to me now Mac?"

Both brothers jumped and spun around in tight circles. "Where you been, boy!" Barked O'Cey. "Don't sneak up on me like that! If you want to see the next twenty three years of your life you best stop playing these games!" Dil smiled a toothy grin. O'Cey scratched his chin, studying his five foot four younger brother. "You not too big enough to stop any animal from eating up your boney body."

Dil puffed out his chest proudly. "Welcome to the land of Rhea, brothers!" The two large men looked disgusted at their younger sibling.

"How you know this fool!" Screamed Mac.

"The book!" Dil beamed a self-satisfied grin. "The book Bill give me."

"The book! I'll teach you to play so dangerous, laddy!" Mac reached out to grab Dil. Before he took two steps, Dil twirled his staff over his head. The staff stopped quickly, coming to point at a bush beside Mac. "Burn!" Immediately the bush burst into flames. Mac squealed as he rolled to his right to safety. O'Cey's mouth dropped open.

O'Cey quickly regained himself and yelled at the laughing Dil. "Put it out boy!"

"How?" Laughed Dil.

"With water, you crazy!" squealed Mac as he got to his feet.

Dil raised his staff again pointing it at the blazing bush. Slowly turning it in a tight circle covering the bush and Mac. A dark cloud instantly formed over both of them. The fast downpour soaked Mac and the fire. The flames died out quickly. Mac dripped with water.

"Stop it now boy!" Screamed his soaked brother. "See O'Cey, he is crazy!"

Dil lowered the staff and when the tip touched the ground, the rain stopped. O'Cey plopped down on a nearby stump staring at Dil again opened mouth. He shifted his gaze to Mac then the charred bush and back to Dil. After a few long seconds he spoke in his fatherly voice. "Dil, come here." O'Cey rubbed his dirty face with his big hands. "You too Mac!" They both came to the command of the eldest, with hanging heads. "We must get along." Looking between the two of them. "OK!"

"O'Cey you see what Mac does!" Pleaded Dil. "He always . . ."

"NO!" Shouted O'Cey. "Enough! We start over, NOW!" Looking from one to the other. "Agreed!" Both nodded. "Now Dil, where is it that we stand now?"

"We have to be in Rhea, according to that book Bill give me." Standing proudly, Dil grinned from ear to ear. "I read the whole book too."

O'Cey rubbed his thick beard, a broad smile crept onto his face. "Well Mac, what you think? Dil makes magic." Dil laughed.

O'Cey shifted his look to Dil. "So you do be a wizard?" O'Cey's head fell back as he laughed.

Mac laughed. "Yeah, I guess he is a wizard. Looks like I will be a toad when next we argue. O'Cey, just think you'll be a wart on me butt."

"No Mac. I just joke better than you." Water splattered as Dil patted Mac's broad back, then he held up his foot and wiggled it.

"What do you do now?" Mac jumped back as he stared at Dil.

Dil smiled. "You said you kiss me grubby foot if that be a door." Mac laughed.

"So I did, but not Mac." Mac laughed again. "I will not kiss that smelly thing little brother."

"Enough! Kiss and make up." Laughed O'Cey. "Mac you think we found where Dil belongs?" O'Cey proudly looked at Dil. Dil walked back to the doorway and reached down pulling the key. The door to their world winked back to stone.

"Agreed!" Mac grinned as he looked at Dil. "How do they dress here wizard?" Mac looked down at his dripping kilt. "How you know magic?"

"Our clothes will do fine here. They dress medieval and they use gold, silver and gems." Still grinning Dil poked his chest out a little more. "You can call me the Blue Wizard if we stay here, ok?"

"Settled! Mac go get our gear and . . . ." Nearby screams interrupted O'Cey. He jumped to his feet with his ax in hand. "What the!" They all ran toward the sound of a small battle. Two men armed with bush axes and one with his new deadly staff. Out the tree line and up a hill, they ran toward screams of help. When they topped the hill they saw five strange looking beast attacking a small party of humans.

"Have care Dil! Mac to arms!" The two warriors charged, screaming their war cries. Dil twirled his staff as the helpless people turned to see what the new commotion was. The archers had released their last arrow when the new sounds joined the fight. The beasts also turned to the new sounds. Seeing the armed men racing toward them, they turned from the defenseless people. Each creature charged to meet the attackers.

Dil brought the staff down towards two of the creatures. They immediately burst into small infernos. The burning monsters ran screaming over the next hill to the south.

Mac and O'Cey reached the next beast at the same time and each man quickly opened many gaping wounds with their bush axes. The creature fell dead. The last two creatures snarled at the brothers as they ran to meet the intruders. Mac spun in a tight circle, dropping smoothly to his knees. His crude weapon struck his ugly foe at the knee, removing it's right leg. As the howling creature rolled to the ground Mac swung the ax downward removing the hideous green and black head. The people cheered.

O'Cey flipped to the left of his opponent, bringing his weapon up hard, dissecting the left arm at the shoulder. The creature's blood curdling scream was enough to freeze any hardcore warrior. O'Cey bound back to his feet spinning his blade with his whole body. The large bush ax seemed to be looking for a target. His over the head swing came down hard slicing his foe's head in two. The people cheered again as their last attacker fell. The repulsive large body fell limp to the ground, it's black blood poisoning the soil.

The people ran to thank their saviors. O'Cey turned to his brother. "Mac! I stay here with blue boy you go back and get our things." O'Cey laughed as Dil stopped at his side. Mac and O'Cey each grabbed one of Dil's shoulders laughing and shaking their little brother.

The Blue Wizard laughed in return.

"Stay put I come quick!" Mac took the key from Dil then turned to run back to the door. Lookin back he laughed. "The wee one is a great wizard now!"

"Don't forget to pull the key!" Dil yelled as Mac reached the top of the hill heading for the tree line. Mac threw up his hand to give his answer back.

The people had started to assembled around the newcomers as soon as the distant screams of the burning monsters went silent. Dil turned and whispered to O'Cey. "I may be able to talk to these people, O'Cey. I do know some of their ways from reading the book."

O'Cey nodded with a grunt. "Book! Book! Book! I see this book for meself Dilman you hear?"

"Sure thing brother." Dil grinned. "What you suppose those creatures were?"

O'Cey grinned. "Did not that book of your tell you of them?" Dil held a finger to his mouth. O'Cey growled. The bearded warrior fell silence. His nose turned up.

The people surrounded the remaining two of their heroes. They all stared at the wizard as much as they stared at the giant man with the beard.

"Thank you my new friends for giving aid to my people, I am Conal, chief merchant of Brant." The short man looked at the battle field and pointed. "The wizard asked as to what those creatures were. They are named Nimenole Trolls. Evil creatures too. Our archers had slain as many as they could."

The brothers looked around to the small gathered crowd. Dil cleared his throat before he spoke. "I am Dilman McNure! This is me eldest brother, O'Conner McNure. The other swordsman is also me brother, he be O'Malley. We were summoned to Rhea from a place far away." O'Cey snorted. Dil shrugged as he finished. "We were summoned to give aid to you. You the good people of Rhea."

The crowd murmurs are filled with awes. Dil turns with a smug look toward his older brother. O'Cey grunts again. "You be lucky with word wee one."

Conal repeats his words. "Again, wizard I say, many thanks and also as many thanks to your most impressive giant warriors." The people muttered the same thanks echoing Conal.

Another man standing by Conal spoke. "I am Leister of Brant. I see the other warrior left. Has he gone to fight elsewhere? Please tell us he has not run away?"

O'Cey stamps a charge toward Leister. Dilman holds a hand to block him as he looks over his shoulder to the direction where Mac had run. "No he shall return. He has a task to complete."

A cute red headed young woman to the right of Conal spoke. "Master Wizard, will you and your big hairy warrior stay and help remove all the evil that plagues us?" O'Cey had noticed she was stroking a belt knife as she talked. He also noticed the bow and an empty quiver in her hands.

O'Cey takes a few quick seconds to look around the battle grounds. He sees other creatures dead by several arrow shots. Growing tired of the small talk, O'Cey buts in. "Aye we come to help you!" he growls. "If not, you would be troll bait now! Or do you think not lassie?"

"O'Cey please!" Dil cleared his throat again. "Allow me? Ok?"

"Ok for now but these piss ant are getting on me last nerve!" O'Cey throws a wicked grin at the smaller man. "But I will speak out again before the great wizard don't put his grubby foot in his own mouth." At the last of his words O'Cey makes exaggerated hand movements as if bowing to his younger brother.

Dil scowls at the big man. "It's a deal brother. The foot still do be waiting on its kiss." O'Cey grunts and turns a scowl at the people. Dilman looks around to each of the people surrounding them before speaking again. "Yes, we will help, but please give us a little more room." The people all backed up at once.

O'Cey had enough of the people bunched around them. He scoffs making their move quicker. "Me little brother, the great wizard said we will help. But we cannot do it alone. You will take up weapons with us." O'Cey studied the crowd. "I see people here are short. Anyone taller than you people."

A smaller man behind Conal spoke first. "We are but merchants my lord, and we are small in comparison to the large warriors that defended us this day." Everyone nodded together.

O'Cey looked at the tallest among the people just under Dil's height of five foot four. "Do there be any warriors among you?" Studying the crowd he counted four female archers all with empty quivers. "Can the women archers shoot straight or do you just let loose their arrows and turn their targets into porcupines?"

Before the angered females could answer Conal interrupted. "Yes they can shoot. They are among the best in Brant's defense!" His broad grin spoke of pride for one if not all. O'Cey nodded. Conal then realized what he said and his smile shifted into a sad look. He turned to look at each of the four young women archers standing behind him. "But hear me giant man of the sword, they are also my daughters."

Conal looked at O'Cey's scowl and quickly turned away putting his right arm around the cute red hair girl. "Arrie here, is my eldest." Again his proud radiance exposed. "I sired no sons and a merchant needs protection on the roads. Sadly I was forced to have them take up and learn the bow." He lowered his head as if ashamed. The people started speaking at once. Most praising again for their deliverance, others bragging on the four women and their talent.

"Ok! Everybody be hushed!" O'Cey's patience was thinning fast. He pushed his way in front of Dil and the people cowered away from the rough speaking warrior. Conal raised his eyes to look up at the big man standing over him.

Arrie spoke with a clear voice. "We will help as we can, my lord. We will proudly serve with the wizard and his great giant warriors if it brings an end to the evil and the return of peace for all of Rhea." She eyed her father. "My father will have to understand our choice in this matter because if we do not help, then all could be lost." Her sisters all nodded their approval to her words.

O'Cey nodded back. "Good, it be settled! When me other brother returns we test your bow." O'Cey turned heading away from the battle field. He was walking away from the portal and if any of the townspeople strayed in the woods, they would see Mac when he returned. "Let's scout a camp, Dil, uh, I mean wizard." Dil cleared his throat, then O'Cey spoke his new full title. "Uh, I mean Blue Wizard! Ok!" They walked as far as they could to cover any questions of how they arrived in this place called Rhea.

Dil simply grinned and walked. The sun was falling fast behind the rolling hills.

Chapter 4

Vanish

Hunter returned his big blade to its sheath. "Tunk, food ready yet? I need to turn in early. Gotta get some things from the office before we go."

"Yeah, food's ready. Let's eat!" shouted Tunk.

Jinx grabbed two plates tossing one to Hunter. "Hunter just remember what I said about the trouble." Hunter nodded. "Don't stay long or we'll have to come get you." He started dipping a heaping plate full of red beans and rice, then gave Hunter a plate full.

"No sweat, just be ready when I get back." Hunter stirred his food. "I want all of you ready to pull out if there is trouble. Who knows, we may need to move out fast."

"We'll be sitting on ready Hunt!" Tunk spewed food as he answered Hunter. "You just watch yourself." Tunk wiped his mouth with the back of his right hand. After the meal was finished, Hunter was the first to get settled into bed. The others followed soon after the dishes were cleaned.

The night passed quickly. Before sunrise, Hunter was rolling his bedding and Tunk was up rebuilding the fire. "Tunk, I'll be back as soon as I can. Ya'll just be ready in case we need to move out quick."

"We'll be ready Hunter, you can count on it." Tunk helped Hunter finish saddling Sequoia and filled a feed bag. "We'll wait for three hours after daylight then we'll come find you." He handed the bag to Hunter.

Hunter swung with ease onto the giant beast. "Sounds like a plan. I'll tie Sequoia on the hill just inside the trees." Turning the big stallion in a tight circle, Hunter look down to see the other two rolling out of their beds. "I'll be back soon. See ya." With a gentle bump of his knees Sequoia jumped and they charged up the hill, crashing through the trees. Ian watched as the long fetlocks danced with every drop of its large hoof in the dancing fire light.

Ian continued rolling up his bed. When he finished he looked at the cook. "Tunk, why does the big horses you three ride have hairy feet?" Tunk laughed, but before he could explain Hunter started the truck. Ian rolled backwards over the ground pulling his large knife and set himself for an attack. "Weasels!"

Jinx laughed. "Tunk, that's what Hunter was talking about."

Tunk tried to stop laughing, but couldn't. "It's ok Ian! Hunter'll take care of it!" Tunk continued to get breakfast cooking on the fire. An occasional snicker left him every time he looked at Ian.

"Ian, let's see to the horses." Jinx took Ian to tend the horses. "Ian this will be your horse. His name is Nickle." Handing him a feed, bag he pointed to a tan quarter horse. "You do ride, right?"

Ian nodded. "Yes, we have animals near this size. Most are used as work horses by the farmers and merchants in Rhea to pull wagons or plows. Then the soldiers have theirs to ride." He looked cautiously at the two remaining war-horses. "I will try to stay away from any of yours. They are so large."

"That'd be a good idea Ian." Jinx laughed. "Especially that fool one Tunk rides." As if on cue, Nightmare rolled his eyes to Ian. Ian jumped back. Jinx laughed again as he picked up the water bags. "Come on, let's feed and water all of them, then we can eat." Jinx poured water from the bag into small collapsible leather buckets. He handed Ian a few more feed bags.

After the horses were cared for and their meal was finished and camp was cleared away, they all made ready for a hasty exit.

Ian nodded, "I guess three men as large as you, do need such large horses." The first rays of the new sun cut through the darkened sky.

*   *   *

Hunter looked at the three sedans and the limo in the drive as he drove toward the office. The door to the office was in splinters. Two men in dark suits were snooping around the fenced area and looking at the boxes. The gates were still closed and locked. He turned the big vehicle around so the rear faced the three patrol cars, front pointing to the road. Getting out of the truck he saw the limo driver standing near the rear of the big car. The driver smiled raising his right fist thumb side to his heart and nodded.

Hunter returned the nod as Jansen stormed out of the office. "That's him, that's him!" He screamed with his fat stubby finger pointing at Hunter while looking in the trailer door. "Arrest him, Johnson!"

A slim middle aged man who was just a few inches shorter than Hunter, walked down the steps. "That's enough Jansen! Mister Tadd Hunter, I presume?"

"You presume correct. Now who are you and what's going on here!" Hunter kept walking toward the office.

"I am special agent Johnson of the FBI, sir." The slim man stepped between Hunter and the office. "If you would place your weapons on the ground!"

"I've done nothing wrong and choose to keep them!" Pushing by the agent, he went into his office. Johnson followed with Jansen on his heels.

"He's dangerous Johnson, arrest him!" Squealed Jansen. "Put the thieving injun in cuffs, Johnson! Now!"

Hunter saw two more agents inside. He quickly turned to Jansen. "Shut up weasel!"

Jansen jumped away from Hunter. "See, I told you! He's dangerous!" The little fat man squealed and his face turned solid red.

"That's enough Jansen!" Johnson turned to one of the men. "Agent Smith, escort Mister Jansen outside of here please."

The young agent pushed the little round man to the door. Jansen grabbed the broken frame and looked back to agent Johnson. "Don't listen to his lies! Arrest him Johnson!" Agent Smith had to shove Jansen's body out the door. Jansen tried to lean his head through the door to look into the room. "Tell him the truth you filthy redskin! Do you hear me!" Hunter stomped his big right leg and Jansen jumped back and fell down the short steps.

Hunter grunted and shook his head. He tried to forget Jansen as he looked around the trashed room. Stopping his search, he stared the agent. "What have you done to all our work?" Hunter walked around the desk and took his seat, rummaging through the mess as if cleaning. "All our hard work ruined! It's like the past all over again. My people pushed by the white man! Again he has destroyed our lives!" Hunter sat glaring at the door Jansen was ushered through. "Why?"

The little man ducked behind agent Smith in case Hunter charged out the door to get him. "Don't play the racial bit with them!" Jansen shrieked. "You did it and you are going to prison!" Hunter continued his search.

"Whatever fool!" Hunter slammed both hands on the desk. The agents in the room tensed. Jansen hid farther behind agent Smith. "Johnson, if that weasel has anything to do with ruining my work!" Hunter looked out the window from his chair. "I play no games Mister Johnson. His kind has always done as they pleased with whomever they pleased!" Hunter pointed to the head peeping from around agent Smith.

"Sorry about the mess. Let me explain and then I have some questions if you will." Hunter nodded.

Jansen jumped from his hiding place. "Johnson you don't have to explain nothing to him! Arrest him like I said!"

Johnson turned and stormed the door way. "Smith get him out of here!" Turning back to Hunter. "As I said, let me explain. There was a jewelry heist in New York and we traced it here." Johnson helped pick up some of the papers as if helping Hunter straighten up the mess. "We're just following leads. Jansen told me a tale. He had papers and witnesses." Johnson shrugged his narrow shoulders. "I will also need to question your two friends, Hawkens and Wolfe."

Drumming on the arm of his chair, Hunter turned to look at the agent. "I don't know anything about that, but I'd say Jansen would."

Not being looked at by Hunter's killing stare, Jansen grew a spine. He jumped from behind his protector. "And how do you know this?"

Johnson looked from Hunter to the door that Jansen was trying to peep in. Johnson looked back to Hunter. "He claims the same of you three." Looking back to the door agent Smith was grabbing Jansen. Johnson points for Jansen to follow the young man back outside then returns a hard look to Hunter. "As I said, I will need to talk to you about this as well as speak to Hawkens and Wolfe too."

Hunter stood from his chair, satisfied the objects he searched for had become in their possession, so he started toward the door. "Well you could, but Jinx is taking Tunk to the airport. Something happened back home so he's flying out today. I guess some kind of family emergency."

"When!" Pulling a cell phone from his coat the agent quickly dialed a number. Without looking at Hunter he runs out the door. "This is agent Johnson! FBI! I need you to call the airport and have all the flights stopped. I'll contact you later! Yes, from here to anywhere deputy! Stop them immediately!"

Agent Smith ran to the steps when he heard Johnson raise his voice. Hunter quickly scanned the room one last time. Johnson was passing orders from the doorway. "Smith, take two of the men with you and tell Brown to stay out here and watch this place." Turning to look back toward Hunter, he snaps his head back and glares at Jansen.

Jansen was frantic. "See I told you, don't trust them! Didn't I tell you, Johnson!" Two engines started in the yard. In no time two of the sedans raced down the drive.

"Shut up, Jansen!" Johnson entered the office and kicked what was left of the door. Johnson quickly turns and grabbed Jansen. Shoving the fat man out the door. "Brown! Hold this fool! Keep him out of my sight!"

Hunter met him just inside the office door. "Johnson, calm down. I have Jinx's cell phone number in the truck. I can call him no prob. They'll come right back. "

"Let's go!" Looking sternly at Hunter. "No tricks, I still don't know who to believe!"

"Sure. As I said, no prob." Leaving the office Hunter watched as the dust was clearing from the cars speeding away from the site. Hunter walked slowly to the large truck thinking to himself '*One car left, two men. Great!*' The tires squalled on the paved road, Hunter smiles. '*Take your time they'll be too far to help catch me.*'

As if he read Hunter's mind, Jansen grunts. "Taking your time won't help big man! All flights are grounded!" Jansen waved his hands as if to speed Hunter up. "You and your cohorts will go to jail soon if you had any part in this! You hear me!"

Hunter stopped and stared at Jansen. After a few long seconds he started walking. Agent Johnson's stare silenced Jansen from speaking again.

The walk seemed to last a lifetime but Hunter finally reached the black truck. Opening the door, he glanced back. Agent Johnson spoke, "Tell this Jinx, to head back here with Wolfe." Hunter nodded. "Right now it looks as if he's running."

Reaching in the cab Hunter quickly sidekicks Johnson in the jaw. The man fell hard. Hunter quickly turned the key starting the engine with his left hand. Diving in the door he slides his large body in place. He was already in reverse before Johnson sat up. Hunter seated himself as he floored the accelerator. The big truck engine spoke to the agent as he slowly stood to gain his footing from the massive kick. The big truck crashed into the remaining sedan. Slamming it hard into the limo. Quickly he shifted into drive showering agent Brown with loose rocks as he was running to help the dazed Johnson. Hunter raced down the drive while his mind sped to think of troubles that now lay ahead.

Just after Hunter hit the sedan, the limo driver jumped into the long black car. "I'll get 'em!" The big car leaped to follow chase.

"Yes! Yes! Catch him, stop him!" The red faced Jansen was jumping up and down, "Go fool! GO! Gooooo!" The high pitched squeal caused the driver to frown as he spun the tires in pursuit.

The long car caught up to Hunter as he was sliding onto the paved road. The limo followed into its own power slide. The driver locks his breaks, the big cruiser stops sideways blocking the drive and wedging it's front end in a deep ditch. The blocked drive was now impassable.

Hunter slid to a stop and jumped out. Looking at the limo, the driver smiled and saluted with his fist to the heart. Hunter smiled and returned the salute. The driver lowered his head to rest on the steering wheel.

As he turns to jump back in the truck, a familiar voice sounds off. "Hunter!" Hunter whips around to see Bill standing in the woods on the opposite side of the road. Bill was smiling. "Here biggun, catch! Find the blue wizard! Give him this!" Bill threw the orb. "Your hard journey is now about to begin."

Snatching the clear blue ball from the air, Hunter quickly studies it. "What wizard?" When he looked up again, Bill was gone. Hunter stood staring in the woods.

The driver blew his horn, Hunter quickly shook his head to recover from his stupor. His current situation came back to him. Hunter waved as he jumped back in the truck and returned to his flight. The sedan was speeding up the drive.

Racing down the road, Hunter had a quick thought, "Turn left, it's goose chasin' time." Not taking the right turn to head toward the door, he went left. The big truck ate a big hole into the new growth of trees. After a few seconds, a false trail was laid. 'This should buy me a little more time.' Hunter quickly backed out the freshly cut path laughing as he carefully crossed the road. After the first few yards were past he topped a hill then rounded some trees. He stomped down on the accelerator again.

*   *   *

Tunk looked up the rise into the woods. "Something's wrong. Hunter should be back by now!"

"I agree. Mount up and be ready!" Jinx grabbed Ghost and slung his long legs into place. "Ian hold your reins and be ready with the key!" Ian nodded, as he headed into his position.

Tunk jerked his head to the woods when he heard the truck racing toward them. "Jinx, should we take the horses on through?" Jinx nodded. "Open the door Ian. Sounds like somebody's in a hurry!" Tunk was on Nightmare's huge back. "Hurry! Open the door Ian and get through!"

As Ian opened the door, Sequoia was shattering tree limbs! As the big war-horse came busting through the tree line, Hunter yelled, "Open the portal! Chopper's coming!" Coming in sight of the camp Hunter saw the door was open and the whole camp had almost passed through it. Sequoia raced in as Nightmare disappeared. The large steed jumped through. Jinx was knelling by the door when Sequoia flew out. "Pull the key make us disappear! FBI's coming in fast!"

The door closed as the beat of a chopper's blades were heard echoing through the small valley. None saw the two agents and Jansen running down the hill into the secluded site. "Check the area! They have to be close by!" Hanging up the phone, Johnson stared as he circled the strange pillar.

Jansen walked up to it and rubbed it. "What is this thing?"

"I was going to ask you the same thing, Jansen!"

"I don't know! They kept this a secret from me!" squelched Jansen.

"No matter sir, look at this!" Agent Brown stood by the dead troll.

Johnson walked up with Jansen at his heels and knelt by the dead creature. "Brown, what do you make of this?" Johnson looked away from the dead creature as Smith returned with the other agents. "Circle the entire area! Find them!"

"Got me sir." Brown held his nose trying to stop the stench from the dead thing.

"Jansen! Where are they and what is this?" Johnson scowled at the little fat man.

"They created some kind of a generic freak," squealed Jansen. "See, I told you they were shifty!"

"If you know where they could be, tell me now!"

Jansen shook as he looked at the dead mass. Within the hour, other agents began flooding the area. Johnson's stare could have burned a hole into Jansen. "What do make of this Mister Jansen!"

Jansen wiped his eyes. "I told you that they could not be trusted! They are tricky!"

"And you are not!"

Another chopper joined in the search from the sky above. The search on the ground stooped as each man spotted the thing in question. Agent Johnson turned to the men staring at the dead creature, their search was abandoned. "What are you doing! Search the entire area! They couldn't have gone far!" The men separated and started combing the area.

*   *   *

The limo sat unmoving in the center of the road. It's occupants looking to the right at the tire marks. Bill looks at the driver as he thumbed a small white cylindrical object. "Jak old friend, I believe they finally found their way now."

"They were not the easiest now were they?" Laughed the large black man.

Bill laughed as he relit his pipe. "How long will it take them to find the others?"

"I hope soon." The driver started the limo's engine. "What do you think?"

"Not long I hope. Rhea has fallen to the evil one and they will have their hands full." Bill blew a smoke ring. "Besides Jak, we have spent too much time in this world, let's go home." The limo eased down the road. "And you know our new warriors may need some guidance. No, they *will* need guidance."

The driver laughed. "I'm sure going to miss that fool, Mister Jansen."

Chapter 5

The Outlands

Ian quickly tethered the pack horses before running back to the doorway. Jinx was already astride Ghost and he tossed the key to Ian as his monstrous steed thundered by. Ian stared at the key before walking back to check the quick picket line. Suddenly he realized he was alone.

Ian stood at the edge of the tree line that concealed the door way, he scanned the flat plain to the east. Streaking across the horizon in front of him were three small specks. One of the specks to his right began to move left. Another to the left was still getting smaller, then it turned right heading toward, the third speck. The rider in the middle was heading straight ahead also shrinking. Ian watched as all three met in the center. A few moments later the trio were racing back toward him.

As approached him, Ian waved both arms. The riders quickly encircled him. Ian looked from one to the other as they stopped with him in the center. Jinx laughed. "What you say Ian, a photo finish or what?" The young man just looked at him searching for the words to say.

Tunk argued. "No way fool! I want to see the replay!"

Ian looked even more puzzled at Hunter. Hunter laughed. "It's hard to explain little man." Ian shrugged off Hunter's answer as the huge man dismounted Sequoia. "Where do we go from here?"

Jinx stayed astride his giant war horse. "Looks clear out there Ian, but we'll be in the open. Do you know of a better spot so we can stop and get some grub?"

Ian looked over the horizon and nodded. He smiled as he pointed. "To the northeast toward Toll, there is a forest." Ian nodded, "That's the nearest place to where we go from here."

"We need to get underway then!" Tunk dismounted and tied the pack horses to Nickle. "Ian, you lead them for now in case we have unwanted guests."

"I can fight too!" barked Ian, as he patted the Bowie knife and sword. Tunk grinned.

"Mount up, let's go!" yelled Hunter.

After several hours, the tree line came into sight. Jinx shouted from the lead. "Hunter, about another thirty minutes ride."

"My guess too." Tunk rode ahead to catch up with Jinx. Check it out. I'll come in with Ian and the pack animals." Quick clouds of dust rose as the large horses raced away. Hunter scanned the ground around them as they rode. About a half hour later they were in the trees and dismounted. 'Ian what's on the other side of these woods The scouts rejoined them as Hunter and Ian were hobbling the mares.

"This forest is very large. To the north is Toll, the village I am from. Further east is more flat land and to the south, swamps."

"Is that where the Nimenoles come from?"

"Yes, they can travel into these woods and go anywhere." Ian nodded, "They can come and go without being seen until it is too late."

Jinx jumped from Ghost. "Looks clear to me. Only saw some old tracks leading away from here."

"I saw no sign to the south either Hunter, just old tracks." Tunk was off Nightmare and digging into one of the pack horses for the meal. "Is anyone hungry other than me?"

"Starved! I didn't eat this morning. Just be ready. The woods hide many things." Hunter pulled a feed bag hanging from the high front pommel and placed it on Sequoia. "Ian help Jinx with the animals, I'm gonna take a quick check in the woods." Hunter disappeared into the shadows of the forest.

A short while later he returned. The meal was almost ready. "Is it always this still here Ian?" Hunter stripped the saddle from his horse. "It seems too quiet for me. I didn't see any signs of life in the woods, but I have a feeling something is in there." Hunter pulled the blue ball from his pack and Ian's eyes lit up.

"The orb of Sumra. I thought it was just a story."

Hunter smiled, then wrapped it in a cloth before returning it.

Ian started back in the conversation with Tunk. "No, you are right. Usually, there are wild animals roaming here. Birds too, but nothing is flying or singing." Ian searched the grounds. "It is strange. Somehow it does not feel right."

Hunter finished brushing Sequoia as lunch was ready. Tunk banged an empty pot. "Come an' get it!"

Jinx looked at Tunk. "We're not home bro, watch the noise."

Tunk dropped his head. "Sorry guys, I forgot."

As they ate, Hunter pointed in the direction he walked. "Saw some tracks, maybe three days old. Some were large like that troll thing and maybe about fifteen men. But I can't shake the feeling we're being watched."

"Trolls do come here, but they travel with care. Usually wolves roam these plains. Wolves are sworn enemies to them." Ian raked his scraps in the small fire. "That may explain the feeling. The men were most likely Rodona's foot soldiers. They are usually in the towns in southern Rhea. Her horsemen, or as she calls them, rangers, patrol the Outlands."

Tunk swallowed a gulp of water. "How come we haven't seen any wolves Ian? Are any wolves left around here?"

"I do not know. I do know the rangers track and kill them any chance they can. Maybe the wolves are gone or dead?" Ian still scanned the open plains.

Jinx put the fire out. "Ian how far is your home from here?"

Tunk started packing the mess kits away. "That is where you want to go, right?"

"Yes! We could find more help there. Maybe?" Ian drew a map on the ground. "We can be just outside of Toll before dark. It sits right here." Drawing his last line, he stabs the spot on the ground. "There's a long high ridge, here. It is this side where we'll arrive first."

"Good." Hunter reset the saddle on his monstrous animal. "We do need the daylight tomorrow to check things out before storming into a hornets' nest."

Tunk walked back to his saddle. "Does everything feel alright now that you've eaten Ian?"

"No, it feels different for some reason." Ian looked into the forest and sniffed. He drew his sword. As if on cue, a snort came from the forest. The rest of the group turned towards the sound, armed and ready. "Trolls!" Ian shouted as he pulled his sword. All four swords had sprung to life simultaneously as five hideous shapes came to life from the shadows. Tunk quickly flipped his sword to his left hand and pulled a tomahawk with his right. A spinning death took flight from his hand. The lead troll never saw the blade, as it buried deep in its right eye.

Hunter's large Bowie knife twirled into the next monster's throat. He jumped to intercept the next of the advancing unwanted guests.

Jinx's spinning sword blocked a quick thrust from the threat moving in on him. He recoiled. Then striking as fast as a viper, Jinx threw his whole body into his assault. His deadly three foot blade sunk to its hilt into the chest of his attacker. A nasty gurgle left the creature's mouth as Jinx twisted the blade and kicked it free. Before the troll fell, Jinx swung his blade slicing across his foe's grotesque face. Looking around before the black and green beast hit the ground, he saw that Hunter and Tunk were in full control of their contests. He quickly moved to cover the rear to take control of any other surprise attack. "Keep your eyes on the woods Ian. I'll look after our flanks!" Ian raised his sword in acknowledgment.

Hunter was blocking a flurried attack from the smaller troll. Looking down a couple inches into its blood shot eyes, he baited the creature to move in closer. Hunter blocked the big black sword. He swung a fast elbow in its flat tusk filled face. The beast staggered back. Quickly it regained its balance, throwing its head back to release a roar. Hunter answered with his own battle cry. The troll stood back and looked at the strange giant. Hunter jumped, then launched his attack. The creature was taken back as the big man's blurring sword danced all around it. A quick dip to the right allowed Hunter's blade room to slice upward removing the ugly face from his foe. The death screams made the last troll turn and look away from Tunk.

Seizing the moment, Tunk buried his sword up and under its ribs. Quickly he twisted the blade and ripped it from his dying foe. The troll's rib cage burst as the razor sharp blade sliced it's way to freedom.

Hunter finished his adversary off with another swing, the headless body fell hard. "Ok look around guys, there may be more hiding!" Hunter started stalking deeper into the forest.

Ian was studying the place from where the Neminoles had suddenly appeared. He had moved into the thick trees before the others were in motion. He did not see the last troll hiding in the dark shadows. It snorted as it jumped towards him. The smaller man rolled to his right, slicing his sword downward on his attacker's left knee. The shrill cry of the one legged beast falling brought the others running to Ian's aid. The creature went silent. Ian jumped to his feet as Tunk kicked the troll onto it's back. The creature was impaled by its own black scythe.

Hunter was the next to get to Ian. "Nice move little man." He patting Ian on his back. "I don't think we need to teach you any of our moves."

Ian shrugged. "I told you I can fight too."

As Jinx ran up to them all he saw was Ian grinning. "I say we need to leave now if we are to make our destination."

"I agree." Hunter scanned the surrounding forest. "Let's go. It feels like the forest has more eyes."

Tunk looked around. "I can't stop feeling there someone's watching us too, Hunt."

Hunter nodded. "Let's move. Maybe they have seen something today to make them think now."

The four quickly cleared the signs of their stop. They drug the dead bodies to the plains to ensure they would be seen before heading for Toll.

Ian led the way as the others periodically studied their rear. They road in silence. The long day wore on.

*   *   *

Mac returned with their gear and a herd of horses. "Everything's ready for our journey. I couldn't leave the other horses." Handing his brothers a sack each. "I brought more clothes."

"Good! Mac, we got four archers. Giv'em a horse and full quivers." O'Cey and Dil walked into the woods. After they changed their clothes they rejoined Mac.

O'Cey grabbed Mac by the back of his neck. "We make Dil happy brother, look at him." They both looked at their youngest brother. "The Blue Wizard do look right now in his robes." Dilman stood straight, looking over the people. Looking noble and wise in his full length dark blue robe.

"The lad do look happy now." Mac smiled as Dil waved his staff at them. "Let's see these archers work." Grabbing extra quivers of arrows, O'Cey called the sisters aside. "Mac, these be the lasses I told you about."

Mac handed each sister a full quiver of their handmade arrows. "Here lass, I wish to see your skills." Mac looked for a target, finding a good tree about one hundred and fifty yards away. "There that tree." "Shoot at the knot on this side." The sisters looked questioning at each other.

Each took a shot hitting the tree but each missed the knot by a wide margin. Arrie shook her head. "That's a hard shot."

O'Cey scoffed as he pointed to Arrie's bow. She nodded, then handed her prized possession to the large man. O'Cey aimed then released the arrow. It stopped just to the right side of the knot. He grunted before passing the bow to Mac. As Mac notched his arrow, O'Cey barked a laugh. "Show me the center Mac." Looking at the disbelieving trio, "Mac do be the better shot than I."

Mac took a deep breath as he drew the bow. Holding for a few seconds he released the arrow. It stopped just hairs from the center. He studies the bow clutched in his large hand. "This do be a good bow. Now can you shoot a long bow?" Handing a long bow from his back to Arrie. "I brought extra. We can practice a bit later." All four pretty heads nodded.

O'Cey went back to the others and found the archer's father. "Conal, your daughters will ride with us." Conal looked sad. "Da no worry look, O'Cey'll keep 'em safe." O'Cey looked at the mass of people then turned back to Conal. "We need cover for the night. Do you know where we will go from here?"

Mac rode in on his huge war-horse. "We need to leave. These people look to be lambs for slaughter. We need to move quick." O'Cey nodded. Mac returned the gesture and turned the large mount.

Conal watched as Mac rode into his people then he spoke. "We are close to Toll. Travel to the where the sun comes go to a small grove near the village. We can sleep there, then be in Toll just after the next sun rise."

"What way is to where the sun comes?" O'Cey looked in the suns mid-morning position.

The merchant looked at the bearded man towering over him then pointed. "Where the sun rises." Conal smiled.

O'Cey barked his rough laugh. "Good then! East it is! Let's go!" Conal wandered off to rush his people.

Within an hour, Mac returned from his short observation ride. His giant Shire Stallion snorted as it halted in front of O'Cey. Mac laughed. "Did our wizard make those wagons? I see they be loaded."

O'Cey laughed. "No the people had'em. The wizard did good overseeing the loadin of the people."

Conal walked his new mount as O'Cey stepped into the stirrup. The warrior was silent as he mounted the huge draft horse. "We ride to the east grove Mac. We can sleep in its cover." Looking at Dil. "Our wizard can rest well there."

"Will we be in Toll when the sun peaks on the morrow?" O'Cey was looking down on Conal. The merchant grinned as he nodded his reply.

Mac had ridden up to the conversation. "Sounds to be a good plan. Let's move!" He barked. The horses were already pulling the loaded wagons. The refugees of Brant were anxious to leave the killing field.

O'Cey spun his horse. Dil sat in the lead wagon waving at his elder brother. "I see the wizard do be ready now. Let's move!"

Dil waved again from the lead wagon, his horse tied to the rear. The wagons creaked as they settled into a steady motion. The refugees of Brant cheered. Mac rode the hill to the rear looking for a safe departure. Finally they were under way toward Toll. To safety.

*   *   *

Night was coming fast, when they saw the rolling hills of Toll. Hunter pulled up after cresting the first hill. "Who do you suppose those two following us, are?" Ian wondered as he studied the rear.

"Don't know." Jinx turned left to go around the last hill. "But time to see!"

Tunk nodded as he turned right. Hunter looked at the puzzled Ian. "I'll stay with you. Back up and be ready."

Ian nodded as he faded off a bit to the rear of Hunter. The two riders topped the hill traveling fast. Jinx and Tunk closed up the escape route of the intruders. The shocked duo stopped in a cloud of dust. Hunter was on top of the lead rider with a steady Bowie knife at the small mans throat. Tunk and Jinx moved in closer. Hunter had grabbed the front man's reins. "Who are you and why do you follow us?"

Ian rode up to intervene. "Ecott! Nuel! Is that you? What are you doing here?" The second rider had a look of wanting to jump out of his skin if he could.

The boy looked shaken as he stared at Ian. "Ian! I knew it! I told you Ecott!" Looking at the other rider. "See Ecott, it is Ian!"

Jinx had closed in on the pair. "That only explains you know Ian. Were you going to shoot him through the heart with one of your shafts!" Jinx grabbed the second rider. "Now answer the question my brother has asked you! Answer it! NOW!"

The lead rider's horse was still in Hunter's iron grip, his voice was shaky as he spoke. "My name is Ecott, of Brant. This is my brother Nuel." His nervous eyes tried to keep from Hunter's cold stare, only to fall quickly to look at the ground each time. "Conn made us ride as his archers."

Before his older brother finished, Nuel blurted. "Ian, they got our family! Conn said they will die if we do not ride for Alexar!" The first rider looked at his brother.

Ecott turned back to look into Hunter's dangerous eyes. "We have raised no arrow to any innocent person on Rhea!" He turned to look at Ian. "Ian, you know us. We would not do that." Holding on to his pleading stare at Jinx. "But we will raise them against Alexar. They hold our family!"

Jinx tightened his hold on Nuel. "You admitted you ride with this Conn! Right! Ian, who is Conn?"

Ian spoke. "Conn is one of the captains of the army of the evil wizard Alexar."

Nuel looked at Ian. "We did ride with him but he made us to do so! We looked for help from anyone that will face them!" The young man looked in Jinx's stone face. "Once we know our family is in a safe place, then we will be able to fight them."

Ecott looked to Ian for help. "Ian, you know us and you know we will fight to our last breath if need be! You know we will not harm helpless people!"

Ian look from one brother to the other. "Hunter, I do know these two. I also know if they wanted, they could have easily shot their arrows through each of us." Ian then looked from Jinx and Hunter. Tunk was still sitting quietly to the rear. "I will stand up for them."

Tunk rode in between the brothers. "Where did you just come from?" demanded Tunk.

The two jumped at the new deep voice. They both turned to see a third large man. The brothers shared astonished looks with each other at the sight of the third one. Ecott looked from one big man to the others. His mouth gaped as he looked. "Ian! Are they the avenging giants from the prophecies?"

Ian grinned. "Yes, they are the seed of Thorn."

"Ecott, Nuel?" After they nodded to him Hunter continued. "How did you two come by us and why are you here now?" Hunter was glaring at Ian so he would not interfere. Ian remained silent.

"We left Brant as ordered by Conn to patrol with six Nimenoles. We had no choice. They hold our mother and father!" Ecott looked from Hunter to Jinx then stopped at the third stranger. "We came across tracks of refugees and the trolls ran ahead to attack them. As we topped the hill behind them, we saw a wizard attacked the trolls. We ran from the fight as the wizard's warriors quickly butchered the other trolls."

"Who was this wizard?" Ian looked between the brothers. They both shrugged.

Nuel chimed in, "We knew of the small forest to the side of the Outlands. There we saw more dead trolls." Looking down at the giant hoof prints, Nuel pointed. "So we followed those tracks."

"That is so stupid, it's got to be true." Laughed Jinx. "Let me see, you saw a wizard attack the company you road with and he had two bad ass warriors. Then you saw slaughtered trolls and you followed. To what? Maybe your own deaths!" Laughing harder Jinx released Nuel and dismounted. "You two are either the bravest fools I have ever seen or the dumbest." Tunk joined in the laughter. Hunter kept his cold stare as he studied the two newcomers. Jinx turned his back to relieve himself.

Tunk stayed between the two. His laughter died as fast as it came on him. He growled as he grabbed both with a death grip by the neck. "If at any time I think you lie, I will kill you myself!" Letting the two go, he finishes. "Understand!" Shaken by the sudden move, they both gave a trembling nodded.

Jinx finished doing his business on the ground. He yells as he swings back in his high pummeled saddle. The brothers jumped at the quick movement, Jinx laughed. "I say this, if Tunk don't kill ya for that, I surely will."

Hunter turned Sequoia to finish their journey. "Ian, darkness is falling quick. Let's go!"

As they rode up the last of the hills, Ian pulls up on his reins. "This is it. We camp in the brush."

Hunter looked at the men in the party. "Ok, Ecott go with Tunk. Scout the grove." Looking at Jinx Hunter nodded. "Go with Ian and take a peep at this Toll." Looking at the sun, "Daylights going fast, so hurry. I'll set up camp with Nuel. We'll enter Toll in the morning."

"Good idea. No telling what lay waiting there." Tunk dismounted and motioned with his hand for Ecott to follow.

"Yeah, easier to fight by day." Jinx yawned as he nudged Nightmare ahead. "I say night is for sleeping."

"Try to be unnoticed!" Hunter called out as the two rode toward Toll.

"Yeah I don't suppose those massacred trolls won't be noticed, right?" Laughed Jinx. "How 'bout that wizard's works."

Ian followed Jinx, he turned to look at the others. "Hunter we can camp this side of the hill and remain unseen, I have camped in there before." Ian pointed to a cut out, hidden by a hedge row. Hunter nodded as he dismounted.

Nuel dismounted, keeping his eyes on the man towering over him. Hunter looked down at the amazed Nuel and growled. "Follow me."

Ecott and Tunk entered the tree line. Tunk pulled his sword as he lead Ecott. Ecott notched an arrow, then place a second in his teeth. Jinx and Ian continued to ride toward Toll.

Hunter and Nuel had the camp setup by the time the others arrived. A cold meal was being set out. There was no fire that night.

"Good job Ian, we sure can camp here and not be seen." Hunter turned to the others. "We'll eat hard tack and jerky."

Ian ate with the two brothers, away from the others. He spoke in a low voice. "Remember this, if you plan anything against these giants, you have no fear of them." Ian took a drink from his water bottle. "I will kill you, myself." The brothers grimly nodded.

"Ian are they the giants of the prophecies?" Ecott stared at the trio of large men.

Nuel nervously spoke up. "Hush brother! Even if they are not, do you want to face them?" The three ate in silence.

Chapter 6

Toll

Before the sun's first rays of light could be seen, the small but growing war party was up and busy breaking camp. Tunk walked between Ian and Hunter. "Ian, how far is this Brant from Toll?"

"From here, four days ride. If the Huntress will let us pass through the Forest of the Whispering Pines, we can be there on the fifth. If not, four more days. Then beyond Brant another two days is Sumra."

Tunk nodded with a shrug. "Hunter, what say we just toddle over there after we fix any problems here in Toll." Hunter smiled as he turned to see the brothers finishing stowing their bed gear. He turned back to Tunk and Ian. "I know where you are going with this Tunk, and I say yeah. Let's ride to Brant and help free Ecott and Nuel's family."

"Cool! Ian, now what is this Sumra' you mentioned?" Tunk scratched his head. "And you called that thing Hunter's got what? The orb of Sumra', right?" Tunk looked at Hunter.

Hunter rubbed his chin. "Bill threw that thing to me and said to find the blue wizard. You think the wizard Ecott and Nuel saw is the one."

Ian answered. "I do not know that wizard. I think we will need to talk to a seer about him."

Ecott had walked up as the three were talking. "We do not know the wizard and we only laid eyes on him that one time." The three nodded to Ecott's explanation. "I do know Toll is under the eye of the Gauvin's Marauders. So I will thank you now if I do not live to see you help Brant. I heard you talking just now."

Hunter put a big right hand on Ecott's shoulder. "It'll be ok Ecott. You'll be fine." Looking at each of member of the blood of brothers. Jinx and Nuel were not in the circle. "Jinx come here. You too Nuel." As they joined Hunter turns to Ian. "Explain this Sumra' to us."

Ian spoke clear. "Sumra' is the last haven other than the forest of the whispering pines. It is where the last of the tribes of Thorn still have a strong hold." Ian smiled, "They wait for the seed to arrive and the giants to lead them against Alexar."

"Ok, we'll talk about that later. What do you know of the orb." Ian shook his head. "Ok then I guess we need to plan in case there is heavy resistance in Toll. Ian can you draw a map of Toll?" Ian went straight to work, scratching on the ground.

Hunter squatted down when Ian finished, and drew battle positions for the new archers. He looked up at the brothers. "If you two wish, you can stay here. We won't think you cowards." Hunter stood after he spoke.

"Master Hunter, we have not lied, we'll help even if you cannot free our family. My brother Nuel and me will be glad to be archers for the giants."

Ecott dropped down on one knee in front of Hunter. "I swear on my family, my Lord. I swear to serve Rhea through serving you."

Nuel nodded as he knelt by his brother. "I also swear to my Lord's service."

Hunter blushed and looked at Jinx and Tunk's giggling taunts, then quickly back to the kneeling pair. "Get up you crazies, I'm no ruler for you to bow before!" The brothers just looked at each other for brief second.

Bowing his head in shame, Nuel's voice cracked as he spoke. "Last night we saw the mark of Thorn on each of my lords. You are the Giants and we are your servants." He looked to Ian, "And the amulet around Ian's neck, spoke him to be a seed, too."

Ecott looking at each of the foursome, a wide smile spread across his face. "You are the seed." He looked as if he made an amazing discovery. "Are you not?"

Hunter look at the two massive men at either of his sides. His brothers in arms. Lifelong friends. Jinx shrugged. Tunk was mocking a bow. Ian was grinning. Hunter shook his head and a brief stare at the kneeling brothers brought him to his senses. "Get up! And you too!" Hitting Tunk and Jinx at the same time. "Don't egg 'em on!"

As the brothers stood Ecott spoke, "who do we say we ride with?" A confused Hunter looked at Ecott.

Ian laughed. "I know, if anyone ask tell them you ride with the blood of brothers Thorn!" Hunter threw his arms in the air, spun around, then stormed to the sacks of food.

Animals fed and watered, a quick cold breakfast, and the band was ready. Jinx looked as the first streaks of sun cut across the dark sky. "We need to head out now if we want to have an early surprise on any of our enemies that might be sneaking around down there."

Tunk nodded as he mounted his giant Nortic stallion. "Hunter, the pack animals are hobbled and hidden. Their fed bags will keep them quiet too."

"Let's ride!" Hunter jumped on his large war-horse. "Freedom for Toll!"

The camp came alive with quick low toned shouts for freedom. "Remember to sound loud battle cries." Nightmare reared as Tunk kneed the giant stallion. "When the battle comes yell your war hoops loud, it'll help confuse our enemies!" The brothers nodded in unison.

The troop headed out of the shrub cover and up the rise, leaving the pack animals safe in their night sanctuary. Jinx was in the lead, Hunter just behind. Hunter looked at Ian. "Ian, ride in with Tunk!" Hunter looked at Tunk off to the his right.

"Hunter!" Jinx nodded. "Something's going on up ahead. See the smoke on the horizon, looks like there's fighting already in the town." He spurred Ghost ahead in a dead run. The others followed suit, the last hill came and went quickly. After topping the rise, they saw a small group of riders on horseback, another group on foot moving into the Toll with weapons in hand. The houses on the outskirts of the town were burning and more soldiers were seen moving inside Toll.

Hunter shouted. "Archers to your places quick, we need cover!"

"Gauvin's marauder's!" exclaimed Ian.

Jinx pulled his sword as he raced on. "Let's go!" The riders charged toward Toll, toward the invaders. The loud sudden war cries turned the marauders attention from Toll. Five of the mounted soldiers spun their horses to intercept the armed men coming down on them.

Tunk laughed as he caught up with Jinx. "Jinx look, a welcoming committee!" Another blood curdling yell came next. Jinx laughed, then yelled. Ecott and Nuel veered far right to their posts, in range to fire a quick round of shots. The arrows dropped two of the riders, the remaining three kept heading toward the blood of brothers. More arrows stopped two of the foot soldiers moving on Toll. The other three stood their ground as if to protect their comrades in the town.

Hunter, Tunk and Jinx, looked at Ian as the foot soldiers fell. Ian yelled then laughed. "I told you they were good with the bow.

Hunter and Jinx locked swords with the first two horsemen. Tunk rode on with Ian staying behind him. They headed to intercept the third rider.

The archers fired another round at the three remaining foot soldiers. Then another at seven more horsemen as they charged out from Toll. Five of the riders crossed over two of the foot soldiers as they fell dead. Two horsemen also fell to the bowmen.

The marauder challengers fell to the Band of Brother's deadly blades. The archers moved closer. More foot soldiers pour out from Toll.

* * *

As the sun broke on the horizon, the people of Brant were on the move. O'Cey turned in his saddle to Arrie. "Lassie, how far to go, it be south east I know?"

"Toll is in the next valley." As she pointed to the smoke filled sky, Arrie pulled her bow. "Looks as if trouble has found them too!"

"Arrie, keep the wizard safe!" Mac spurred Thunder. "Coming O'Cey!" They raced ahead toward the smoke filled sky. Mac turned in time to see his brother's large frame passing by. Dil and the archers raced to join in the fight.

O'Cey bumped his brother as he passed. "You too slow Mac, watch me an' learn to ride lad!" The bearded warrior roared his gruff laugh. As the archers dismounted, they eyed the group challenging the warriors coming from Toll.

Arrie yelled. "Gauvin's Marauders, but who are those men! Sisters let us show those men how to shoot!" Quickly they were on the ground and notching a deadly round.

O'Cey and Mac, smiled at the quick glance they had of the swordsmen battling below them. "We go help'em brothers!" laughed O'Cey. The brothers screamed their battle cries, as they stormed down the hill.

Dil laughed. "Lassies! Don't be shooting the men wearing leather! They be our friends!" His staff began to twirl. The sister's drew their notched arrows and quickly released their flying death along with the male archers. Dil's staff stopped, as six arrows cut through the air.

Six men stopped to guard Toll and they all fell to stand no more. Ecott and Nuel quickly turned to face the new bow slingers. The ground rumbled then erupted into flames around the seven mounts charging Hunter and Jinx. The new war cries and the fire turned the band to see who was behind them. "Hunter, the crazy brothers are here to play too!" Jinx let another war cry.

Tunk resounded his war cry as he saw them too.

As the three look back to the men coming from Toll, they see two riders fall screaming as the flames devoured them. The others were able to jump to safety from the inferno.

Tunk met the next wave of battle. Ian joined in as Tunk dropped his adversary. Five remaining mounted marauders stopped their advance and looked at one another and again Dil's staff comes to life. It stops to point at the bewildered horsemen. A twirling whirlwind lifted three of the men from their mounts. The men screamed until they were smashed into the bro ken stone wall surrounding Toll. Again, arrows filled the air killing the last two.

The six warriors come together.

Tunk laughed. "Hey Macky, did Dil do that!"

Mac beamed. "Aye! Tunk the wee one truly be a wizard, now!"

"No matter, we'll talk later!" yelled Jinx, as he spurred Ghost forward. "We gonna let the archers and Dil, um, the wizard do all the work, or do we free Toll!" Ghost was off with a slight lead. The other five just behind. The six race into Toll as one. The archers take to a run just behind their champions.

Dil stopped all the archers before entering Toll. "Two of the sisters watch our backs from here. Whatever tries to sneak in, stop them! The other two sisters cover the swordsmen." Dil kicked his mount into a run behind the brothers. The women set to their posts. The brothers look confused, then followed the wizard into Toll.

Inside Toll, three more riders charged the newcomers. O'Cey teamed up with Jinx and Tunk and the three raced in to face them. O'Cey and Jinx meet the first two riders. Jinx passed a quick motion to O'Cey. "Show time, big boy!" Tunk sweeps wide to meet the third. Both men stopped their adversaries battling from horseback. Tunk quickly encounters his man. He blocks the broad sword of his man and ran a left handed Bowie knife into the man's throat.

Six men were in the street beating an old man in front of the Black Thorn Inn. Ian races in behind Hunter and Mac and the three charge to meet these brave soldiers.

Two arrows fly amid the charge, one strikes the soldier holding the old man. The old man drops free to the ground and his oppressor drops lifelessly to the ground. The second arrow stops a swordsman facing the large charging warriors. The man fell while trying to protect the pack beating the old man. The new threats move in quick.

Hunter jumps from Sequoia as the man facing him strikes first. Hunter blocks the sword coming at him. Mac quickly removes his man's head as he lands from Thunder's back. The other two enemies stop in their tracks as the foreign warriors split to face them. Ian now in the lead. Five other marauders run from inside the inn, and an arrow cuts the air driving deep into the left eye of the first man. The sword play lasted no time, with no contest.

Two foot soldiers remain alive and they both turn to flee. Tunk sees them and yells, "Runners!" O'Cey and Jinx help in cutting off one of them from his exit. Tunk reached his prey in a cloud of dust. He dives on the man running in the lead. Rolling to his feet his blade comes alive as the man tries a fleeting display with his sword. Smoke from the burning buildings fill the streets.

The brother archers had taken up positions on opposite ends of the Black Thorn Inn. Dil watches over the warriors, slowly turning his staff. Before the last man falls, the wizard's staff stops. Dark clouds quickly form and a steady rain falls, slowly extinguishing the fires burning throughout the town.

Jinx grabs Ghost's reins, as Mac and O'Cey swing into their places sitting in their high pummeled saddles. "Hunter! We'll search the other streets!" Hunter raises his sword to acknowledge O'Cey. Gliding on the large white stallion, Jinx thunders down the street just behind the whooping brothers.

Ecott and Nuel notch arrows and face opposite directions. Two of the women with bows ready, slowly walk the soggy streets, searching the building tops.

Hunter watched the sisters on their patrol into Toll, then he noticed the other two guarding their rear. He slowly turns to help the old man to his feet. "Ian, take the two archers watching out front, and get the pack horses." Two horses walked alone in the center of the street.

As the women archers grew closer to Hunter, the closest softly spoke. "Hey Ol' Sam."

"Arrie! It is you!" The grin on the old man's face reminded Hunter of Jed. "Is you father alright?"

"He's outside Toll as we speak." Nodding to Hunter, "I'll ride out to get the refugees from Brant."

Hunter returned the nod. "That was good shooting. Welcome to the family."

The archer gave a questioning look, as she mounted. "I ride with the Blue Wizard and his big warriors!"

They all looked at Dil, and he made a slow arch with his staff and his free hand. The rain stopped. Hunter grinned as Dil spun around to walk toward them. "I'm proud of you, boy!"

"I told you Hunter!" Dil grinned.

Hunter laughed. "Yeap you did! I knew you had it in you." "

The pretty archer spoke to the wizard, "You know one another?"

"They are me brothers too!" Dil couldn't grin any bigger. "We all be family!"

Dil was standing at Hunter's side with a big toothy grin on his face. "What thought have ya Hunter!" Hunter turned to receive a welcome hug from Dil. "Surprised to see us?"

"Not at all Dil!" Hunter laughed. "Not even at your magic? It's fantastic, little brother!" The giant grinned at the mounted archer. Her puzzled look made Hunter laugh again. "We are all family." Arrie scratched her chin as she looked at the wizard, then back to the large dark skinned giant warrior. Hunter nodded, as she rode out. "We are the Blood of Brothers Thorn!" Hunter grabbed Dil by each shoulder. "It is good to see all three of you, boy!"

O'Cey and Mac roar together as they walked up, bringing another laugh from Hunter. "I should have known those two clowns wouldn't miss any sword play!" Jinx and Tunk rode in, completing the group of old friends.

Townspeople started to appear in the streets and Toll seemed to come to live again. Hunter smiled as he looked at the old man. The man standing in awe of the five giant warriors, gathered around a wizard. A wizard dressed in a shimmering dark blue flowing cloak.

Hunter nodded to the old man. "Sam is it?" The man nodded in return. "Is there a place where hungry people can get some food and talk in private? And maybe a room or two?"

Jinx spoke up. "How 'bout a bath or two as well?"

Sam beamed, "why yes, my Lords! You stand before, the Black Thorn, the best inn and food around!" Sam turned to hurry inside. He stops at the door with a quick look back. "I'll get it ready now!" As he turns to enter the door, his shouts fill the streets. "Toll is thankful to our liberators!"

Arrie returned with the wagons full of the refugees. The people of Toll welcomed those from Brant. Just behind them Ian rode in with two of the women archers. He dismounted and walked up to stand by Hunter's side. "I will help the six archers tend the horses."

"Good." Hunter nods. "After that everyone come back to the Black Thorn. We'll eat and discuss what to do next." Ian nods and walks with the others with horses in tow. Ecott and Nuel went with the wizard, only after Hunter's nod told them to follow.

Conal and a dozen men of Brant, walked up to the group of swordsmen. "We will be pleased to assist the giant warriors any way we can, Master O'Cey." Jinx joined in with Mac's laughter.

O'Cey growled at them both. "Whatever! Go help the archers, then! And you two can laugh all you wish!"

Tunk snickers. "Yes Master O'Cey."

After all the horses were tended, everyone gathered at the Inn. Conal was there also. Old Sam had escorts on standby to lead each member of their rescuers to the wash room then to their personal dining hall. The large room in the rear of the inn, looked crowded with the five gargantuan strangers.

After introductions were made, they ate a meal fit for several kings. During the feast the room was silent. The only noises to be heard, were the scraping of empty plates. As soon as everyone had their fill, the large round table was cleared by a steady flow of servants. Slowly, all of the meal's remains left the room. Jinx left his chair to check as the door closed behind the last worker.

Hunter rose with Jinx's approving nod. "I see we've got quite an army forming now. And it looks like a good one to me. Formidable to challenge any one that would dare face us." He praised all of the liberators involved in freeing Toll. They spoke of improvements and training for their new comrades in arms. Talks wandered to some plans of freeing Brant. That talk grew into hot topics, everyone voiced their own views. Battle plans were laid out.

The talk slowly turned quiet. Hunter was pleased with the outcome of the discussions. O'Cey and Mac nodded as one then began to beat the tables with their club sized hands. "Aye! We make more of this fun, right Hunter!" O'Cey rolled his burly head back with a deep roar of laughter.

Mac beat on the table louder. "Aye, I agree brother, kick more ass!" Mac laughed harder as he steady drummed the table top. Tunk laughed as he joined in beating the table, he looked at Jinx. The newcomers looked at the large swordsmen in wonder of what would happen now.

Jinx shrugged his broad shoulders. "Stop that playing youngling's!" He yelled. He busted out laughing, then he started beating on the table. As soon as he started his part of the noise, Jinx stopped quick. "A little more work today, a good meal, a good night sleep then we will par-tay again!" A loud knock on the door brought a quick hush to the loud swordsmen.

O'Cey growled. "It best be important!"

Mac and Jinx chimed in together. "Enter!" After the words passed, they gave each other a high five across the table, laughing as they gave a head nod to each other.

Sam slowly opened the door and shuffled into the dining hall. "Please forgive me my lords." Bowing so low he almost kissed the floor. Jinx and Mac laughed again. "I know it to be still early of yet, but I took the privilege in having to prepared rooms for our brave freedom fighters to rest." Raising only his eyes, Sam looked at Hunter. "Lord Hunter? I know it is early still, but I thought all of you may have tired from the battle." His toothless smile split his face again.

Hunter nodded. "Thank you Sam, but we have much work to do. During our talk, Ian said your son is a blacksmith?" The old man beamed again as he nodded as he slowly stood erect. "Good, can you get him for me and a good leather worker too?" Without a word, the old man was out the door like a flash. Hunter laughed. "Cool Sammy, handle it then." Turning to the others he laughed again. "That old man is fast. How did they catch him to beat on him?" The room filled with laughter.

Hunter shook his head. "Ok, we'll divide up to make the weapons we talked about. Like you said Tunk they will give us a little more of an edge." More discussions broke out on what to make.

In less than an hour Sam returned with two men. Pointing to a stocky middle aged man on his right. "My lords this is my son Sann, the best blacksmith in all of Rhea." Turning to a short fat man to his left. "Lord Hunter, this is the son of my brother, may he forever stay in peaceful rest. Oh yes sorry, this is Efrin, he is a tanner and the most talented of all leather workers you could find."

"Many thanks, Sam," answered Hunter. Looking at the snickering bunch around him. "Sam I'm no lord, just call me Hunter, ok?" Sam nodded with a hurt look.

Tunk slapped O'Cey on his wide back. "Lord Hunter! I'm taking O'Cey here and we are going with the smithy to get started. If this will be to my Lord's liking?"

Hunter grunted at Tunk and threw his hands in the air. "Bite me Tunk." The rest of the strangers to Rhea laughed. The archers looked from one to the other with questioning looks. Hunter grunted again. "Ok, fool, you two get to it then!. Jinx, don't you have things to do too?" Jinx nodded. "Good, get to it then! Mac take Ian and go with Efrin. We'll all meet up before dark." Hunter looked down at Sam. "Thanks for the rooms, but we won't have any need for them until tonight."

"They will be ready Lor, umm I mean Hunter." The old man grinned, as he backed from the room bowing repeatedly.

Hunter was up and walking to the door. He paused as if remembering a forgotten thought. "Nuel, take two of the young lady archers and find a Fletcher, have him make his best arrows for us." Shifting his gaze to each of the six archers. "You all done well today. Thank you for your protection." His look stopped at Dil, a big grin overtook his face. "And you boy, you done more than I can ever say! I am truly proud of you."

Dil beamed. "Thanks Hunter! Do you have something for me to do?"

Hunter nodded. "You know it! See if you can help the townspeople with your gift." The blue wizard's whole body shook from his excited nod. "Ecott, take the other two young ladies and make rounds through Toll just in case someone is trying to move in on us."

Hunter turned back to the door. Conal cleared his throat. "And what does the great warlord have for us to do?" Hunter looked questioning but the words stuck '*warlord? Cool has a ring to it Hunt.*'

Conal finished. "I mean sir to aid in your, I mean our task. Sir?"

"Oh ok. You wish to join us?" All the men of Brant nodded excitedly. "Ok! Check the condition of the wagons then take your crew and get provisions for our journey." The man of Brant nodded. The war party broke up and everyone set off to complete all the necessary tasks.

As the sun started its descent, some of the new army had come together in a large paddock in the center of town. Toll was on its way back to life. Every one of its people smiled and nodded in acknowledged of their liberators as they passed by. O'Cey was talking to the members of the band gathered on the green. "So far of what I see of our opposition, they were too weak, but O'Cey knows that will change. We all best be ready."

"I agree," Jinx answered. "We need more swordsmen."

"I agree with both you," voiced Mac. "Is there any and too many people to trust."

"As it stands we are a growing force for Alexar to contend with," Ian spoke up. "And there will be more to come with us to help." Ecott and Nuel nodded their agreement. "We just have a need to go too Sumra'. We find many there."

O'Cey blew through his thick whiskers. "That may be boy, but now if we get swamped, can any of these good archers fight hand to hand?" All six archers were present to hear the question. Looking around at each of them, he barked a laugh. "I thought as much!"

Hunter was standing off from the gathering. "O'Cey, we'll just keep up with their training. It's all we can do right now." He studied the members of the group. "At sunrise we'll pass out weapons and start training. Anyways, when the bolas are made, everyone will need to be shown how to use them. Those that can will carry them"

Dil joined the group as Hunter was finishing. "I rode through the outskirts of Toll while everyone was doing their part here. It looked pretty bad. Farms burned. Death everywhere." He shook his head. "I did all I knew to do, but I know there is more I need to know and learn, but from who?"

The sun was melting away and the long hard day was passing on. Sam walked outside to stand in front of his inn. Seeing the gathering, he walked down the broad dusty road to the meeting. "Lord, uh, I mean Hunter." Sam shrugged his shoulders before slapping his fore head. "Hunter, I have baths drawn and the food will be set out in the same room as earlier. That is, when you are ready."

Hunter smiled at the toothless grin on the old man's face. "Thank you Sam, we're on the way." The inn keeper bowed then hurried back to the Black Thorn. Hunter smiled at the memory of Ol' Jed.

After everyone was clean and fed, Sam entered the dining room. "Excuse me but the people have been asking me questions and I did not know the right answers. But ahh I mean." Sam's eyes went to the floor.

Hunter studied him for a few seconds. "It's alright Sam. You can ask anything." Sam remained silent, "Go on Sam."

Sam looked up with true fear in his eyes. His head bobbed in rhythm with each word. "Yes sir, ahh, are you the giants of the prophecies?" Sam looked at the solid stares. "I mean how is it? We have heard of the three giants yet there be five of you here before my eyes?"

Before anyone could speak a voice behind Sam softly spoke. "My death shall be avenged, the seed shall spread anew life throughout the land. The three giants will strike fear in the hearts and death to all that oppose the righteous people." An old man stepped around Sam as the whole band looked to see where the voice was coming from. Sam gasped then bowed deep.

"Master Seer!" Ian rose and bowed his head. The brothers followed his lead along with Arrie and her sisters. The old man clad in a white tunic calmly walked into the room. A black swordsman, larger than most of the people they have seen so far, came in close behind the Seer. All the swordsmen noticed the man's hand clasped firmly around his sword, ready to use. O'Cey's wicked smile crept over his face.

Jinx turned to Hunter, "Does he look like the limo driver or what?"

"Yeah, could be his twin." added Tunk.

Hunter looked the old man in the eyes. "Are you the Seer?"

The seer chuckled. "I am a Seer and you are the seed. All of Rhea thanks you for coming." Looking first to Hunter, "You giant one, have the mighty eagle flying over you."

Tunk looked amazed at Hunter. "Mighty Eagle? How'd he know your spirit guide?" Jinx looked as cautious as Hunter, who shrugged off Tunk's question.

The old man looked to Tunk, "Don't wear the look of shock, oh Deadly Wolf, for I know you all." The old man smiled then looked at Jinx. He nodded. "And I see the Great Hawk is here as well. I welcome your presence to our land"

He walked over and placed a thin hand on Ian's shoulder. "And I see you have been given a new life to young one. You have done well." Hunter, Jinx and Tunk looked from one to the other, then watched the Seer as he moved. It seemed like he almost floated to the end of the table. "I also see you have brought a young wizard who possesses a strong spark within." Dil looked in his cloak and blew a long breath, looking puzzled when his face reappeared.

He looked at O'Cey and Mac. "I thank the wizard for bringing you great warriors." Smiling at Dil and his brothers. "I welcome you three to Rhea as well. You are needed very badly. I also thank the archers you allowed to join you." He moved to an empty chair at the end of the table. "Oh forgive me, may I join you?" All nodded so the Seer eased into the chair. "I think that it is time for us to have a talk." The table went deathly quiet, the black man stood silently behind the old sage. His hand still resting on the hilt of his sword. His eyes taking in the whole room.

I wish not to seem rude, but may I talk to our new warlords alone please?"

Hunter nodded to the group. "Thank all of you for what you have done today. There are beds ready and we have many long days ahead so rest well when you can." the room emptied quickly and quietly. The wizard sat with the five large warriors looking at the old man and his body guard. Ian stood at the closed door.

His story opened. "Thorn was our great and beloved leader. He made several of what he called 'journeys'. On his first journey, he was gone from us for a long time. When he returned he wore the hair such as the Great Eagle wears." Motioning to Hunter. "He also returned with a wife."

He looked at Hunter with a broad grin of admiration. "He appointed a third of his warriors to be known as the Cherok tribe." The story changed as he looked at Tunk. "After the seasons changed, he went on his second journey. He returned quicker from this journey and wore the hair as that of the Great Wolf. Appointed half of the remaining warriors the Sosa tribe." Turmoil was starting in Rhea and the tribes fought it off.

Looking now to Jinx. "After his third journey, he brought the Catak tribe and wore hair as you, Great Hawk." He signaled for a drink and Ian served him. He took a long sip of the rich wine.

Before the goblet touched the table he continued. "On his next to the last of his journeys, Thorn said his seed had grown and they knew him. We the searchers of his meaning came to agree he had sons. Rhea was unstable, but his tribes held strong."

"Many years passed as he longed to journey again. The Seers and the Wise ones protested this journey, but he left anyways. One of our Seers known as the Wanderer, followed on this crossing. Thorn's last trek lasted most of a change of seasons. After this return Thorn spoke to all the wise ones in Nod. 'The eagle and hawk will take flight one day, their talons long for flesh. They will be joined by the wolf in the fight for freedom. Freedom for my future people of Rhea.' "

"We pondered these words for too long. Our conclusion was his seed were to teach their offspring to become his great warriors. I hear you are great warriors and the warriors in which we did seek for so long." He took another drink, then sat in silence studying his captive audience. His smooth voice came back to life. "The uprisings during that journey changed the counsel in the fortress, Edaun. Someone evil worked inside Edaun and throughout Rhea. This evil was turning the people against Thorn. Some said he did not care for Rhea any more but for the new place in which he walked. Battles sprung up and the Neminoles rose out of their lairs. Giant trolls attacked the innocent and old."

The old man cleared his throat, Just before his death," He looked to Ian, "Thorn declared there will be a Brave Falcon known as the Key Bearer. His task will be to bring the seed to us. In his hour of deep need, he will find the ones to bear the fight. The giants will avenge my people and remove the evil that was to fall on Rhea. My death shall be avenged. The evil will leave Rhea. Its curse will be removed." Shaking his balding head, the Seer grinned, "Even I did not consider the seed and the giants were one in the same."

Jinx moved restlessly and broke into the history lesson. "OK, OK. It seems you may know a lot of what someone said. But who are you?" Jinx looked from the old man to the black man, and pointed at him. "And you! I know you! We all know you."

The swordsman looked deep into Jinx's eyes. "You know me not. I am as my father and his father and my brothers. We were, and we are, protectors to the seers. I am the eldest of six and I am called Nate." The big warrior's expression did not change. "One of my brothers, Dak, was killed crossing the Outlands with his seer before Edaun fell."

The Seer was dry washing his hands as he looked at the empty table. "I know not of the Seer of Dak's protections, his fate, or his whereabouts since that happened. Maybe he was killed. We do not know."

Hunter's elbows were on the table as he brought his hands together locking his fingers into a steeple position. The index fingers rested in front of his lip as he looked to the Protector. "Nate you said you have four remaining brothers. Are they all here in Rhea now?" Hunter spoke slowly, trying to chose the right words.

"No. One of them is with the Wanderer. The others stay in their own corners of Rhea, with their seers as well."

Hunter nodded, "How was your other brother killed?"

"Dak and his Seer were falsely summoned to Edaun, just before Alexar had taken the fortress." Nate looked sad in the remembrance of his fallen brother. "Alexar was trying to stop the telling of the prophecies." Hunter shook his head seeing the man's pain.

Jinx looked at Nate, "I still know you. We all know you." Nate grinned and shook his head.

Tunk could not take it anymore and blurted out. "You look like a man we called Limo, to me." Tunk laughed as the words left his lips. No one returned the laughter. Tunk looked around the quiet room and stood up. Nate tensed. The seer waved him off. The others in the room looked at him as if he were a fool. Tunk faked a yawn. "It's getting late. Does anyone else want to turn in. We can talk on this more tomorrow." No one moved. He flopped back in his chair with a groan.

Jinx looked around the table then laughed. "Seer, we say crazy things without thinking. Forgive my friend and forgive me as well. All this is still a shock to us." The Seer looked from one giant to the others and smiled. Jinx finished with, "Fun is our middle name!"

"As danger is your given and death being your last," grinned Nate.

Hunter's eyes touched the Seer's, as he slowly lowered his hands. "If I am understanding you right and what Ian has told us of the lost tribes, then we need to travel to Sumra' and reunite them."

The seer nodded and closed his eyes as he recited. "When the righteous returns, then peace will grow and the just shall reign again. We feel you are to retake their lead."

Hunter returned the nod. "You do speak as you know us."

The seer cleared his throat. "I know you, I have seen your names."

"Our names?" Tunk sat up from his slump and looked from Hunter to Jinx.

The old man nodded. "The book of life is filled with names on its sacred leaflets. As you turn the pages you can see each life as they are lived out. But when you turn to a page and the writing ceases to be seen, so also ends that life. Sad that they shall be remembered only by a small few and then forgotten."

Jinx rubbed his face as he spoke. "What does this have to do with us? No one knows us, so we won't be missed."

The Seer laughs. "I have seen your lives and know each of you; even the wizard and his kinsman. The life that had been taken from all that knew them, will be forgotten after a while. But a hero's name will live forever in the memories of all left behind. They become legends for those yet to come."

Jinx laughed, "What?"

The Seer smiled. "It is simple. You are the chosen and so are the others as well. Someone has allowed your talents to grow and to be brought here to give us aid. You three wear the mark of the

Thorn and you are the giants. You are the seed. Now you have a duty to perform and I am here to help guide you if you wish."

"Where we are needed then we must go!" Jinx placed a big right hand in the middle of the table. "I don't need a guide but Tunk and the McNures do."

Hunter looked to Nate then placed his hand on Jinx's. "We had planned to go to Sumra' after Brant. We welcome you and Nate."

Tunk placed his hand on Hunter's. "I go where my brothers go! I don't need a guide, but I may need a pretty baby sitter though."

Mac laughed as he got up from his seat. "Brunette preferred, right brother?" Jinx grins.

"Excellent! Brant needs you worst than Toll ever did." The Seer smiled as he nodded, "I conclude with a proverb . . . 'the righteous warriors shall prevail!' "

The Seer rose from his chair. "If this resistance force will allow us to travel with them, we will go also. Just remember, you travel where death and evil have no boundaries." "

O'Cey looked from the seer to Hunter, slapping his hand on Tunk's. "I go with me brothers too!"

Mac dove in almost knocking everyone from the circle. "Right! I'm not gonna let you four have all the fun!" O'Cey rolls his head back as he releases a hardy laugh.

Hunter looked around his four large friends and then to the stack of hands. "Seer, I will go anywhere and into anything with these men." He looked at the wise man, "And we do welcome you and Nate to join us. Besides you can explain more of Edaun's past to us and more of what we may expect to see or do." Hunter smiled as Dil put his hand on top of Mac's. "Besides we have the Great Blue Wizard with us, so we have go and help as we can."

Hunter stood and pulled his hand free, keeping his eyes on Dil. "I know you Blue Wizard and I know you to be true." He looked back to the Seer. "Can you help us with re-uniting these tribes?"

The old Seer grinned. "I may be of help there, but the Wanderer would fare better as far as you are concerned to the tribes. He is well known to them."

Mac pulled his hand and slapped the table. "I say you be in with us Seer! You can travel with the Band of Brothers says I!" Getting up from his chair quickly he looked deep in the Seer's eyes. "Where should we go to find this lost wanderer? If he be lost, we will find him!"

"He is not lost." The Seer laughed as he rose from his chair. "He will show himself. He roams into every corner of Rhea and his travels take him anywhere a man can go." His laughter passed quickly. "Whenever and wherever he is needed, he always shows himself. I know not where to send you to find him, so I say follow the path you now take and he will appear." The old man turned to leave. "I will join you on the morrow and I also pledge my help to you in this quest." Turning back to face the circle of warriors, "I also pledge to stay out of the way and I'll make no battle plans."

"Settled then! It is getting late. We have an early day tomorrow." Hunter followed the Seer and Nate to the door. "We will stay in Toll one extra day. Plan on pulling out early day after tomorrow." Their wizard was close in tow to Hunter.

The Seer and Nate vanished into the shadows down the long corridor. Hunter and Dil stood waiting for the others.

Tunk followed Hunter and Dil in the hall. "Can someone tell me why morning always has to come so early?"

Hunter laughed. "My guess is it comes that way just to aggravate us. What you think Dil?"

Dil shrugged. "I say it does, because it does." Hunter and Tunk laughed as the three headed down the hall to find old Sam and their rooms.

The night went quiet. All the archers took turns as night watchers, but they saw no one wanting to return. Word of the battle and death had spread to all that stood against the liberators of Toll. The night stayed quiet and passed quickly. Before sunrise the blood of brothers were gathering again in the large dining room.

The staff of the Black Thorn were working hard, ushering food in to the waiting warriors. Jinx was nowhere to be found.

The room was still as quiet as the passing night, until Jinx entered the door, breaking the silence. He dropped a large wooden box. "There's forty eight bolas, throwing knives and tomahawks in here." He opened the box and started passing them out. "They'll have more bolas finished today. Sann's making more knives and tomahawks too."

Hunter nodded. "Good. After we eat, everyone split up. Tunk, Jinx and Mac take the archers, and teach'em how they work. Work a good four hours?" Hunter shifted in his chair, dipping his plate. "Practice bolas first, then swords?" He looked at O'Cey. "How bout working one on one with Ian on his training?"

A normal growl left O'Cey as he answered, "Aye, I will have the lad a blade master afore you know it Hunt!"

Excited murmurs accompanied the sounds of the filling of plates. Silence quickly entered the room once again as everyone was concentrated on attacking the food on their plates. After the meal was finished, the whole battle squad filed out on to the street. Each of the giant warriors took their share of archers for training.

Hunter pulled Arrie aside. "If I know O'Cey and Mac, they have been teaching you how to handle a sword, right?"

The pretty little archer smiled, "Yes my lord." Hunter scowled at the words. Arrie smiled again as she pat his large crossed arms. "I only tease you Hunter. I apologize. I saw how that title upsets you. I will use it no more." Hunter nodded. She continued, "They say my sisters catch on fast too."

"Good you go with Ian to train with O'Cey. He is a great teacher. Not the most pleasant but he does put on a show as if he hates everyone. He can train you better than any of the rest of us." Hunter turned to Dil, who stood in his shadow. "Wizard, find the Seer and bring him on to the green where we met yesterday." Dil quickly nodded and ran back in the inn. Hunter saw the beaming grin spread across the young man's face when he called him wizard.

Hunter watched as O'Cey started his lesson in a shaded paddock, beside the livery. His other friends were set to their lessons. He was engrossed in his observation but still Hunter heard the quiet steps as the Seer approached, closely followed by Dil. The board walk in front of the Inn moaned slightly under Nate's large frame at the Seer's side. After a few silent minutes of watching Ian spar with Arrie, he headed toward the green. O'Cey's bark was easily heard. "You two maggots need to use your whole body. Don't forget, use everything feet, elbows even spit if need be!" Hunter watched the young woman grab the wrist of Ian's sword arm.

Arrie cut her eyes to Hunter. "If he spits on me, O'Cey will face my bow!"

Hunter laughed as he walked off with the Seer. Dilman, the wizard, and the silent protector were close behind. Hunter broke the silent march. "Seer we plan to do all we can for the people here, but this talk of the giants and seeds, how can it be we are who you seek?"

The Seer stood in the center of the green, scanning the horizon. "Hunter, answer me as to how you came to Rhea?"

"By that door thing."

"Think my son, how is that possible you mystically show from faraway to here. Could it have been by accident? Or was it planned?" The Seer smiled as he turned around to look at the troubled Hunter. "How can you believe someone may have foreseen this and set forth his plan and now you are here?"

Hunter shook his head. "This is strange to me, strange to all of us. I guess I try putting too much logic into figuring it out. Someone did tell me to stop thinking too hard." They talked on as the sounds of mock battle blended with the sounds of Toll's people enjoying their peaceful day of a life again.

The sun climbed quickly in the sky. O'Cey barked his lesson at his pupils. Noon approached and he roared again. "Okay Orc bait! Let's go eat!"

The group headed into the inn. Tunk hands Hunter a bandoleer filled with throwing knives as they reached the front door. "Just picked 'em up." Hunter studied the sharp thin blades. "What you think Hunt?"

Hunter drew one of the blades from the long row. His hands was a blur as he threw it across the wooden crossways. The blade sunk deep in a knot on the farthest post from the Inn. "They feel good and are really balanced. Nice! How many so far?"

"Bout fifty and they say they can triple that by tomorrow afternoon." He handed Hunter a tomahawk. "Look at it close."

Hunter studied the miniature ax and nodded. "It's the design we had talked about, remember?"

Handle slightly curved away from the cutting blade. A star shaped point at the top of the handle over the blade. "Yeah, we were drunk then, but it does feel good." Looking at the knobbed end of the handle. Hunter nodded as he fingered the Thorn emblem burned on the end. He ran his thumb over the sharp blade and studied the head of the weapon. Blade wide and curved and a wicked point on the other end. "Nice job, Tunk." His hand blurred again as he threw the new weapon to stick beside the knife blade. "Cool! These people do make excellent weapons."

Tunk retrieved both the new weapons and handed them back to Hunter. "Do we have time to stay, or not?"

"Don't know, well I guess so. Can one more day hurt? We'll check with the others." Entering the building Hunter looked at Tunk. "How many people are working on this stuff?"

"Looks like half the town. I went back to Sann's after breakfast. I couldn't believe the number of people working in there." Tunk laughed. "I believe he'll have even more help as this goes on. We need to get in there and eat or the McNure brothers will eat it all."

The war party had gathered around the large table for their noon meal in the dining hall. Hunter made his announcement of the weapons and if they should stay in Toll one more day.

Jinx nodded his approval. "I say that'd work out great Hunter. We can help setup Toll's defense. Mac, O'Cey and me have worked out a few things."

Hunter nodded. "Good. Do what you can for them."

After the meal O'Cey and Hunter went to oversee the afternoon lessons on the green. The others helped to prepare the town for future attacks. Twelve men from Brant went with them as well to help build.

They took turns training the townspeople in case of more attacks. Mac took the first in the class. "Your best defense is keep the scoundrels out. Fightin' hand to hand an' sword, is not for the week of heart. It be bloody and you die. You be fare shot with short bow so we will get you to know the long bow."

The sun was dropping quickly from the skies and the students were showing signs of exhaustion. O'Cey's loud bark overshadowed the dull cracks of the practice swords. "Alright troll snacks, time's up!" Hunter shook his head and laughed. O'Cey smiled his crooked smile. "Afore light on the morrow, I be here! You too! Be ready!" The archers slowly accompanied Ian into the inn.

Tunk and Mac met Hunter and O'Cey on the green. They talked of the day's progress. Jinx saw the small meeting and headed to them from the blacksmith shop. Tunk was telling his story when Jinx interrupted the low buzz of conversation. "All the weapons are made and they will continue to produce more." Jinx seemed excited about something.

Tunk looked shocked. "What if they fall into our enemy's hand? Then they'll be used on us!"

Jinx shook his head and smiled, "they'll have places set up to safely store them." He laid out the plan to the others. "If the battles last longer than we see as of now, we'll need all the arsenal we can store up. The smithy will see to delivering the goods to the drops in every town. He and local merchants will take care of the details."

"How will we know where to find them?" Hunter was looking at the blacksmith shop.

"What else! There will be a thorn, on a plaque near each spot." Jinx laughed. "Sounds cool, huh?" The whole circle nodded. "At

D. E. Hendley Jr.

each place the owner, picked by our people here, will answer to one of the prophesy riddles they told me. For example say when will the eagle fly?"

Tunk shook his head. "Wouldn't the thorn eventually be figured out?"

Jinx laughed at his questioning friend. "I didn't say the thorn would be in front of the safe house Tunk. A shop owner near the designated spot will point to a person then another until the right spot is named."

Hunter nodded. "Ok. I'll approve this, but only if we are sure the safe house will not be breached."

Jinx laughed. "You worry too much. We already have that worked out. The pointers to the safe house will tell only if he hears the right words."

O'Cey had stood long enough. "Stop the riddle fool! Tell us as it be."

Ian was smiling as he pushed his way into the circle. "The righteous will come, and the giants will be avengers of the slain. The people will arise and the eagles will again take flight."

O'Cey scratched his head. "That sounds like a lot to remember and say."

Hunter nodded. "Make sure that the thorn is concealed in a mixture of art or something that we can identify with; just so nobody else figures it out."

Tunk nodded as he rubbed his stomach. "Good job bro, now let's eat!" He patted Jinx on the back.

"No, that isn't the answer." Jinx laughed. "The question by us is, when will the eagle fly? They answer, when the giants free them. When the next come back, then they are free."

They walked in silence back to the inn. As they entered the common room, they all noticed the Seer was there sitting at a small table with Dil. The Seer waved Hunter to the table. As Hunter made his way to the table he heard the Seer say, "I'll talk more of this with you in the morning, young wizard. Just remember, you do need to go and train." Dil nodded as he left his chair. As he turned, he grinned at O'Cey and Mac.

O'Cey elbowed Mac. "I like to see the wee one happy, don't you brother?"

"Aye, but you best not tell him I say as so!" Mac's broad grin beamed a proud showing of their younger brother.

"Let it go Mac! We be in a new place, a new life that brother argument ends now! Understand!"

"I am proud of him too O'Cey, but if I don't ride the wee one, he will not try as hard to impress me." Mac laughed. "But I will try to do better by him, brother."

Hunter walked up to the Seer, Jinx and Ian walked on either side of him. Tunk entered the room ushering Mac and O'Cey toward the same table. Ian took the seat in front of the old wise man. "Master Seer, I have some questions and you may be able to help me to understand."

"Sir, we also need more answers too." Hunter helped himself to the seat beside Ian, also facing the old man. The large black man behind the Seer carefully watched. He was poised to spring into action if need be. Hunter noted the man's deadly look, but show of fear was absent in Hunter.

The Seer watched the wary look of the giant man before him. He quickly studied Hunter's eyes. He saw the care for the weak as well as a cold stare of a deadly warrior. The Seer nodded to the massive man as he wave a hand to ease any growing tension. Turning slowly to his protector he smiled, nodding him to relax.

He spoke as he turned to face the troop. "If I can answer you with the truth I shall. If not, then we will have to see if I can find it. I also feel a need to speak with all of you." Tunk had made his way to the table. The Seer nodded for all to sit. He then looked to Ian. "You may proceed, young Key Bearer."

"During my studies with the wise ones and the seers, I was taught of prophecies of the Giants and the Seed." He looked from Hunter to Jinx, then to Tunk as he took his seat. The Scottish warriors stood off to the right talking with the wizard. "These are the seed of Thorn. I have seen his mark on them, but I see five giants have come to us. All are deadliest of warriors as I have ever seen and all live by the sword." Looking down as he dry washed his hands. "I cannot see my way. How can there be five when we were taught there is to be three?" Dil moved toward the table with his brothers. Ian looked as the new trio also took seats. "Seer?" Dill looked questioningly at the wise man. "Master, what of this wonder of a wizard?"

The old man smiled as he studied each of the faces. The large guard kept his close watch, noting every detail. "Simple answers, my son. I do not question what has come to me out of a dream." Looking at the three brothers, "When extra aid shows itself, we will take their help." Nodding to the wizard and his brothers, "When that help turns up at the door, let them in." Waving for them to sit and join them. "I invite them in because they also were sent to us. A wonder of a surprise, so allow them to do what they can if they will."

Ian stumbled with his words. "No, that is not what I mean," still rubbing his hands. The Seer raised his hand for silence.

"You wish me to explain that which I cannot, and I will not try. If Rhea is blessed with more champions, we welcome this as the true gift that it is. All that is present before me, will deliver a great blow to the evil that clouds over us." Smiling the old man finished. "Mine is not to question why, yet maybe Thorn knew not of the other swordsmen. To me it matters not. Or maybe he knew and allowed the secret to do as it has." Laughing, the Seer slaps the table. "A great surprise and I welcome it. Yet, unless they are one with the same evil that is trying to cover us I wish them gone." He laughed again. "Alas I say, they be friends."

Ian smiled, "Sir I do not question my new friends involvement or loyalties. I ask simply does the prophecies speak of them?" Pointing to the brothers and the wizard.

"I know what you are trying to say. As I said, I question not, for I see them here so be it as it is. Listen to me Ian you are also the seed."

O'Cey took a seat from another table and his brothers followed his lead. The Seer smiled as they took their seats. O'Cey interrupted in a rare and soft voice. "With all the foretell here, I do wonder if me brothers and I fit in this Seer?"

The Seer thought before speaking. "I do recall it is written that The Wizard of the Orb shall one day rise. He will take up fight against evil. He loosens his wrath and helps to cut a path for freedom. Now it works out the magic users and the seers have their protectors so should not a wizard be protected or in the instance be double protected?"

Ian nodded. "I do not remember those words. I have read and studied all the books and writings. It was not of Thorn's prophesies."

The seer smiles and watches Dil as the wizard looks the room over. He continues. "I know, it is from books of the sages and magic users of Nod. It was written many years before Thorn was sired by Stagg. We thought it to be another time" He nods as Dil meet his gaze. "So I say it is good timing as I see it. We need all the help we can receive."

Mac laughs and grabs Dil. "He do be the Great Wizard old man! O'Cey and me do be his wrath to release."

O'Cey roars. "Aye! See to it wee one, loose your wrath! It do be so in the foretelling!" A small eruption of laughter floods the table. The silent guardian allows a quick smile to show. Hunter takes note.

Dil laughs as well. "Aye, me brothers do be my wrath! I say, let them do their havoc on the evil!" O'Cey roars again as Mac beats the table. "And my other friends can strike their own fear too."

The Seer chuckles. "I do not feel for all those that oppose this force. Those gathered before me are the most deadly I have encountered." His protector's deep laughter draws the eyes of all seated around the table. He snaps to attention and scowls at the onlookers.

Tunk waves his hands for silence. As quietness returns, he takes his turn. "Sir, ah Seer, can you explain all this to us. We are new here. New to this place. New to your time." Tunk looked around the table. Every one focuses on the old man again.

The old seer simply nods. He clears his throat then speaks. "Rhea has always been plagued with evil and bloody uprisings. Some die by the people uniting and following a champion. Others have been smothered by the great leaders in our past. In my lifetime I have known two of such great leaders. Stagg was a barbarian warlord of Sumra'. He was a great leader, he came to power defeating the dragon walkers of the second age. He took rule over Rhea and held it with a strong hand. He later built the first fortress, Edaun. Or as known today as the ruins of old Edaun."

"In his prime, he, as he called it, journeyed. On one of these journeys he brought a wife back to Rhea. She was, ahh, let's see. Different. Yes, yes, different from the women here." He looked from each of the giant warriors. Then he smiled at Hunter. "She wore the kind of feathers as you do." Pointing to

Hunter's Eagle feathers. "She wore the animal skin also like those as you three are wearing now."

The Seer drank from a cup sitting in front of him. After what seemed like a long pause to swallow, he continued. "Stagg said she was named Running Fawn."

"She could have been from where we come from." Jinx smiled and winked at Hunter. Hunter looked up from fiddling with the bandoleer and shrugged.

The Seer nodded. "She said a word to us. Oh yes, Chero, ahh now I remember. Cherokee, yes that was it. Yes that is what she said." Hunter's searching eyes studied the old man's face. The Seer smiled and nodded as he continued. "The seers found her to be very wonderful. Her works with herbs was amazing, even her knowledge of warfare. She called all the seers, medicine men." Hunter nodded as he draped the finished knife belt over his shoulders. The seer grinned at him. "I see you and your friends are great warriors. You are warriors of the same people as she? The blood of your people run strong in each of you." Looking to the Scottish brothers. "I see the warrior blood is strong within you three as well." O'Cey grunted. Mac and Dilman grinned.

Tunk nodded as he flexed out his broad chest. "Seer, we are of different tribes, but we all are of warrior blood."

The protector laughed. "Any fool can see that you all are a great force. Even the protectors of the wizard are mighty swordsmen. I have seen each of you and the deadly path you have cut."

The Seer waved his left hand and the man behind him went still. The protector's wary look stayed searching the faces of each man before him.

Jinx saw the tension in the lone swordsman's actions. "As I see it big man, you are not a threat to us." The protector didn't acknowledge the man trying to communicate to him. Jinx looked to the Seer. "Hunter is of the Cherokee blood."

"This is truly odd to me if he is only of the same blood." The three giant warriors exchanged more of the puzzled looks they were now growing used to in this strange land. The old man studied Hunter's chiseled face, then gave a casual nod. "No matter as to that for now. Stagg set up the laws and pinned the evils of his day to the ground. He had a son with Running Fawn. They called him Thorn." Hunter, Jinx and Tunk each looked at their exposed tattoos. The old man nodded. "Oh yes I am glad to see the giant brothers proudly show his mark. I also have even seen Ian's new mark as well. He now wears the mark flashing from his neck." Ian felt the coolness of the medallion resting on his chest.

O'Cey pulled the gold ring tied to the bottom of his long beard. The Seer looked in wonder as he looked at the wizard. Dilman smiled as he exposed the same imbedded in his staff. He next looked questioningly at Mac. "Do you also hold the mark.

Mac slowly pulled his sword. The protector tensed.

Mac barked a quick laugh. "No worry, you not me enemy." He showed the gold ring with a thorn on the hilt of his trusted weapon. He then quietly slid it home.

The old man shook his head. "So you are all connected? Wonderful!"

O'Cey spoke quietly. "These trinkets have been ours on our births. How or where they come by in no known to me."

The seer sat thinking in silence before continuing. "Thorn also journeyed as his father had. After each of his journeys he divided his warriors into his tribes. Each tribe was to watch over the people of Rhea. One from the east, another from the west and the last within Edaun itself. Each tribe member wore their locks in similar fashion. Their styles as the three of you wear. Each style identified the members as to which tribe they were associated with."

"Makes good sense." Hunter sat a little more relaxed in his chair. "All troops should be known together as well as apart. Mark them somehow."

"He does sound like some kind of military genius." Chimed Jinx.

The Seer nodded. "I said that to tell you that people here will join the fight. They will identify you, but we must go to Sumra'. Go find and unite the remaining of the tribes that were built in Thorn. Rhea knows your hair and knows of the once strong justice the tribes once carried. Thus it will identify you as of the tribes. They will also see your size, and what do you suppose they will think of that? Giants?"

Hunter nodded. "But will the tribes be willing to follow strangers? We may wear similar hair, but they will know we are not of them."

O'Cey looked puzzled. "If the tribes be as strong as you say, why are they not doing the job for themselves?"

The Seer waved off the question. "Oh yes. My brothers, the other seers are now sharing the news of the giants arrival. Rumors of you have taken flight and spreads as wildfire. I know the news of a blue wizard and his mighty protectors have spread as well and as fast. All of you will be expected. The tribes look to the East. They are looking to see when the prophesies of giants coming will unfold."

O'Cey grunted. "I say Seer, if the tribes were as great of warriors, why were they defeated?"

"They were not defeated. They, as we know it, left as Thorn asked them to. The Seer adjusted in his seat and spoke casually. "Alexar had and still may hold great allies. We will discuss that at a later time."

Hunter finished another strap. He stood to his full towering heights as the Seer looked on in wonder. Slowly, he placed the holders, adjusting the heavy leather to fit around his neck, over opposite shoulders. The belts crossed his broad chest and back. A blurred movement sounded a thunderous clap on the heavy table. The dead silence was awakened as all quickly spun around the table to see where the sound came from. A newly made throwing knife still quivered in a post fifteen feet from where they sat. Hunter slowly looked to the Seer then to the Protector. "I have heard what you said. I have talked and heard what Ian had said. I have seen with my eyes the world here. I say if we are those they seek, then we must not disappoint the ones who wish us not to be."

O'Cey roared, "Aye and O'Cey say the McNures ride with me brothers in arms." Hunter nodded to his friend and comrade.

The Seer also nods in agreement. Then smiles in satisfaction. He continued. "Thorn did grow to become a brilliant warrior but not the wise leader as his father Stagg. Stagg was killed in his old age, but still in the battle for old Edaun. Thorn reluctantly took his place. Staggs' old warriors repelled the last of the Orcian army. After the last battle, the warriors followed under Thorn and killed most of the fleeing Orcs; then marched on the trolls of Neach and Sumra'. The Orcs are few this day because of the tribes. A good many of the Trolls were able to stay hidden and a large number did survive and multiply." The Seer smiled. "Now a days they take no pity on the people of Rhea. The beasts come and go at will."

The old man took a drink from his cup, then spoke again. "Edaun is now ruled by worst of evil and Alexar is allies to an unknown number of those creatures. There are others who pose an even greater threat out there at Alexar's beck and call. Your road will get harder as the days go on."

Hunter nodded as he retook his seat. The wooden chair groaned under his weight. "That is all good for your history lesson but how is it you seem to have known of us before today. These giant seed, what is that?"

The old man laughed. "I do know of all you, for I have seen the pages." The strangers to Rhea looked from one to the others. Others in the room sounded as if in awe. The Seer calmly continued. "Okay it is not time for us to begin that journey but we will soon." He rose from his place of sitting before the staring crowd of listeners. "It is getting on in time and the night will pass us by if we continue to sit here. I will say for now it was a good day and time to retreat to my room. We will talk more of these things at a later time."

The Seer pushed his chair back under the table then spoke again. "Only remember this my friends, the enemy you have faced thus far is not the full strength of the evil possessed by Alexar." He turned. The whole room watched as the duo quietly left the room.

The band stayed in the dining hall. They all ate their meal in silence. The only sound heard was scraping of the plates. When finished, each retreated to their own rooms with the same thoughtful silence. A bed awaited them for a well deserved rest.

Morning quickly came without any problems during the night. Toll awoke to a peaceful morning.

While sitting to his morning meal Hunter studied the somber face of the Seer as he quietly entered the room with Nate, close at hand. Tunk was seated to the left of Hunter. "Hey Hunt, you reckon we have a little time to talk more with the Seer?"

Hunter shrugged. "We only have a short while, but we need to start with the town's defense. I would like to know a little more of what we face, but we need to try and make Toll ready. Time is running short."

Nuel spoke up. "The archers can load the gear in the wagons, Master Hunter. We will practice first then do what is needed." As he talked he pointed at his brother and the four women archers. They each nodded their approval.

"Good. Most of our gear is ready to load." Tunk motioned to the door. "And take the new batch of weapons and distribute them out to the others. Stow all the extra in that munitions wagon I showed you." Nuel nodded, then hurried out the door.

Jinx grabbed Ecott's right shoulder, easily spinning the smaller man in his tracks. "You do need to be aware of our horses. They still ain't use to you!"

Ian spoke up. "No worry there Jinx, I will go with them and help. Those beasts do act as if they do not want to eat me now."

Jinx grunted his answer and released the archer's shoulder. "Go then, but just remember, they will hurt you."

Hunter noticed the Seer was looking so he smiled into the patient face of the old man. The wise man simply nodded in return. Hunter then turned to Ian. "Ok Ian, do what you can but you need to be careful of the horses as well." Looking over to the other large warriors then back to the silent wise man. "All our war-horses are high strung and very temperamental." The old man nodded quietly again, but continued to study all the gigantic warriors crowding the room.

"Jinx and O'Cey's hay bags are more mental than the rest!" Laughed Tunk. Mac laughed as he slapped Jinx on the back of his head.

Jinx growled. "But O'Cey and me are even more mental than they will ever be, Tunk my friend."

The Seer was nodding still, but Hunter knew the man didn't have a clue as to what they were talking about. Hunter grins again.

Mac pushed from the table. "You don't need me right now so tell me a shorter version later Hunter. I need to go finish training the townspeople. You stay here to talk. Talking bores me."

Jinx nodded to Hunter as he pushed from the table. "I'll help Mac." Hunter waved as Jinx turned to follow Mac.

"I do want to hear more before we head out into what lies ahead." Hunter settled back into his chair. Tunk moved beside him, as the crew of men herded out the door.

Conal stopped before leaving. "We will go to get the supply wagon stocked up for the trip."

The pupils of O'Cey had eaten quick and were already on the green to train again. O'Cey had the lessons planned out and was planning on working them extra hard before he would let them load the weapons wagon.

The Seer began his story as the door closed. "After Thorn repelled the last of the troll attacks, he had to make many repairs to old Edaun. So he decided instead of rebuilding his father's outdated stronghold, he would build the new fortress. Not long after, the new Edaun was complete. He began to travel, as he called it."

"What is this traveling?" asked Hunter.

The old wise man spoke on. "The portal that brought you to us, Thorn used them. On each return from his three travels, he came back to us with the hair as you three wear. Each became a symbol of his three tribes. He set up a new tribe from each trip. They are the tribes in which you now will seek out."

"Thorn made other journeys later, but I know not of these or their reason. Thorn did say as he was getter older that the seed had grown and will soon be ready. That is when the evil fell on Rhea. Thorn was soon caught in liar webs of the wizard Alexar. During the last of his travels, lies spread and people began to listen. Alexar was able to use the absence of Thorn to start turning the people against their ruler."

Hunter interrupted, "You did say you wished to join on our journey." The Seer nodded. "Then we can learn more of the history, during our journey. What we really need to know is about these trolls, their habits and the warriors of Alexar. The Nimenole things we will face and what to expect."

"Yes, yes you are right. There are not as many old trolls as before, but Alexar's Nimenoles are now plentiful. The regular trolls were not as easy to control but this new breed they are meaner, smaller, quicker and smarter. They are deathly afraid of large fires but fires draw attention and are extinguished. They are not fond of large bodies of water as well." The Seer smiled. "Hunter you and the others are greater in height by a head than the largest of the Nimenoles. The older breed of the trolls are also as few as the orcs."

The Seer cleared his throat and took a drink from the large mug sitting in front of him. After a brief time in thought he continued. "Now the true soldiers of Alexar's Edaun are a well trained force. The ones you have faced are not of those soldiers. They are local brutes and thugs made into soldiers. But if one was to remove the control from their leaders these outlaws may disband. When they have no leader, you will see a difference."

Hunter interrupted. "But they may run to another leader."

The old man took a long drink of mead before he spoke again. "That may be true, but without heart, most thugs hide. All we need is for this resistance to grow in all of Rhea. If you win, most of the people on our side will reunite with the warrior tribes. Then this evil will do nothing but fall."

Hunter laughed. "From what I have seen so far, the people will be following us and soon."

"Yes, yes but they also have been misled by others. Winning all of Rhea will not be as easy as Toll. There have been others to rise up and the people followed only to be led into disaster. Then death comes to many a citizen."

Hunter nodded. "We will win them by securing their freedom."

"Yes, I know but, Alexar will do all he can to remove your creditability." The Seer rose from his chair. "We do have a ways to go and I think we need to ensure that Toll is on its way to control itself."

As the two warriors walked outside the Black Thorn. The townspeople looked at Hunter as their leader. People nodded and said, "My lord." Calling him the new warlord. Hunter looked at Tunk. "I guess we need to get use to being called 'My Lord,' huh?"

Tunk laughed and started a flamboyant bow. "Yes, my lord." Townspeople saw this and started bowing. Hunter scowled and turned to storm off. The Seer chuckled from behind them.

Conal of Brant, walked toward the foursome with a small party of followers. Quickly the Protector eased between the Seer and the men.

The men stopped and bowed their heads as Conal spoke. "Good master, we, pointing to the eleven men standing behind him then to himself, would like to ride with the blood of brothers. We could take care of the camp for you and your war party as you need. We have been training with the blade master O'Cey, and will do as we must in battle. We can take care of ourselves."

Hunter looked at the Seer. The old man nodded. Hunter looked back to the men assembled before them and then to their spokesman. "What do we call you?" Conal shrugged. "We'll call you the Crew." The men nodded as one and all wore wide smiles.

Another man from the crew stepped forward bowing his head, "I am Leister, I am also a Fletcher, I offer my skills to the service of the Giants."

"We could use a good arrow maker. Each of you will continue to train with the warriors." Hunter looked from Conal to Leister. "Ok, the camp duties are for you and the crew. I say you train and stay out of the way. Understood?"

The whole group nodded. Conal spoke, "Done, good master."

Hunter returned the nod. "If all is ready, find Ian to get some weapons. Train more with O'Cey while you can today." With that, the men set off on their way.

When the whole troop reassembled outside, they all set about their training.

Chapter 7

Something in the Air

In a corner office in Pierre, South Dakota, two men sit opposite across a large desk. Each man stares quietly at photos spread across a layer of papers. One of the men showing gray at the temples rubbed his unshaven rough growth of facial hair. His tall, slender body slouched as his elbows rested on the desk, protecting an open file. Agent Johnson's eyes were swollen from the lack of sleep. Slowly, he folded his hands covering the open file laying beneath his searching gaze. He looked across the collage to the other confused man. Slowly Johnson shook his head. "Jason, let's try this one more time. What do you think happened after that trailer incident?"

The younger agent, Jason Brown, spoke while rubbing his own tired eyes. "I am still as confused as you are, sir." Sitting in a leather high back chair across from his supervisor, the young man's eyes began searching the papers and photos. Again, no answer jumped out at him. "I say as you said before, this Jansen character cooked up the thefts and the laundry scheme. As far as the others, I can't fit them into that. If you want to know anything about that creature and the other strange objects, he looked Johnson in the eyes, I can't say, and I think we need to bury them for a while. As far as where this Hunter guy vanished to, I can't do anything but call him Houdini."

Johnson's nod was interrupted by a soft knock at the door. They stopped the conversation so nothing they said would come out to make them sound crazy. Both men turned to face the new comer as the door opened without permission. "Sir, sorry to interrupt you but you were right, Jansen was trying to board that plane for Mexico."

Johnson shook his head in discuss of that name. "Thank you Smitty, where is he?"

"Bill's got him down the hall. You know he actually cried like a baby when we grabbed him." The younger man laughed as he held the door open.

Johnson let a small laugh escape his weary lips. "Good! Come on in and close the door." Agent Smith entered and closed the large oak door. "I say sit down for a few minutes and let him sweat." Johnson smirked, as Smith headed towards the desk. "No, nevermind, I can't wait. Go get him and bring him in here. Cancel that. Drag the crying fool in here!"

"Yes sir. My pleasure." The younger agent laughed as he turned back to the door. He turned the knob and looked back to agent Johnson. "Sir, I say my two cents worth is this Hunter and his crew are innocent. But that's just my opinion, sir." Johnson waved him on. Agent Smith opened the door and walked out just enough to wave to the other agent down the hall.

Johnson and Brown grinned as Jansen's squeals echoed through the empty hall.

A few minutes later, a red faced, Paul Jansen was pushed into the room. The four agents watched as Jansen recovered then waddled into Agent Johnson's office. Johnson shifted his stare at the collection covering his desk. He spoke without looking up from the mess laying before him. "I'll speak only once and do not think me to be stupid Mister Jansen. Now sit down." Shaking, the short, fat man almost missed the leather chair emptied by agent Brown. "Another thing Jansen, do not say a word until I ask you to speak! Understood?" Jansen's head bobbled his reply. Jansen straighten himself in the chair with a groan. "Jansen, I went back to the site. I was disturbed by what I saw."

Jansen blubbered, "I can explain!"

"Shut up! I'll ask, you answer!" Johnson jumped to his feet slamming his hands on the desk. "I saw a crane at the site where that slab once stood." Jansen looked down from the cold stare coming his way from the aggravated agent. "The crane was overturned and that slab broken in half! Not you tell me why?"

"I don't know, vandals, maybe?" Jansen shook as he spoke.

"You're right. A fat, little greedy vandal." Jansen sunk as low as he could in the thick pad of the leather chair.

"I didn't mean to break it! I was trying to take it to a lab so my people could study it! Mister Johnson, I swear! You believe me right? You do sir, don't you?" Jansen was still shaking. "There was a flash of light when it broke free. The men got scared and ran when . . . ."

"Get a grip you weasel. I know you had something to do with the theft of the jewels. That I can prove easily. I can also prove you have received other stolen goods 'cause we have recovered those from your store house. I'd say there was more but you've already moved loads, didn't you?"

Jansen shook his head and his whole body quivered. "No, no it was them! Not me!"

"Shut up, Jansen!" Agent Johnson walked around the old desk to face Jansen at close range. "If those other men were here then I would know that for sure by now, wouldn't I?"

The little man jumped in his chair. "I don't know," Johnson held his finger up to his mouth. Jansen clamped his mouth shut.

"I wasn't asking for an answer. I believe I could work it to prove you managed to have them kidnapped or maybe disposed of." Johnson laughed. "Then again, that would be hard to do. I did get to see Hunter in action so neither of those could have actually happened. I've seen all of their military papers and I know that it would not be possible for a worm like you to have pulled either off, but for you sir I am willing to lie. Now do you understand me Mister Jansen?"

"Yes sir, I'm sorry." Jansen grinned, "I was just defending my . . ."

"Enough! Why were you leaving for Mexico?" Jansen fell back to the protection of the chair.

"Business, Mister Johnson." Smiling again, Jansen put on his best airs. "That's all. I wasn't running away, honest."

"Honest? That word doesn't seem right coming from your mouth!" Agent Johnson turned, grabbing the open file. His tone mellowed a bit. "Do not think of me as being stupid again Mister Jansen."

Johnson looked at agent Brown as he laughed. "I bet he thinks he is smarter than you sir."

"When donkeys fly out of my butt!" Johnson's stare zeroed back on the cowering Jansen. "Now, to the test on the creature we found." Dropping the papers in Jansen's lap, the little man jumped. "I have found nobody in this country to give any kind of name for it. No one has a clue what it is or where it came from. And now that all the other diggers have vanished, you try to run. What am I to think?"

"I know it looks bad but the students have all gone home!" interrupted Jansen. "The dig ended the day before all this chaos took place."

"Chaos? You call this chaos?" Agent Brown laughed. Johnson grinned at the younger agent.

Johnson shook his head. "I do not mean them, Jansen. I was talking about this Jinx and Tunk as Hunter called them. To top all this off I have learned your driver is missing in action too. And no trace of the old man they called Bill. You know him from that damn dig site too. I'll be damned if they all haven't just up and vanished too. But the good news from all this is, we did find your limo. Bad news is, it was empty. Sitting alone at the Montana state line. The whole car was wiped clean" Johnson inhaled deep and slowly released the air before speaking. "Now Mister Jansen, what is going on here?"

"I have no clue, but they all are in on this! Any fool can see it! They planned this, can't you see that?" Jansen rubbed his chubby face with the back of his stubby hands. "They all are trying to set me up!"

"Whatever! I'm no fool, Mister Jansen!" Returning to his chair, Johnson regained some composure. "Well sir, if they are in it together, it worked!" Johnson grinned at the wide eyed stare on Jansen's round face. "More good news, I went to the local judge, tossing a folded paper to Jansen, well bad news for you. We will be holding you by court order until we can piece this out. You proved to us that you are a flight risk." Johnson walked to the closed door, while Jansen stared at the paper work. As he opened the door. "You can think all about where you stand, as well as who you can blame for this. As I see it that you will have quite a while to think of a good story while you sit in a small solitary cell. I do hope the accommodations will suit a man of your stature."

Johnson turned to the young man who opened the door earlier. "Agent Smith, could you escort Mister Jansen to his new living quarters if you would? And Billy, turning to look at the forth agent, if you would be so kind and see to it that our guest is taken care of during his stay." The two man laughed as they acknowledged his orders.

Without looking at Jansen now cowering in the chair, Smith answered. "Yes sir, my pleasure, and you need to call the home office too sir. They called earlier."

"Great, that's all I need now. We have no answers for them right now. Almost like farting in the wind. We ain't got a clue on the goings on around this mess." Agent Johnson nodded at Jansen. "So much for that any way, just get him out of my sight. I think that a windy fart would smell better than his personality." Agent Brown laughed as he reached to helped Paul Jansen to his feet.

Jansen jumped to his feet screaming. "You can't do this to me!"

"According to the local judge we can and we will. This will stop you so you can't decide to run again." Johnson smiled as Jansen fell back into the chair sobbing.

The slim young escort, Bill Jones, looked at the crying man in the chair. "I do think that this is the clue you need sir." Johnson nodded in agreement. Jansen got to his feet scowling at the four ridged agents standing over him.

Johnson stared deep into Paul Jansen's eyes. "I want answers. I know you are responsible for the heist. I can make that stick. I may be able to stick all the disappearance of the others on you too, but I want to hear you confess."

"No! I had nothing to do with none of it!"

"Get him outta here!" Johnson threw his hands up. Jansen ducked as if he was being jumped on.

"Yes sir." Smith and Jones both grabbed the screaming man pulling him from the room.

Watching the door as it closed, Johnson shook his head. After a few seconds he returned to the window. "Where oh where are you Hunter?"

Brown laughed. "You need to say come out, come out, where ever you are."

Johnson looked at the younger man, and a twisted smile appeared on his face. "I know what you think and right now I agree." Turning the agent retook his seat behind his desk, he opened another file sitting in front of him.

A quiet knock on the door didn't faze his reading. Agent Smith slid into the room. "Sir? I know we can prove Jansen's involvement in the theft, but why did the other three run?" Looking at Brown the younger agent continued. "We know they weren't anywhere near this New York job. Their records show they are spotless. So why, where and how did they vanish, sir?"

"I can't answer that right now." Johnson looked between the two men. "Right now we need to know what that monster was and where did it come from?" Johnson rubbed his grizzled chin.

Brown nodded, "I say something's in the air, sir. I've never seen anything like it."

Johnson got up and returned to the window and laughed. "It's like it's from another world. Why is that slab bleeding?"

"I don't know." Smith answered. "But sir, don't forget to make your call."

"I don't really want to but I guess now is as better a time than never." Johnson returned to his chair and picked up the phone.

Smith talked quietly with Brown. "We followed the horse tracks found racing down from the hill. Straight to the slab chipping the slat flooring. There were more horse tracks near the limo and leading to another slab." Brown grinned. "Cool, sounds like a road trip. We all going sir?"

"As soon as I finish this stupid phone call." Johnson held the phone receiver. "There's a chopper sitting fueled and ready for us to board now."

Brown nodded. "Cool! I'm ready to go. Just make the call so we can get out of here." Johnson nodded as he dialed the number.

*   *   *

A small frame draped from head to toe in a dark blue and white trimmed hooded cloak, stood by a rock worked pool. The calm dark blue water looked like a sheet of glass with the reflections of the stars painted on the light blue dome ceiling. The hooded figure looked into the dark waters. "Gauvin, something stirs." A larger man, dressed in chain mail and leather, walked gracefully to the pool.

"Change in the weather is normal now, my lord." The hood shifted to look at the muscular warrior, silently approaching the wall to look in the pool.

"No! Something else feels different. If you had the sense you could feel it." The man of war looked into the waters. "Something stirs in the air." He returned his gaze into the pool. A bony arm escaped from the sleeve of the robe and hovered over the still water. A long index finger swirled the waters. "Well of wisdom, waters of vision, show me what you will."

"My horseman have seen nothing in the whole realm, my lord."

The robed man slapped the waters and the spray from the water dripped from the warrior. "So I should put all my faith in the eyes of your murderous dupes. The whole bunch only see spoils to take and women to rape!" The bony hand slaps the waters, again.

"Or do you truly possess a power to see all or feel all! So do you, lord captain?"

"No my lord, I do not mean to say I do. All I know is all I say to you. I only state what I know and hear." The six foot soldier bowed his head. "My apologies. I am yours to command as you see fit. I serve the one who rules Edaun."

The hooded figure returned his finger to stir the waters of the pool again. "Waters of vision, forgive this raging fool I call my Captain. Show me oh Pool of Sight what you will." The dark waters of the pool began to bubble. The waters seemed to come to life. Small ripples formed, then quickly died to become still again. As the waters calmed, they became cloudy, then a mirror again. Quickly, images formed, an Emerald Knight upstaged by a Crimson Knight. A giant leather warrior springs into combat.

The two gaze into the pool. The Captain is unaware that his right hand rests on his trusted sword. Neither take their eyes from the scene. Silently they watch the dance of death. "The leather clad warrior defeated him, Gauvin. Who is he?"

"I have never seen him, my lord. Never seen any of them as I can say." Gauvin became aware of cold sweat beads on his forehead, and quickly wiped them with the back of his left hand.

"He appears to be a great warrior, Captain." The hood turns again to face the warrior still caressing the sword hilt. "Do you think so of him as well?"

Gauvin shrugged as he becomes aware of his hand. "It is easy to beat a man that can't move easily to fight back, my Lord." Slowly, Gauvin lowers his hand, letting it rest on the pool wall.

The scene changes as two different warriors battle and defeat a pack of trolls. Alexar screams. "Who are these other dolts that dare to come with a challenge of your forces, captain! I want the soldiers of Edaun to find them!" Guavin grins as the wizard slaps the wall. "They are to die!" Alexar goes into a rage fit when he watches a wizard attack with the warriors. "Does this youngling wish to challenge me!"

The waters change again. Four riders, three larger that the forth. They stop at woods edge and a quick battle leaves eleven trolls dead. "Who are these strange new warriors, Captain Gauvin? How is it that they defeated a fist of trolls with speed? What say you of that?"

"They say the trolls lack the attitude they once had. Easy marks, easy prey." The ancient hand makes a flipping motion towards Gauvin.

"Look now Captain, is that not Toll?"

"Yes, my lord." Gauvin scowls as he watches the defeat of the troops at Toll. "See how easy Rodona's marauders fall." Smiling Gauvin looks at the robed figure, "Mine would not have been defeated as easily."

"Silence fool, I think yours would be laying dead as well and just as easily!" The wizard's hood snaps toward his captain. Gauvin looks away. "And I so I say, all these new warriors, will challenge you soon enough! I see they have all united and they have a child sorcerer with them as well." Alexar spit in the pool. The pool bubbles and a bony blue hand sticks out from the center of the water. "Search all of Rhea and find them! Find them Gauvin or I will have your head!"

Gauvin bows. "As you wish, lord Alexar." The soldier turns and as graceful as before, heads for the door.

Alexar reaches into the air and a large fish appears. He places it in his bony hand. The hand returns to the murky waters of the pool. "Gauvin!" The raspy voice turned the captain at the door. The cloaked body seemed to float towards him. "Send Rodona to me. Now!"

Smiling, Gauvin turns to leave. "Yes sire, as you will." Looking back at Alexar, "And should I send her horsemen to search Rhea as well, sire."

Alexar nods. "Yes but do not send her color guard." Gauvin snorted a laugh as he left the room, leaving the door opened.

Alexar returned to the pool. Time was lost as he stared into the waters. Within minutes, a five foot nine muscular woman appears. "You have sent for me, my lord?" removing her head dress, exposing her shaven head.

"My dear Avandarian, have you heard from your men in Toll?"

"Not yet sire."

"Have you heard of any movement of trolls through the Outlands south of Toll?"

"No, not of yet sire." Rodona looked annoyed at the figure standing before her. "Should I know or hear something from them? They are locals hired from that area and not my regular warriors, sire."

"Well you are hearing now, they are all dead! They have been slaughtered, my dear."

"The people of Toll could not have killed them, there must be some mistake Lord Alexar!" She shot a distasteful look at the man, "I had them trained some by my color guard!"

"What! You dispute me, woman!" The cloak danced as the figure challenged the female warrior. "I make no mistake!"

"No sire, I meant . . . I mean . . . ."

"Silence woman!" Rodona glared at the ancient robed man, as she rubbed her dagger. Alexar watched her movement. "I see. Do you wish to attack me woman? If not, remove your stare from me!"

Immediately Rodona looked to the floor. "No my lord. I live to serve Edaun. My apologies if I sent a mistaken message to you sire." Looking to the pool. "I did not know of my warriors, my lord. I was taken by the news. How did this happen?"

"They are all dead, I saw their fall as did Gauvin." Rodona's head snapped back to Alexar.

"He attacked my men? If you say to me he had them slaughtered, I will kill him myself Alexar!"

"No, foolish child! It does appear the Giants are here." A look of shock came upon her face.

"This cannot be sire!" She looked into the waters. "I serve the true ruler of Edaun, do I not?"

"As you say, I am the true ruler." Alexar stood still and spoke softly. "Oh it is true. You must assemble your best and ride woman! There seems to be those who will dispute this and it also seems they may have hired evil giants to do their bidding."

Alexar turned and headed toward a balcony overlooking Edaun; Rodona followed. "Gauvin has readied his forces and they ride south. These so called giants are creations of Nod to discredit me."

They stopped on a balcony overlooking a courtyard. Flowers encircled a cut stone patio. The circular stones encircle a large tombstone shaped pillar in the center.

"But sire, I control the land to the south!"

"Silence." The bony finger touched her pouting lips; Rodona recoiled. "You do my child, and you shall continue to do so."

Alexar turned and waved his hands over Edaun. Rodona quickly rubs the touch from her mouth. "All this can be yours to command." He turned to look at the full figured female. "Just give to me what this old man wishes." He reached out to rub her breast plate and Rodona quickly backs away. She looks out over Edaun then back to Alexar. "All I ask is for you to consent to me, fair one." Alexar crossed his arms and they disappeared into each other's sleeve.

Rodona bowed. Slowly she put her helmet back on. "I am a warrior sire, not a wet nurse to an old man. I am pledged to serve the master of Edaun with the sword and my life."

A faint chuckle leaves from under the hood "I have heard it said that only a superior warrior can have you." Alexar looked back over the garden walk. "I say go then. You go ride to you death and let these so called giants slay you!"

"As you wish, my lord." The warrior turned heading for the open door. "Woman, willing or not, I shall have you! Eventually, I shall! If your horsemen fail, you will return and then I shall take you into my chambers!" Stopping at the door she looked back to the cackling wizard. "Whether willing or not, you shall be mine!"

Rodona scrubs the vial touch from her lips again. "If the giants slay me, seek my corpse, then do to me as you wish." Rodona spits. "I serve Edaun, I am not a toy for a dried up wizard to try and have his way with!"

Stalking through the open door she passes the guard. Softly she curses the name of Alexar as she entered the hall. She did not bother to close the door in her rage. Several times she stopped to glare back at the open door and rubs her sword hilt. After the long walk of the hall she regained her composure and proceeded into the courtyard.

Alexar returned to the pool. "Well old Seer, you answer me, if that is possible? You are proof of my dowsing and it does works." He pulls his hood back and it falls on his narrow shoulders. His mouth twisted into what some would call a smile as he runs his bony fingers through the few strands of hair upon his dried up head. "I made it work on you. Could it work on her? Is it possible to make it as true as I have you?" The pool bubbles to life again. A fish skeleton popped out and landed on the floor at Alexar's feet. "Maybe that means yes, I will have to study on it." Alexar kicked the bones across the floor.

A loud gasp from the open door made the wizard spin around. The hall guard stood looking in the room through the open door. A look of horror appeared upon the young man's face as he saw the sight of his master's ghastly head.

Quickly Alexar sails across the room as his hands went into the opposite sleeves. "Do you fear my appearance? Do you now, boy!"

The guard quickly looked at the floor. "No sire, I saw the door opened and I was closing it my lord." He nervously looking into Alexar's beady eyes, then quickly back to the floor. "I was just making sure you were well, my lord."

Alexar smiled a wicked grin, his large hawksbill nose twitched. Removing his hands from their hiding places, he lifts his left hand to rake his fingers through the twigs on top of his head again. "Look close fool, you will never see this sight again!" The guard blinked as he looked up. Alexar's right hand flashed the twisted blade and it found it's mark deep under the man's ribs. The man stumbled back as Alexar pulled the blade out as quick as he inserted it. The guard crumbled with a look of shock on his face as he drew his last gurgling breath.

Alexar pulled his hood back over his head with a nasty cackle. "Guards!" Looking at the body his laughter deepened. "Guards!" Bending down Alexar wipes the blade clean on the young, dead man's clothes and cackles again. As he stands, he straightens his cloak. The sound of running feet now fill the hall.

The first to arrive is a burly man in leather armor, sword in hand. "Are you well my Lord?"

Alexar waved him off. "Look! This fool tried to kill me!" The solder looked down to the fallen man. "Be a good servant and see that someone removes this heap of dung from my sight!" The cloaked figure turned to go back to his room. "And see to it that a trustworthy man be in his stead!"

"Yes my lord, Alexar." The leather bound man bowed his head as others arrived. "I know not why he would do this my Lord. He was a good soldier."

"Something in the air, my son." Alexar retreats back into the room. The large oak door slams, muting his scratching laughter.

*   *   *

After the noon meal was finished, the new defenders of Rhea' were under way again. Crossing the plains northwest of Toll, Hunter rides to the Seer'a side. "Sir, can you tell me of Alexar's power?"

The Seer nods. "The land called Nod is a small island north of Rhea. Seers, wanderers and wizards live out their lives there. Some come to live and aid the people of Rhea. The ones found to be of evil are contained or eliminated. Some escape the judicial tribunal and even enter Rhea. They have been tracked in the past, but there is no one to oppose that as of yet. Alexar, like the others, can control elements and the mind. Strong warriors such as Stagg and Thorn were able to fight his power." The Seer adjusted in his high pommel saddle. "Alexar is the wizard of waters."

"So is he a conjurer as Dil has proven to be?"

The Seer laughs. "I can conjure simple spells, Master Hunter. With heavy training, the Blue Wizard will be one of the strongest wizards Rhea has seen in many years." Hunter looked back toward Dil and smiled. "It is up to the blood of brotherhood to help keep him alive until he can reach his full potential."

"Alexar is most powerful using water." The Seer's look turned serious. "In the old days of the forgotten past, our fathers connected with stronger powers. They created staffs and orbs to aid." Hunter looked at the old man as if to speak but the Seer held his left hand up to stop the words. "Say nothing of any such items, they would be better off in hiding just of yet, but in the right hands." Hunter looked amazed. "I have sensed it's presence, but know this, Alexar will sense it as well." Hunter nodded. The old man looked to the archers, riding in a large ring around them. He shifted his look to Jinx and O'Cey, then toward Mac on the far left in front. Ian was in the rear with the pack animals riding with Tunk. "These items can not fall to Alexar. Your wizard must live to grow stronger."

Hunter nodded. "I do plan to keep all alive and to see Rhea return to peace."

The old man grinned. "I know this but strange things are taking on now, I fear something is in the air."

"Like what?"

"Alexar now knows you are here." The Seer shook his head. "The time has come." Hunter looked at the old wise man. "Our wizard will be powerful, but he needs to travel to Nod for a short while. The council will help him mentally prepare to face another wizard in battle; a wizard such as Alexar."

"Does he or his brothers know this?"

"He and I talked of it in Toll. He is to talk with you and his brothers."

"The objects I spoke of were carried away by the wandering seer. They were to return as need called."

Hunter laughed, "who is this?"

"Who? Alexar?"

Hunter laughed, "No. This wanderer, you speak of."

"Oh yes." The Seer returned the laugh. "He is a brother; he too is a seer and a, as you say, a conjurer. You will soon meet with him. He is away preparing now."

Hunter laughed. "I believe I have met him." He looked at the Seer. The old man laughed in return and shrugged. "Damn Bill, it's got to be you."

The Seer looked puzzled before he spoke. "Remember, the time has come and soon to be the worst." A sadness spread over his face as he finished. "Just remember this Great Eagle, show no mercy when the end comes. Believe what you see, trust no one!"

"Even you, the seers or the wanderer?"

"Make your choices little brother, trust your feelings." Hunter looked around to each of the group. "Trust what you see, Hunter." Hunter looked back to the man, he simply raised his hand, for silence. "We'll talk more later when you are ready. Now you must prepare. Go join the other to set your plans now. Our wizard needs more strength." Hunter nodded. "Just remember this, trouble lay ahead." He pointed to the horizon. "Show no mercy." The Seer slowed his horse and turned, heading to join Dilman.

Hunter nodded again and waved Tunk to join him. Tunk caught up as Hunter quickly popped the reins; kneeing Sequoia ahead. Together they rode to the point to join Jinx and O'Cey, flagging Mac on the way.

As Hunter and Tunk rode to match Nightmare's pace Jinx looked at them. "Hey, Hunter. What the ol' coot have to say now?" O'Cey laughs.

Hunter shook his head. "Bunch of nothing, mostly riddles. Well, truth is, about the same as the council has been saying all this time to me."

Tunk look toward the Seer. "How we gonna help if we ain't got a clue?"

"We'll gang up on him tonight. Right now, he said we need to plan for the trouble that lay ahead." Hunter nodded toward the western horizon.

"Boy, trouble is all over here!" laughed Jinx.

Tunk joined in. "Who don't know that Hunter?"

O'Cey barks back, "we'll do what we can, my brothers."

As Mac caught up with them, Hunter looked at the two brothers. "If you are sure 'bout that O'Cey, he said Dil should go to Nod for quick training."

"What? Dil will go nowhere without his brothers!" growled Mac.

"Well, it's not my call, Mac!" Hunter scowled at Mac. "I also want Dil, to be able to protect himself at his full potential!" Hunter looked at Jinx. "As we have seen, evil runs over Rhea, that's why we find so many fights. We'll meet the regular troops of Edaun and they'll fight much better than what we've faced so far.

O'Cey slapped his left leg and the loud noise stopped Mac from speaking again. "I know Hunter cares for the wee one too Mac and I say he go. Mac you go him as his protector. I know you are the one to do that." Mac nodded then lowered his head as not to challenge his eldest brother's last word. "Now, that be settled, what do we need to be ready!"

"Thanks O'Cey. First, I say send two archers with Mac and our wizard. We will make all the plans and preparations tonight. Just make sure we keep a close eye all around us." Hunter spun his giant war-horse, heading away from the whole party. Jinx cocked his head toward Hunter while looking at Tunk. Tunk nodded and heeled Ghost and the giant white stallion leaped into flight. They pulled up on either side of Hunter in quick time.

"What you thinking about, Hunt?" Tunk rode alongside Hunter.

Jinx pulled up on the other side. "Yeah bro, what's up?"

All three turned, looking back in the caravan's direction. "It just doesn't feel right." Hunter looked at each of his longtime companions. "The old man said several times for us to show no mercy." Hunter pulled Sequoia's reins. Tunk and Jinx circled so each could face the other.

The three huge war horses, restlessly stomped the ground. Hunter rubbed his forehead. "Remember when I said, the counsel made similar remarks?" Hunter looked at each of the men in front of him. "The elder at the council said to remember the old way. They also said show no mercy, same as the Seer."

"The only thing I can think of is a scalping party," laughed Jinx. "What else drove fear into white people?"

"Maybe, but will we be able to be that ruthless?" Hunter looked up at the passing clouds. "I didn't mention the last vision.

The chief said we were of his blood. Could it have been this Thorn guy they talk so much about?"

Tunk grunted. "Maybe. Don't matter who he is. All that matters is we do what is needed when we need to do it." Tunk scratched his head. "As I figure it, we're cousins and Thorn was our grandfather through his travels." Jinx nodded.

Hunter smiled. "My thoughts too." All three turn to the sound of drumming hooves.

Ian pulled up. "What's going on."

"Just talking Ian." Jinx clamped a big right hand on Ian's shoulder. "We are thinking right now Uncle." Tunk and Hunter laughed. Ian looked puzzled, then quickly regained his composure. "Should I join you then?"

"No Ian, you can join with the ones to come." All four men turned to spot the Seer mounted behind them. "They must deal with their past now Ian. You can help later when the time calls for you to do so."

Hunter looks from Jinx to Tunk. "Another thing I still say is this wanderer is Bill." Looking toward the Seer, "He also knows more than what he says."

Tunk looks at each of his friends. "Back to no mercy. How do we do that Hunter? We aren't barbarians."

Jinx looks back at Tunk. "If we want to survive bro, we will have to learn."

Hunter reluctantly nods. "We need to drive fear into the cold hearts of the people that follow this Alexar."

"Yeah, as I see it, they fear only the wrath of this Alexar person." Jinx pulls his Bowie knife. "We need to show them we are the ones to truly fear. We are the new defenders of these good people. We need to teach Alexar and his henchmen to fear this!" Holding up the large blade. "How else but to show no mercy!" The other two pulled their knives and they touched blades.

Hunter looked around them. All the others had surrounded the three. In a loud voice to ignite and new spark. "No mercy!" The small army erupt in cheers.

Jinx chuckled. "Kill'em all! It's time to clean house!"

Tunk looked at Jinx then at Hunter. "I'll do what I have to when needed, no worries bro."

Hunter lowered his blade and smiles at Tunk. "That's all they expect out of all of us Tunk. I know you are always there when we have needed you and we know you will do what needs to be done. I thank you my friend." Hunter reached out and grabbed Tunk's right wrist. Tunk grabbed Hunter's with the same hand.

"Yeah blood and guts ain't your kind of thing but you have always covered my back when I needed you bro!" Sheathing his big blade, Jinx raises his fist thumb side to his heart to Tunk. "You know we'll be watching yours as always."

"That's cool with me." Tunk places his blade in its sheath and raises his fist to salute Jinx then Hunter.

Hunter returns the salute to each of his friends. Turning Sequoia with his knees, he displays the salute to the whole Blood of Brothers. "Today we ride into the enemy's world! Look sharp! Look out for each other! No one is alone from this day on!" The war party all return the salute. "Archers pair up and take the flanks. Ride about twenty paces from the other duo!"

They all turned back to the trip and began their ride in silence. Each person searching the horizons. Heads swivel studying through ground covers. No obstacle or resistance were found. Dil and the Seer quietly talked for the next six hour ride.

As the sun started hanging low on the horizon Hunter pulled on Sequoia's reins. "Set up camp here, Conal! Leister gather some wood! Everyone else fan out and check the landscape!" Hunter dismounted. "We don't need any surprises!"

After the meal was finished everyone gathered in a circle around Hunter. "Listen up! Everyone needs to be ready at all times for any unexpected attacks. Tunk and Jinx will assign guards and rotations for the night. Everyone else turn in until their time comes. The first guards will wake you for your watch and so on."

The Seer walked into the center of the circle. "Remember for the people of Rhea we will need to be as one. Change is here and you are the change." Everyone nodded quietly in agreement. "Something is in the air, and it is called freedom; freedom for the captive people of Rhea." Again the group silently agree, with fists raised to their hearts in unity.

Chapter 8

Whispering Pines

Before day break the Blood of Brothers fed and pulled out of their quick made camp. Tunk rides along with Jinx and Hunter. "You know, it was too quiet last night."

Jinx laughed. "I heard it too."

Hunter shook his head as he grinned. "Jinx you have a way with words."

Tunk returned the smirk. "I say we are as ready as we can be. My guess is something fix'n to happen."

"I agree. Tunk take two archers and ride left flank. Jinx take the other two on the right." Jinx and Tunk had turned as one, each nodding their archers in motion. Hunter quickly studied the growing army. "I'll take the spear head with O'Cey and Dil, I mean the wizard. Blue Wizard if you will. Conal and Leister get your bows ready and ride with us." Looking to the last of the swordsmen, "Mac you and Ian take your archers to the rear. The rest of the Crew get your bows ready. You four get into the wagon and guard the Seer with Nate. The rest get in the other wagon to watch the rear."

The war party rode in silence. Everyone knowing their task that morning, did what was needed. The crew was busy moving things around in the wagons as they rolled onward. The sun was reaching noon when a vast forest came into view. O'Cey reined Banshee to a stop. His monstrous black and white English Sire draft horse stomped the earth awaiting a run. "Hunter we can stop to feed here. You can see forever in all directions." Hunter quickly scanned the terrain in all directions, then nodded.

As soon as the party stopped, the crew sprang into action with their methodical works. The animals were all tended to and the meal almost finished. The Seer moved his emptied plate of dried meat, hard bread and dried fruit. "We will be arriving at the Tree of Forgotten Lives before the sun starts to disappear."

Mac looked up and flipped the crumbs from his long mustache. "What be that tree?"

"It is said to be the tree of wisdom. A blue tree that sits on the edge of the Forest of Whispering Pines, straight ahead west of our location. The protectors of the forest call it the Tree of Forgotten Lives."

"Blue, you say, like me brother, the wizard?" snorted O'Cey as he finished his water bag.

"That is correct. It is under the protection of the Huntress and the Avandarians," Ian interrupted. "The story is quite interesting." Looking at the Seer, "I apologize sir for my interruption."

"That is quite alright Ian." The Seer smiled before he continued. "It is said from the wars of old, that all those who died rest within the tree to offer their wisdom and comfort. If you sleep beneath its branches, you would have dreams of comfort and answers to help in problems and quests to come."

The Seer looks at Hunter. "I feel it is now time for the thing I said not to mention." Hunter simply nodded. "Give it to the wizard. He will know it's purpose." Hunter nodded again, then walked to his saddle bag.

Pulling out the goat skin bag, he walks to Dil. He removed the blue orb and handed it to the wizard. Dil took it and a broad smile cut across his face.

Dil stood holding his staff in front of him. He raises the staff and jabs it's point to stick in the soft sod. Slowly he raised the orb over the end of the staff. The staff came to life. A pale blue glow emitted from the orb. Slowly, root like fingers stretched from the end of the staff toward the blue ball, wrapping and weaving around it. When it was finished, the orb shined through the lattice wrappings of roots which connected the staff to the orb.

The wizard raised the staff and a flash of blue light surrounded the entire war party. As the light winked out, Dil looked as if he aged several years. Mac jumped to his brother's side. "Little brother, are you ok?"

Dil laughed. "I feel great brother, I am now the Wizard of the Blue Orb. The Orb of Sumra."

Jinx stared at Dil as he handed his plate to one of their attendants. The man stood dumbfounded and the plate hit the ground. Jinx laughed. "Coolness! All we need now is to be visited by the one of those spooks from that wise tree now!" Jinx turned to Hunter and laughed. "We do need more visions, right Hunter?"

Tunk laughed with Jinx. "Whoa now that was awesome!"

Hunter handed his plate to Leister. "We need to be moving. That flash could have been seen for miles. It's a beacon that would signal anyone and we don't need to get caught here in this open yet."

The crowd followed his lead, checking their tack before mounting. The camp people finished their duties quickly; packed and were ready to move as the last warrior mounted. They headed in the direction of the mystical tree.

The sky slowly grew dark as heavy clouds rolled in from the west. A soft steady breeze blew, dropping the temperature. Jinx stopped his horse to look at the movement overhead. "I see it rains here." He laughed as he spurred onward.

After a few hours, Tunk shouted to the riders coming fast toward them from the south west. Jinx kicked his steed to catch the point where Hunter and O'Cey rode. "Who do you think they are, Hunt!"

Looking at a squad of mounted warriors coming fast toward them, Hunter shrugged as he dismounted. The Seer and Ian were there with Nate in tow. The large protector answered. "Nimenole Trolls!" All were looking across the flat field.

None of them looked as the others joined them. "What be those things they ride?" No one looked at O'Cey as he pulled his trusty blade.

"Pumoarans. So that's what Alexar calls them." Nate unsheathed his double bladed ax. "They are deadly without their troll riders."

The leader of the Nimenole, one of three humans, signaled for attack formation. Without slowing their, speed the screaming trolls spread out into two lines. The trolls were preparing to meet the new strangers that now stood before them. Hunter quickly scanned their location, "Tunk, how far are they?"

"Half a mile, and closing fast." Tunk had climbed down from his mount. "We can't fight them from horseback, they'll be too short for us!"

Mac laughed as he dismounted. "Yeah, all we would do is fan over the ugly heads, while they whittle us down."

The rest of the new growing army were standing around the giant warriors. All of the horses were safely behind them. Hunter issued quick orders as the Neminoles continued their death race. "Archers set up here, quick!" Hunter saw the camp crew produced long bows and assembled behind the kneeling regulars. "Two rows, good! Stop their front line, now!" O'Cey grinned at his trained archers, then elbowed Hunter.

As the Nimenole Trolls grew closer Jinx laughed. "Those Pumoarans look like wild boars to me!"

"Look at their legs and feet cat like paws!" laughed Tunk standing in front left of Jinx and to the right of Hunter. He watched as thirty two trolls and three soldiers raced toward him. "Man! Be careful, they move like a big cats too, and gottabe just as dangerous!" Tunk's right hand held his sword high. The big blade cutts circles in the air as he sounded his war cry. His Bowie knife held low in his left. Jinx and Hunter let their cries blend with their blood brother as arrows whistled over their heads.

The warriors spread out on the front line, each shared with equaled volume war cries. Two rows of archers lined on the left and two more to the right. Ten Pumoarans tumbled. The Seer and the young wizard stood in the rear. Nate stood solid in front of the man in his care, double bladed ax ready. As Dil was circling his raised staff, a blue halo held the air outside the circle.

"Archers ready!" Ecott sounded, all drew their bow strings for the second wave. "Make it count! Take out the Pumoarans!" Eighteen deadly broad tips filled the air. In a whisper of time, a third volley filled the atmosphere. Half of the strange animals flipped from under their riders as trolls took the broad tips in their grotesque faces. Each rider somersaulted as the mounts crumbled from beneath them. Each troll that became unsaddled landing on their feet without missing a step to continue the race to their enemies. Tunk now standing ten feet in front of the others looked back. "These guys are quick! Did ya'll see that!" The attackers were within a stone's throw.

The lone Pumoarans fell as did six of the running trolls, from the other wave of arrows. Dark clouds started rolling in over the battle field.

Four bolas spun at the four runners, all hitting their marks. Two were hit high and lay kicking as the cords cut off their air supply. The other two fought to untangle their legs. A lone human pulled reins to observe the strange melee. The archers had taken out the racing Pumoarans. Time had come for the wizard to drop his staff. The ground erupted swallowing four screaming trolls and throwing the two advancing horsemen to the ground. The remaining nimble trolls now easily ran to fight the new comers. The archers held notched arrows ready, it is now up to their warriors. Each archer hopes were that a troll would stray into clear sights.

The front line of swordsmen stood ridged as they readied for the rapid advancing Nimenoles. Tunk was just able to set his defense as four snarling trolls bore down on him. Hunter and Mac threw tomahawks stopping one of the four running trolls. O'Cey released a bola on another. It fell hard on its horrible face. They filled their hands quickly as Jinx readied a tomahawk. Hunter's hand held only his sword. The blade sang whispers to the soft breeze as he worked the days ride kinks out of his arm. The breeze was soon to become a blowing death to the small troll army.

Jinx threw his tomahawk to the troll at Tunk's far right. "Watch out Tunk!" The archers slowly picked off another two trolls, one long bowman took the horse from the watching rider. The other swordsmen were now busy handling their own. Ian had two kills. O'Cey and Mac had three kills apiece.

Tunk blocked the first volley from each of the two trolls on him. Seizing an opening, he stabbed his Bowie knife, left handed into the troll to his right. As he drew his sword to strike the one coming in on his left Tunk miscalculated the small troll's movement. He wasn't expecting the nasty little beast to go into a roll from a full run toward him. The troll's slender sword slid in through his left thigh. Tunk was already in a downward slice and removed the trolls arm at the elbow this move caused the slender blade to rip down his own leg. The blade sliced out just above the knee. Tunk stumbled back and fell as Hunter sliced the throat of his foe.

Hunter watched in horror to see his friend fall and more of the enemy racing toward the falling man. "Tunk!" Hunter drew a tomahawk left handed and let it twirl at the troll advancing on the down warrior. The tomahawk splits the troll's left eye and buried to the handle.

O'Cey stabbed one of the men in the midsection then ran with Mac to help cover Tunk.

Jinx hearing Hunter yell looked at Tunk as the human he was fighting fell dead. Jumping quick to also protect his fallen friend. Jinx took up a position between Tunk and the last three trolls. "Stay low Tunk, I got your back!" Tunk grunted, holding tight to the bleeding leg. All the archers centered on the one of the last Trolls. Eighteen arrows whistled as one and the troll fell tripping both his partners.

The two Trolls stopped to surveyed the field as O'Cey, Mac and Hunter stood between them and the kill they were denied. They see for the first time they are alone and looking at the party they fought. Each threw down their weapon and turned to run. The creatures only made two steps away then they erupted in flames. The wizard let a barking laugh that O'Cey would be proud of. The last rider looks on in disbelief. No way to escape the war party before him. A soft drizzle of rain falls.

Jinx looked down at Tunk's mutilated leg. Two of the archers were running with bandages and water bags. Jinx looks over to the one armed troll still alive and lashing around in pain. Jinx worked his sword quickly and the Nimenole lay still in silence.

Jinx look back to Tunk to see archers were wrapping the leg tight to stop the bleeding. Then he remembered the last human riding with these creatures. Jinx looks down to the man he had just fought and saw the soldier was still breathing. He knelled down toward the man.

Just before he was on his prey, Jinx snatched his Bowie knife from its home. Quickly he completed his kneeling and grabbed the dying man by the hair, yells another war cry then buries the large knife into the scalp of the screaming man. The soldier of Alexar releases a blood curdling scream. The big blade rips through the top of his head.

The soldier standing alone on the hill drops to his knees. Holding the bloody prize high Jinx cries out again. Looking at the second man moaning in death, he kicked the man on his belly and removes the top of his head. This man's screams of death now fill the air. Jinx chants as he raises both bloody scalps high in the air.

He watches the last of their enemy on the hill sobbing. Slowly the lone soldier stands back to his feet. The only enemy now alive looks sick. Fear painted on the man's face. Does one feel sorrow for an enemy as he stands alone? Jinx studies the man as he chants louder. How many defenseless people fell to this so called warrior? Jinx wonders. The chanting fills the small valley. Tunk joined in with the chant.

The rain drops grow in size and fall in to a heavier shower.

Hunter lets out a whistle. Sequoia rears then races to his rider. Hunter swung into the saddle without the giant horse slowing down and races up the hill toward the sobbing man.

Jinx is still chanting, Hunter screams another war hoop. Again Sequoia isn't given time to slow down as Hunter jumps from the saddle, landing inches from the man. The lone soldier drops to his knees, as he begged for mercy. Hunter only hears the words of the Seer. Echoing words blending in from the men of the vision. The chanting is carried loud to Hunter's ears.

Hunter repeats the words. "No mercy." Hunter wasn't aware of the crying man as he quickly grabs the screaming man by the hair and snatches his Bowie knife from its sheath.

With another war cry the giant warrior quickly removes the man's scalp as the man's death cry fills the valley.

Jinx moves in on Tunk and tosses the scalps on the ground. He quickly checks the blood stopper bandage on the leg of his friend. "You ain't gonna bleed to death on me, bro!"

He looks to the archers. "You both did a good job. Tunk I need to get you out of this field and clean it. with my herbs on it you will be ok, bro." Tunk gives a weak nod.

Hunter sings his death chant. He sings praise to the war party of his visions. Everyone watched the man as he was scalped alive. The whole party heard the man's screams of death. Hunter slashes the soldiers throat as he stands to wave his prize high.

*   *   *

Everyone sees.

Alexar slaps the pool with both hand and curses. "Who dares to attack Alexar's warriors?"

The bony hand extends from the depth of the waters as Alexar spins away. The blue hand balls into a fist and shakes violently before returning to its watery tomb sending water to splash off the back of Alexar. The old man glares back to the pool only to see the vision of Hunter and Jinx holding the scalps in the ripples of the water.

The wizard storms away from sight and loudly curses the name of Thorn. "I will show you no mercy!"

Alexar stops in his tracks and spins back to glare at the pool. He spits, then quickly turns away again. Ranting to himself, "We shall see! We shall see!" He storms from the room.

*   *   *

Off in the short distance of the battle, the Forest of the Whispering Pines silently watch. Its thick branches slowly wave. The Enchanted Blue Tree also waves it's branches toward the victorious war party. No one noticed there was no wind blowing. Victorious songs fill the air. Not one in the Blood of Brothers could see who was singing the praise. Slowly the branches stop and seem to lower in respect of the new warring giants of Rhea.

Chapter 9

Healing Wounds

Jinx kneels at Tunk's side under the temporary shelter, as the troop prepares to leave. The dressings smelled of herbs and spice. Jinx looked at his friend now passed out but alive. He stood up and started walking solemnly toward the wagons. Every other step he looks back at the little hospital room holding Tunk.

Jinx walked to stand by Hunter at the wagons. "I finally got the bleeding to stop Hunter, but he's lost a lot of blood." Jinx drops his medicine bag in his box to the rear of the new transportation of Tunk.

Without looking at members of the crew sitting on the wagon's bench, Jinx barks an order. "You best have care when we put him in a wagon." Jinx turns and gives a cold stare to Leister and Conal who in return nod. Slowly they move the wagon closer to Tunk.

Ian walked up to Jinx wearing the few wraps covering his wounds. "Is Tunk going to be ok?" Jinx just looked at the young man.

The crew had made room for the wounded warrior in one of the wagons. They carefully loaded Tunk for the ride to the forest, then pulled a small cover over the wagon. As soon as it was tied off, Leister started easing the team forward. Ian mounted Nickle and rode at the side of the wagon. Hunter watches with worry for his fallen friend.

Mounting Sequoia, Hunter finally speaks. "We need to be at the forest before night fall!" The little bit of light in the clouded sky was fading away fast. The darkness overtook them as the dismal war party arrives at the edge of the forest. The rain slowed its heavy drumming of the soaked ground. Hunter advanced to the wagon hauling his friend.

Hunter dismounted and tied Sequoia to the wagon. "We'll camp just outside of the tree line. Jinx scout the south, Mac to the north! Take a couple of archers with each of you!" They both nod as they dismounted. Walking in the darkness the scouting parties faded away quickly. "We'll meet you at the base of the blue tree!" Hunter looked in the wagon at Tunk.

Tunk's weak smile was hard to swallow.

"Leister, set up between the blue tree and the forest! We'll need tents to get dry in!" Several members of the crew wave their response. Hunter reaches in the wagon patting Tunk on his right shoulder. "Hang in there big'un."

Tunk was holding his left thigh and watching the look on his Hunter's face. "What's up, bro?"

Jerking his head toward Tunk, a smile quickly replaced the worried look. "Not much Tunk and you? You ok?"

Shrugging Tunk put on a grin to cover the pain. "Hunter, it's bad dude. I ain't gonna be no good no more. I can't feel my foot. It doesn't move right either." Looking at his leg, "Maybe I can work on the rear line or something. I can cook you know."

Hunter faked a grin. "It'll be ok, Tunk." Tunk smiled and gave a simple nod.

O'Cey was barking orders and doing what he could to make a comfortable spot for Tunk. "Nuel, Ecott help tend the horses!"

After a lean to was made, the crew picked Tunk up and out of the wagon. Hunter turned his head when Tunk grunted loud from the pain.

Tunk was placed beneath the Blue Tree. A soft breeze blew, sending the sweet aroma of the strange flowers around them. Strange green and blue flowers grew in large circles around this mystical place. Jinx had returned and made a quick study of the area, before checking his patient.

The nights meal was eaten in silence. The light rain had stopped, everyone full then spoke wishes to Tunk as they readied for sleep. Jinx quietly checked the leg wound again. He was checking on Tunk one last time before turning in himself. "I'll do what I can, Tunk. You'll be ok." Tunk just nodded. Ian laid near Tunk with a bandage around his right shoulder and fore arm.

O'Cey continued the arrangement on the guard's schedule. In the quiet darkness some found sleep fast, but others were restless before drifting off.

All was quiet as the full moon regained its place in the sky. A soft warm breeze tried to ease the day's tension. Tunk felt as if he were watching the darkness alone. He lay in the silence tenderly rubbing his life changing wound. His thoughts were interrupted by a quiet rustle from deep inside the forest.

The full moon cast strange shadows in the darkness. Fighting his pain and anguish made his mind race. The quiet rustle grew closer. Tunk drew his Bowie knife. A lone small figure took shape. It moved carefully toward him and Ian from the protection of the shadows of the huge tree line.

The small shadow moved with the grace of a ballet dancer toward Tunk. Slowly, the shape became more defined. Tunk was in a trance as a beautiful petite woman knelt by his side. He lay his large blade safely aside. The small woman spoke in a sweet musical voice. "Peace to you great warrior." Tunk felt comfort in the warm smile that followed.

Quietly she went to work on the wound, carefully cutting the field dressing from his thigh. To his surprise he didn't try to stop her. After the old dressing lain on the ground, she carefully cleaned the horrible wound with a potion that smelled of honey and lemon. Tunk smiled as the melodious tune she hummed eased his anxiety. Only when he saw the leg did he feel like crying. He wanted to cry at the thought of not being able to help his comrades and at the sight of a leg useless to the cause at hand.

His thoughts halted when the beautiful face shared another smile before continuing the soft tune.

"I will apply a new wrap now." She rubbed his forehead and left cheek. "It will sting at first so be ready strong one." Tunk could only nod. He watched as her skilled hands worked a white powder into his wound and then wrapped his leg at the same time. He covered a wince as best as he could, but kept his eyes on the lovely tiny vision working on his ruined leg.

A whispered gasp came from Ian laying to his right. The woman's soft smile silenced him. Tunk looked at Ian's surprised expression.

She finished with her first patient and without a sound she moved to care for Ian's wounded arm, almost floating. Tunk and Ian watched as their silent healer tended to his wounds. She opened a canister emitting another strange but sweet odor. Again she hummed as she wiped a green paste on all the scrapes and bruises on each of them.

She looked around at their sleeping comrades. Quietly she hummed her song as she applied the poultice to each of their sleeping friends. After what seemed an eternity, she began to dance. She gave the impression of being a small ballerina, dancing back to Tunk and Ian. Bending between them both, she touched each on the forehead, and whispered softly. "Sleep well, brave warriors." She kissed their foreheads, smiling as she rose to her feet. Their eyes drifted closed while the vision of her slowly faded back into the darkness of the forest.

The night passed quickly without any incident.

Ian rose before the sun. He quickly dropped the bandages and studied the soft white scar were the wound was a few hours before. Slowly the rest of the camp was coming to life. Ian grinned as he watched all of them rub the strange dried paste from the healed bruises and scrapes.

Tunk rubbed his leg as he awoke and to his surprise, there was no pain. He wiggled his foot and laughed. Ripping the bandage from his thigh, he yells.

Jinx looks to see what was happening and he yells and starts running toward Tunk. Before he could reach him Tunk, had jumped to his feet, "Tunk, NO! You'll reopen your leg!" Jinx grabs Tunk and looks at the pale healing scar. His mouth hangs open as he drops to his knees for a closer study. "How? I don't understand." A soft giggle from the trees stops his mumbling. Everyone draws weapons as they watch the small healer exit from the shadows.

The shadows from the rising sun add to the mystery of the small beauty gliding into camp.

Tunk laughs and falls to his knees in front of her. "It was you, thank you! My leg is like new again. Thank you! I thought it was a dream. Thank you."

"It was my pleasure and duty to give aid to the giants of the prophesies." Her sweet voice reminded Jinx of the birds singing back home. "The giants and their army are welcomed in the Forest of the Whispering Pines. I am sent to invite all of you to come before the Huntress."

Before she finished speaking Tunk scooped her up and stood hugging the little beauty that saved his leg.

The seer made his way in front of the gathered crowd. "Merveela! It is good to see you again my dear!"

Her face lit up at the sight of the old man. "Good morrow, Seer."

"Good morrow to you, dear one." Looking around to the others, "we must Prepare to leave with haste." Jinx started to protest, but the Seer's stern expression silenced him. "Master Jinx, a healer elf has graced us with a visit and an invite. I say we best not keep her waiting. Oh Tunk could you please set the lady down now?"

Tunk laughed. "I will carry my doctor to wherever she needs to go, old man."

Merveela kissed Tunk's cheek. "I can manage on my own legs giant one. But I do thank you for the offer." Tunk nodded as he gently set the small Elf back on her feet.

Hunter walked up to the healer and kneeled down. "I would like to thank the lady for saving my friend's leg."

She smiled. "I am the one to thank the Giants of Thorn for saving the lives in the days just passed."

In no time, they were packed and moving deep into the forest. Hunter rode by the Seer. "Who is this Huntress?"

"Before the elves fled to a safe haven in Baseen, an Avandarian Council was sent to these forests. A group of warriors moved in to protect them." Looking deep in the woods, "They watch us now. It is said some of the elfin warriors also remain here, but I do not know." Turning back to look to where they came. "No one has seen any of them, but then this is a safe haven to all who travel. Merveela is a healer of the wood elves. She is one of the battle elves brew."

"So these Vanguardian came to take the place of these wood elves?" The Seer let a chuckle escape. "No, no I need to explain in more detail about the Avandarians, instead of telling only portions."

"Ok it seems we have a while, talk to me." Hunter shook his head. "No riddle talk ok?"

The seer shook his head and smiled. "Alexar was planning on taking the elves. With his black arts, he had some sinister plan for them. With the elves gone, his plans were changed. If he could destroy the tree, then this grand forest would follow."

"But it's just a tree, ain't it?"

"You will learn. I understand you know little of this place and I will teach you when I can." Hunter nodded and the Seer continued. "The tree holds hope for all of Rhea. The wise men of Nod helped in its creation; they brought peace and unity to this world. The trees of this forest shelter several healing herbs and many other wondrous gifts as well.

The Seer talked quietly as Hunter listened close. Jinx was in doctor talk with the small healer kneeling on the bed roll behind his saddle. She was chin high to Jinx's shoulder explaining the strange healing herbs of Rhea.

During the ride, Hunter scanned up in the trees. He smiled every time he would see silhouettes moving among the large branches. Hunter spoke to Merveela. "Healer, how many eyes does this forest have?"

She looked puzzled at the question. "I was not aware that the trees could see, my lord." Jinx and Tunk laughed, Hunter shook his head.

"No, I mean the people moving up in the trees." Hunter said after a grunt.

173

Merveela looked up in amazement. "How did you see them? Most that enter do not until it is too late."

Jinx looked back to his passenger. "We've seen them since we entered the woods." Tunk nodded his head. The others quickly looked up and scanned the area.

O'Cey laughed. "They don't hide too good for trained eyes lassie." The elf simply grinned.

After a few hours of steady riding, the party arrived inside a small settlement deep in the shadows of the protecting trees. Before them a banquet was set. A great feast had been set in a council area. "Man look at that spread!" laughed Tunk. He dismounted near several wash basins. The horses were quickly tied and several men dressed in plain soft gray leather tended to the horses. Women in similar gray dresses assisted the members of the war party at the wash basins. Other women in brown attire were finishing the preparation on the tables.

Three large stone tables formed a triangle inside of a large egg shaped ring. In the narrow end of the ring a raised flat cut stone stood alone. Encircling the ring were three high stadium style benches. To the north behind the flat stone lay a stone wall half circling the small arena. At the arch of the wall was a small opening. Behind that the forest gave way to an opening of a well traveled path. The path was now being traveled by the servers in brown; a flow of women going to and fro setting the tables. Hunter's thoughts picked through the words of the Seer and figured this was the place of that the Avandarian council met.

The soft wispy sounds of the women's leather as they moved quickly about their work, added to the mystery of the place. No other sound filled the air. The delicious sweet aromas of the food drifting from the tables fought the whispered sounds for their rightful space.

Tunk looked at another group of tall women moving about. These women stood taller than the other women he had seen as of yet in Rhea. Each of these women held either a bow and quiver or a sword. These women were dressed in the various colors of the forest. As Tunk looked around, he saw the same googly eyed look on all the men of his party, he soon realized he too had a stupid grin on his face. Quickly he wiped it off. To his surprise so did the others and he laughed softly to himself.

Hunter thought of Rhea's standard of height he had seen so far and these women averaged at foot taller. All were pleasant to gaze upon.

Jinx was sitting with the tiny beauty on the short wall, still deep in conversation. He only looked away when Tunk burst into sudden laughter. "What ails you Tunk!"

"The look on all of men's faces, funny thing I was doing it too!"

"What?" Jinx looked at Merveela, then finally realize all the women moving around the area. After a few seconds he laughed. "Never mind bro, I see what you mean. Whoa! Hard body babes everywhere!" Tunk joined in with Jinx. The Seer cleared his throat and the laughter trickled down to silence.

A quiet buzz rose from the servers over the laughter, then suddenly went silent too. All the women stopped in their tracks and looked to the opening. Someone was coming from the shadows; silently coming from the quiet darkness. A tall figure began to take shape. The most beautiful auburn haired woman appeared. Hunter felt his mouth fall open. Her tight leather clothing clung to her picturesque body. She moved smoothly across the yard. The earth tone outfit blended into the forest background. Hunter clamped his mouth closed, wincing as he bit his tongue.

The whole party was staring at the graceful strides of the full figured goddess moving in front of them. No one saw the sword bearing woman with a long bow and sword walking behind the perfect woman until the first lady stops just inside the opening in the wall. The armed woman side steps and moves to stand on the flat rock at the top of the arena. The second woman spoke loud and clear. "The Huntress graces these grounds with her presence! We are all in one in the protection of this dark forest and the enchanted tree of Forgotten Lives!"

The beauty walks graciously to the raised stone and stops behind the battle maiden. The female warrior turns to face the Huntress and bows her head.

The perfect woman as Hunter saw her, steps forward. "We have invited and now greet the new warriors to our sworn protected lands." Hunter, Jinx, Tunk, O'Cey and Mac raise their fists thumb side to their hearts and the tall woman smiles. The Blue Wizard bows. The Huntress bows her head to Dilman then to the large warriors. "We are graced by the presence of walking prophecies. I personally welcome the Giants of Thorn. We knew you would one day come to ride on the evil that infests these lands. We the Avandarians have pledged to protect the land of the elves. In that pledge we will also do as we must to return all of the land of Rhea to become peaceful again. As it was in the days of the Great Thorn. I say our pledge also tells us to do our part to aid in your quest!" The forest came to life with shouts of all the women and men of the Avandarians. The Blood of Brothers look around in amazement to find another host of hidden voices chanting outside in the forest around them. The Huntress raises her hands and the forest goes quiet instantly. She smiles to the serving women. "It is time to feed our guests. They made a hard journey to get here and have an even harder journey ahead."

The Huntress moved to take a seat at the center of the middle table. She motioned for Hunter to sit across from her. Then to Jinx and Tunk to take either of side of him. Then to O'Cey by Tunk and Mac by Jinx. The Seer led Dil to sit by the Huntress. The small healer sat by the Seer and the rest of the war party took their seats as well. Plates which were already filled were placed before them. The Seer blessed the food and then they ate in silence.

When the meal was finished, the serving women quietly cleared the table. The Huntress looked deep into Hunter's eyes and smiled. "Your warriors have made an impression on Rhea." Her beautiful smile eased all of his ill thoughts of this place and the past battles. "All of you have made amazing stories that have proceeded you."

Hunter nodded. "We have only done as we saw fit. We know there is much more to be done."

She nodded, and her beautiful hair flowed with the movement. "Yes, even now, the good people of Brant call out loud for help. Will you give aid on the morrow?"

Hunter looked from side to side. "Is it possible to wait that long? The day doesn't wait and we have wasted a big portion of it already. I thank the Huntress and the Avandarians for this fine meal and your gracious hospitality, but I know people are being wrong there as we speak. As I have been told, it is a long ride around these woods to get to Brant."

Again she smiles "We can lead you through the Forest of the Whispering Pines. It will be a quicker journey. Brant will be before you at first light after the morrow." She raises her wine goblet. After a quick swallow she continued. "But as you were trying to say, we must leave now." At that the crew jumped up and quickly bowed to their host and started for the trip. The Huntress smiled at the hustling men.

"Huntress? How bad is it in Brant?" Arrie had moved to take a seat by O'Cey.

"You can judge that at the first light of day after the morrow. I do know mercy is not shown to the good people there." She rises to leave. "I will say just be prepared for the worst." With the last word, she turned and left the table.

"Wait!" Hunter got up from his seat and the Huntress turns to acknowledge him. "Will you and your warriors help us in the battles to come."

"You are the one to heal all wounds caused by this evil. We can only help if we wish to give up this forest as our home."

"I don't understand."

"We are here to protect this place and we are to stay and do that. You know not of our pact with the mysterious woodlands. If we leave, we will not be able to return."

"Ok. I had to ask but you'll get us there and then we'll do all that is needed."

Raising her voice. "If there is any of the warriors of the Avandarians that wish to follow the Giants of Thorn into battle against the wickedness of Edaun, assemble in the ring! It will not be looked at as you want out of our pact with Thorn to protect the Forest of the Whispering Pines." The Huntress rounded the table to make way to stand on the mound again.

Ten women were assembled in the ring. As their leader walked around them, she cocked her head to Hunter. "The giants are getting my best. Five archers and five maidens of the sword."

She turns her attention to the women standing as statues on each side of her. "Each of you know this, when you leave from the shadows of this forest, you will not be able to return here to live. Your life as you have known will change, you can vow to the citizens of Rhea and live as their protectors or you can hold your heads high and return home to Baseen. Third, you each can vow to serve the giants standing before us this day." Each of the women of war nodded and knelt as one facing Hunter with heads bowed. The Huntress shifted her gaze to the men before her. "It does appear that they wish to serve you Lord Hunter in your campaign to rescue the people of Rhea."

The Blood of Brothers thorn nodded and all saluted with a fist to their hearts. The women stood and gave quick nods of acknowledgment. They then saluted with a closed fist raised to their lips.

Hunter speaks. "I thank each of you for your sacrifice in leaving this beautiful forest. Huntress, we welcome your warriors in joining us and pledge loyalty to the Avandarian and to your cause to protect the Forest of Whispering Pines. Oh and also pledge to protect the Tree of Forgotten Lives."

The Huntress cleared her throat then spoke in a loud clear voice. "I say then it is agreed. Go with the blessings of the pines. The good people need all the valiant warriors to liberate them from the clutches of the evil of Alexar."

The Huntress looks at the male warriors. "Avandarians are trained to show no mercy as well Lord Hunter. Their lives were to protect this forest, not to serve the cause in which you are appointed. They have defended these hallowed grounds and have lived to love it." Looking back to the women, "Now they are willing to follow and serve the seed of Thorn to defend all of Rhea. I am pleased and I give my blessings for their hunt." Looking back to Hunter, "I expect the giants will do their part to see no one is a waste." The five giant warriors raised their fist in unison again; thumb side to their hearts. The tall Avandarian leader smiled then returned their salute and followed with the one her warriors gave her.

She stared deep into Hunter's eyes. "The Avandarians have pledged to Edaun. You are Edaun, not the foolish one named Alexar. We are all pledged to the just. Command us and all here shall follow you."

Hunter cleared his throat from the blow he just received. "We thank you, but at this time you are needed here. These ten are welcomed into our war party." Looking at the volunteers. "You will be treated as equals and treated well. You are now a part of our family and all of you are welcomed in. Thanks to all of the brave Avandarians for the work they are taking on." The Huntress smiles, then gives a pristine nod.

Without a word she turns and exits through a large opening.

The Blood of Brothers quickly prepared for their departure. After quick preparation, they mount up. Twenty Avandarian archers began the journey with them. The Huntress is nowhere to be seen. Hunter rides beside Merveela. "Does anyone come into these forests trying to destroy it and those that protect it?"

The small Wood Elf looked puzzled then smiles. "I am sorry Master Hunter. I forget the seed comes not from here. Creatures of evil cannot overcome their fear and enter here. Humans on the other hand do not have this fear born in them They have tried but their attempt is futile. Anyone meaning harm to the woods or its inhabitants are doomed to die horribly." They rode in silence while Hunter studied the huge trees and the scattered silhouettes high in the branches.

Merveela watched the amazement on the giant man's face. She spoke quietly. "The Avandarians have done their best to hold their pledge to Thorn." Hunter studied his small tutor. "They also have learned to care for the trees and plants here. I see the great warrior can spot even our best at blending into their environment"

"You thought them how to hide?"

A surprised smile spread across her face. "Yes, and they learned it well. But I now have learned there are those in your party that can see the best at hiding."

Hunter smiled at the small beauty. "I see the lands here are well protected and cared for." Again he studied the trees. "Merveela and the Avandarians do all of Rhea proud." Turning his gaze back toward the elf. "Thorn smiles on you."

Merveela stares at Hunter for a short while. Her surprised look made him think he said something wrong. Without warning, she smiles the largest smile he had seen on her. "Thanks to your grand sire, Thorn, we have something worth protecting. I am glad one of his seed has given his approval in our good works."

Hunter returns the smile and nods. "I am impressed by the order and loyalty I see here. The good works done here to keep this forest alive will one day be appreciated by the whole realm. Ian and the Seer have also spoken highly of you and the warriors that dwell here. Again, I know all Rhea gives thanks to all of you." The tiny lady giggles and quickly spurs her horse into a dead run back to where they came. Hunter stared after her confusing and hasty leave. He shrugged at the stare from Jinx.

The party rode in the dark shadows of the thick woods in silence. Tunk rode at the Seer's side, opposite of the protector. A long while after the elf sped off, he spoke quietly. "Sir, Merveela is the only wood elf still in this forest?"

"As I know it, Master Tunk."

"Were all of them as small as she is?"

The old man laughed. "Oh no, she is what they called a battle healer. Some of the children, uh well, those born small as she, were trained early for that task. Think about it, she can pass where others can't, reaching the wounded to give aid without being seen."

"Smart thing. Think she'll join us?"

The Seer shrugged. "Lord Jinx seems capable of some healing."

"He is but, what if he falls to a sword or arrow?"

"Good point. She knows, as the Avandarians know, if she leaves she cannot return." Tunk shook his head. "Besides, she is the last elf, as I know of to be still living here."

Tunk nodded and after a few seconds he spoke again. "It would be tragic if she were killed or captured." The old man nodded.

The large party faded in and out of the dark shadows, as the day passed. The long ride passed slowly. As the darkness grew thicker, the warriors reached a small clearing. The sun was leaving from its little spot in the sky. The lead maiden turns to stop the procession. "We'll camp here. Brant is another day's ride beyond this small tree line." The crew methodically set to work. A fast cold meal was made and cleaned as the last rays of sun fade away.

No guard was set and night quickly passed. Before the sun was able to sneak into the clearing, the party was fed and was underway.

The day's ride was long and quiet and so was each person's thoughts. Each preparing themselves as they saw they should. As the day was growing to an end, the lead maiden spoke again. "We'll camp here in the trees. Ready your mounts for a hasty move on the morrow.

Again, as normal, the crew jumped from their wagon. They washed and went steady to work preparing a quick cold, but fulfilling meal. As was every evening during this new freedom campaign, riders stripped their horses of their gear and each tenderly cared and brushed their four legged partners. Only after the horses were fed and watered did the members of Rhea's new army of liberators eat. The tack was set near each horse and the riders slept near the animals. The Avandarian escorts moved to the west placing guards for the night. Conal made sure the guards were given food for their long sleepless night.

The Seer made a hasty quiet speech. "We will embark against the evil of Alexar on the morrow. Best to all that will descend into the bowels of this evil; sleep well. I will turn in now and suggest we let the skilled Avandarians watch over our war party as we rest to face the morrow."

The camp went quiet as everyone followed the wise man's advice. When sleep finally came to each of the party members, no one could tell amongst the quietness; another night of eternity.

The Avandarian guards awoke their precious warriors.

The night had passed quietly and nothing dared to move on the Forest of the Whispering Pines. The Avandarians kept a deadly watch and nothing stirred to disturb the new tribe of Rhea. As each warrior awoke, they tried to imagine what lay ahead of them. The soft sounds of the forest wind seemed to ease the days of long rides.

Chapter 10

No Mercy

The Seer awoke before the sun rose to see that the war party had already packed their bed rolls. Each member was checking their weapons and the mounts were loaded with only battle needs. "I hope you boys slept as well as I. Something about sleeping in these forest soothes the most bedraggled traveler."

"We did just that Seer, but now I think it's time to eat." Tunk helped the old man with his camp gear.

The Seer gave a low toned laugh. "For men as big as you five, you move about as quiet as Merveela." The small healer grinned and nodded.

Jinx and Hunter were studying strange brown and green lights dimly lighting the camp site. The small lights came from several locations around them. Jinx looked at one of the maidens of the blades standing near one of the trees and pointed at the soft glow. "What are these?"

The woman stood in silence as the baritone voice of the protector answered. "It is a gift from the wise ones of Nod to aid in the guarding of these woodlands." He chuckled. "It helps add to the mystery here and even scares away unwanted guests."

As the group washed then sat for a quick morning meal, no one spoke as the salted meat and hard bread were eaten.

Hunter finally broke the silence. "From this day on, every one fighting for the freedom of Rhea will be known as the Blood of Brothers Thorn."

The seer nods. "That sounds good. Now the people will put you with the prophesies; A name and a cause." The seer stares at Hunter and smiled. "I agree with the giant of the light."

Hunter looked puzzled. "Seer, why do you call me the giant of light?"

The old man grins as he tells his short story. "Last night I saw a man of war become light. Another became the wind and a third became the rock. The trio stands firm and evil trembles."

"I recall another prophecy." The Seer spoke in his quiet calm voice. "If the evil darkens the light, then the wind will calm and the rock will wither to dust"

"What does this mean? We ride to death?" asked Hunter.

"By no means. Battles are as they end. Tell me why the light cannot overtake darkness? As the sun climbs in the sky, does not darkness run?"

"Guess so." Hunter rubbed his face. "But when the day is over, doesn't darkness overtake the light?" Jinx looked at Hunter and shrugged.

"Do we not light fires? Is not the darkness in which we ate alight?" The Seer grinned. "Does the light hide or chase darkness away to other places?"

"He's right. The light shines to eliminate darkness all over." Tunk spoke trying to help understand the prophecy. "But it takes wind or water to break down rock."

The Seer nods. "All I say is if all that will stand in the right and stay true to one to another, then you shall prevail." The Seer smiled again.

Jinx hit his head with the palm of his hand. "O'Cey he gives me a head ache with his rambling talk."

O'Cey laughs. "I do feel your pain brother."

The first rays of sunlight were breaking in the hidden horizon and the whole camp was ready to move. Everyone was fed and on their way toward Brant before full daybreak. They rode in silence, each ready for what may lay ahead. Everyone spent the short ride in deep thought preparing for the battle at hand.

In less than an hour the trees began to thin out. The ground began to slope steeper with every step. As they were descending out of the forest, the air grew foggy. Movement drew Hunter's eyes to his right.

The Huntress appeared speaking softly. "I bid the good warriors of Rhea a good morrow." Every one nodded their bidding to her. "Brant will be guarded heavily. From here the hill increases downward toward the walls of the city. You must descend with care." She lowered her eyes. "I regret that my warriors will pull back here. I have planned to accompany you and give aid from the hill top overlooking the city." The women of the forest gave hurried pats of support to their leaving sisters now riding with the war party. In no time, they all had melted back into the shadows of their beloved woodlands. "The forces of Edaun have started to move. Brant is the gateway to this forest. Gavin's men have taken the town and they hope to take this forest."

Merveela had ridden at Jinx's side. She looked up at the massive man of war to her left and smiled. Slowly she looked at the Huntress. "My bow will also give aid." The Huntress nodded her endorsement. The wood elf smiled at Dil. "I will stay at the wizard's side to offer my protection so he may do what is needed."

The Huntress nodded again. "I will also accompany the wizard as I know the Seer will also." When she finished, she rode to the Seer's side, just behind Dil.

Hunter dismounted as red streaks of light raced ahead of the coming sun. A heavy fog covered the ground below the forest, hiding the town of Brant. "Arrie, can you give us a quick lay out of this side of Brant."

The archer nodded and rapidly drew the landscape on the ground with her boot knife. Hunter pointed out spots for the archers to line out. He picked a spot for Dil to stand and give his cover to the swordsmen. "O'Cey and Mac, take two of the maidens and go in from the north. Tunk, you and Ian take two and go from the south. Jinx and the last maiden will go in with me straight from this side." Hunter held his right hand out and Tunk and Jinx placed their hands on top. O'Cey and Mac followed. One by one the others crowded in to do the same. Most just touched the ones in front of them on the backs. Hunter looked up as the sky was slowly trying to clear. "Thick fog is a good sign warriors. It is a day to die but let's all come back alive." Slowly he broke from the group. "Archers, get ready!"

Pulling two bowls from his saddle bags he quickly mixed water with some colored powder. Jinx and Tunk beamed and stood ready behind their leader. The others looked puzzled. Hunter dipped four fingers in one. With red stained fingers, he drew four lines crossing down his left eye and his strong nose stopping at his jaw. He then drew three black ones over his right eye also down to his jaw.

Tunk rubbed the red paint on both hands and then he put his right hand across his face covering both eyes. He put the left hand on Nightmare's shiny black neck, then smeared both hands on the stallion's mammoth chest. Tunk jumped onto his massive horse's back.

Jinx blacked out his forehead to below his eyes. "Ian come here." Jinx put red and black stripes down Ian's face. "Ecott, Nuel! What are you two waiting on, come here!" The brothers jumped at the fact they were now accepted in the circle. They copied some from each of the giants. Jinx also marked Ghost with black hand prints on its neck.

Jinx grabbed the high pommel saddle and mounting in his style. His muscular legs swung like a gymnast. Stopping in a quick hand stand then easily slid his legs down into the saddle. As soon as his show ended, he turned in his saddle to speak to the war party. "Warriors, it's time to rain doom down on these fools!"

O'Cey and Mac each blackened the left side of their faces and covered the right side in red. Mac let out a deep whoop as O'Cey added his part to help set the mood. "Archers, remember your war hoops. Make them loud and fierce!" Mac beat on his own barreled chest, and growled.

"Freedom for Brant!" Tunk quietly yelled from his enormous ride. Hunter watched the others from atop his huge war horse.

The war party quietly rode from the tree line. Slowly, each descended the steep hill toward Brant. The archers quickly took their places; ringing around Brant on its eastern side half way down the hill. Brant was still blocked by the thick fog. The wizard was gathered by his small crowd as they took a rise on the north eastern edge toward Brant.

Brant was quiet even through the two war shouts. Although no one had been able to look in the city since arriving, nothing was moving. Daylight was slowly creeping into the bowl shape valley in which Brant was cradled. "We may still have an element of surprise on our side. Those brothers are crazy." Hunter stopped as he stared down at Brant.

The sun was now brightening the upper landscape. Brant was slowly coming into a hazy view. "Yep, I think we . . . ." Jinx's words froze as he stared in disbelief. The fog was slowly lifting, opening the sight of life as the people of Brant had now come to know. A horrible sight was developing. Everyone was now in their places ready to storm Brant. Each member was studying their surroundings as they too became aware of the horror below them.

A horror the people of Brant had now known as life; Death and torture. As the horror began to appear, each member sees the truth of the evil before them. A new hate takes it place; a new cry for freedom.

Hunter took a long look at decaying bodies hanging on stakes. Each hung about ten feet above a low rock wall encircling the city. A lone guard stirred as Hunter spotted a naked woman on a lone pole. She was hanging upside down. Nimenole Trolls were sleeping drunkenly below her partially eaten body. A look of a horrible death still on her face. her breasts were sliced off, most likely while she was still alive. A new anger began to boil from deep inside Hunter. He looked at his old friends and saw the same feeling in them. He read the others mounted at their posts just beyond him. Their faces expressed the same anger, the same look of disgust. Rage twisted their faces as each looked deeper into the horrible death faces below them.

The council's words shouted in his thoughts. Great Eagle, take flight! Remember the old ways! No Mercy!

Hunter could wait no longer. A flash of the sun reflected as he drew his sword. "NO MERCY!" Sequoia reared with a snort and in an instance they bolted. A few guards stirred below them. Blood curdling war cries killed the silent air. The whole war party began to vent anger in loud whoops and war cries. More guards came to life.

Seconds after the Roan stallion reared, Jinx yelled. "Looks like it's go time!" Ghost reared and Jinx let his fearsome scream answer Hunter's.

Nightmare leaped through the air clearing a large piece of the ridge. Tunk blended his brutal voice with that of his brothers. Their death blur headed into Brant. Flashes of swords reflected the rising sun as it now shone through the lifting fog.

The archers readied their first wave of arrows looking for the soldiers within Brant. Their goal was to stop the first of the opposition so their warriors can get deeper into this evil and crush the wickedness residing just below them.

As the thunder charge unfolded, more guards quickly sprung awake. The battle cries increased. Heavy hooves shocked the ground as the five monstrous horses resonated on the surface earthquake. The soldiers jumped sleepily to defend themselves. Who dared to do battle against soldiers of Edaun? The archers release their fury through the air. The soldiers woke only to see the first wave of arrows. The Blood of Brother's archers now bid them good morning.

As the war party raced down the ridge, each rider looked into the dead eyes of the people of Brant. Heads lined a second rock fence encircling the city. The eyes pleading for revenge. Twisted mouths remained open and seemed to shout, "Avenge Us!" The Blood of Brothers heard it loud. The battle cries and the thunder of hooves did not cover the screams of the innocent. Only one answer ran through the charging men's mind. "No Mercy!" Their shouts echoed the words.

The archers also heard it and a second wave of arrows found it's mark. They blended their war cries with the charging swordsmen as they released their answer to the evil. "No Mercy!"

More battle cries and more arrows filled the air. Soldiers fell to torture no more. More soldiers fell to rape no more. The time has come for the soldiers and Neminoles to experience the same fate as the citizens of Brant.

The Forest of the Whispering Pines heard the silent cries too. The forest cried out for the blood of evil to flow. It cried for the giants to take vengeance for the slain. "No Mercy!" Avandarian voices flooded the air and maidens of the blade stormed from the forest. The Huntress watched the tree line.

The thunder charge had sounded. The sounds of the coming battle filled the ridge. The forest watched.

The riders drew closer to Brant. Tunk twirled a tomahawk and it found it's mark. A guard was holding a naked child by the hair as he looked out a door. The boy broke and ran for freedom.

The Huntress studied the terrain as the battle began to unfold. The Seer spoke calmly. "What do you think of our large warriors, Cael? Do they have a different way of announcing their arrival? What do you say?" Dil snickered as he made ready to do his part. He raised the staff high as the orb slowly turned.

The Huntress looked amazed. "They did send a shock of terror through me. I thought I was a seasoned warrior." The Seer chuckled along with the wizard. She stopped with a quick shiver. "Their archers are impressive too."

The trolls quickly awoke grabbing weapons as they jumped for action. Their nasty snarls spoke of readiness to attack this new source of a battle. They readied their weapons only to find the ground erupting into flames around them. Their blazing bodies ran into Brant with screams of terror. The Huntress looked at the young wizard. Dil blushed. He gave her a weak smile and the Huntress simply nodded and nervously returned a faint smile. Slowly, she returned her watch to Brant.

O'Cey spotted a warrior entering his range. He quickly unsheathed his double edged knife. The ax welding soldier fell as the blade drove deep into his throat. Two knives left Jinx's quick hand. Ian released a tomahawk and three more enemies fell.

More well placed shots from the archers parted the air just over the warriors heads. O'Cey raises a closed left fist praising the archers for their cover of the charging horsemen. A path had been cut down before them and the town was now open for their entry.

Nightmare rears then leaps across the rock fence. As he lands, he tramples two men trying to guard the waking army. Tunk pulled the reins and the trained war horse spins a death kick to another bewildered swordsman. It stops the man dead in his tracks. Tunk rolled off it's back, with his sword twirling. The blade drops and severs the face of another screaming soldier. The soldier never dropped his raised sword as he hit the ground. Ian had his sword in hand following his partner into the waiting battle. Their horses jump back over the wall heading back to safety.

"Their sword play is impressive, Seer." The Huntress watched as the wizard brought the staff to point at another group of trolls running in front of a building. The Nimenoles were heading towards his brothers at full speed. A strong down burst of wind flung the grotesque creatures against the inner wall. The sound as they splattered caused the woman to shudder.

The Huntress had proven to be a worthy opponent in battle many times over, but what she sees from the troops of Alexar turned her stomach. The ease of the killing from the Blood of Brothers also caused her great concern. "Seer, I do not mean any harm, but I mean . . ." She noticed the youthful face of the wizard looking at her. "These new warriors will stay true to Rhea and freedom for its people, right?"

Dil nodded then looked back to the battle. The Seer looked unconcerned. "I know from a special source these men, all of them, will stay the course." He ended with a fatherly look. "I feel good about them and I would trust my life to them." Nate looked at the Huntress and nodded.

Another wave of arrows parted the gates and Jinx and Hunter quickly spurred their mounts into the path opened for them. Hunter and Jinx rolled off their mounts, both landing on their feet like a pair of big cats. War cries over shadowed the death screams of the men falling onto their blades. Hunter and Jinx continue their dances of twirling destruction and it appeared as if they were partners in a deadly minuet.

Bodies were beginning to pile up and a steady flow of soldiers were coming out to meet the intruders. Some of the soldiers never discovered that they were in the line of fire of the dead eyed archers, until it was too late. The others that were passed over by the rain of arrows were forced to face the deadly swordsmen. All showed no mercy.

Ecott and Nuel could wait no longer and they slowly advanced on the wall. The brothers moved in shooting as they stalked in on the evilness of the city. When they hit the wall they replaced the bows with their swords. They charged in to add their part to the sword fight. Their war whoops filled the noisy air.

The battle lasted a long forty five minutes and sixty four soldiers of Edaun lay dead. Two dozen Nimenole trolls lay crisp or splattered by the wizard's hand. Jinx and Hunter looked up in trees at the same time. The bodies of children hanging by their necks filled their eyes. Small arms gone and half of their legs missing. They would never grow to be an adult. They would only be food for the trolls.

Hunter's mind raced. Another time another place. Mass destruction and killings. Death in the Middle East and bodies piled in mass graves. He came back to reality as the people of Brant slowly peeped outside their dwellings.

The weak had no chance of survival in Rhea. Bodies of the elderly people were piled in heaps. Children, the future generation to any civilization, were killed and hanging in trees. Others were left laying around for food to these disgusting beasts of this world.

Nimenole Trolls abide by a lawless and unmerciful rule. The survey of the scene ended with the tortured women hanging head down from the tree.

Red flashes of anger clogged the two giant warriors minds. A quick glance passed between them. They both released war cries as each drew their razor sharp Bowie knives. Townspeople slammed their doors, retreating from the giant warriors.

They went into motion, one a shadow of the other. Both moving as one with the same goal. They each released another blood curdling war cry. Their shouts were their answers to the silent cries of the dead. The warriors heard the painful cries from the victims.

Jinx was the first to jump and Hunter was a split second behind. They each grabbed one of their now moaning enemies, each moving as a blur. The wanted to show their heartless enemies their brand of 'no mercy'. Scalps began to leave from each screaming man's head.

The fury quickly filled Tunk. He too had looked at the bodies of the innocent people laying around him. The innocent of Brant died for sport. He snapped at the noise his brothers were making. Tunk looked back to Ian as he drew his blade to an exposed scalp. Dropping his stare, he lifted his voice to the dead, echoing his brothers' song.

Ian looked at the frenzy. Anger filled him but compassion took over. He turned away losing his stomach. No one heard his cries to stop. No one felt his pain for Rhea's death. He felt sorrow for the good and the evil. He ran away without lifting a scalp. Tears filled his eyes for the slain people of Brant. He didn't look back as the cries of the dying filled his ears. He ran as hard as he could, leaving Brant through the gate. He ran to the comfort of the Seer.

The Scots join in with their brothers in arms. They felt sorrow for the people and answered the call.

Ecott and Nuel watched. The archers on the ridge watched as the butchers did their job. The archers remained at their post, ready to release a blanket of fire for their comrades.

The Huntress turned away. "Seer, what are they doing?"

"They are showing no mercy, Huntress." He put on a weak smile. "I would say they are sending a message to Edaun and to Alexar. I know he sees this and I know he will now think twice. He knows the giants of prophecies are here."

"But Seer, they are our people too!" She pleaded.

"Yes, but they are corrupted by the evil of Alexar. They are lost to compassion for the people of Rhea. This must be done to show the people of people of Rhea that someone has heard their cries. Someone is here to stop the evil and shows no mercy to those who have killed the innocent. Word will spread fast and all will hear of the terror released upon those who are evil."

After the bloody display was over, O'Cey and Mac signaled the maidens of the blade to help search the city. The slaughter came to an end as fast as it began. All of the barbers now joined in the search.

A short time later, more men were found and dragged from their hiding places. They hid from the threat to their lawless rule. The men were herded to the gate where the charge began. The maidens were set to guard the six prisoners. The women warriors ridiculed each of the soldiers for hiding from the killing field and they each took turns challenging the prisoners of their manhood.

Nuel kicked one of the prisoners. "Why do you hide brave warrior!"

Ecott followed his brother's lead and kicked one of the soldier balled up in the fetal position. "Stand up and face the Brothers of Thorn!" The two men trembled as they giants stood over them.

195

Each of the huge warriors were covered in the blood of coward's friends. The men knew they would die.

Hunter walk up to the largest of the two. His face was tattooed making him look different than the rest. Hunter looks down staring deep into the soldier's eyes. "Who is in charge here?" The man stared at the ground. Hunter raised his voice louder. "Are you in charge?" The other captive soldiers watched in fear. Hunter fished around in his wampum bag and discovered a large rattler from a timber rattler they had killed in a world that seemed so long ago. Hunter paused studying the buttons. Home was a memory but yet he didn't miss it. Shaking his head, he let the quick memory go.

Hunter tied the rattler's tail to the horses mane close to its left ear. The horse nervously jumped. "Jinx I wonder if this animal knows what this is?" *Jinx shrugged.*

Hunter held the reins as he grabbed the man's face and looked coldly in his eyes. "I will not kill you for now, but I do wish to face you on the battle field. There you cannot hide in a corner like a milk sucking child!" Hunter released the man's face and cut the reins. "Now deliver this message to Edaun. Take it to this Gauvin and to Alexar tell them the giants have come! Tell them if any more innocent people suffer, you will see us really turn vicious!" He slapped the horse's rear. Immediately the horse barrels down the street, heading fast away from the smell of death. The strange noise shook in its ear forcing the messenger to keep running.

Jinx looked to Ecott and Nuel. "You two did well little brothers."

"That you did, but now we need our weapons picked up." The brothers looked at Hunter as he spoke to them. "Don't look at me, get to it. Time to go."

"Yes my lord, we are at your command!" shouted Nuel before he ran away behind Ecott. Hunter shook his head. The rest of the archers had come down from their assigned places during the battle.

Hunter turned to the townspeople. "I wish to apologize for what took place here. We've made a terrible mess. I also want to apologize to the good people of Brant for our late arrival."

An elderly man in the front answered, "You need not to worry about it my lord. We will clear away the carnage."

Hunter nods. A smile grew on his face at the excited look on the old man's face. "Good people of Brant, collect all the weapons from your dead enemies and ready them for the new army of Rhea. You will need them to fight Alexar if it comes to that. Pass them out and help one another!" Jinx walked toward Hunter leading their giant war-horses.

Hunter walked over to check Sequoia for any wounds. Quickly he threw his leg across the high pommel saddle, taking his rightful place on the huge beast. "Brothers of Blood! Mount up!" He gently kneed the horse. Sequoia slowly turned in place. The large steed reared then bolted out of the downed gate and up the ridge.

Ian looked at the Seer through redden eyes. "Blood was everywhere!"

The Seer cradled the boy's head and he spoke softly. "To rid the evil from this land, we must be strong. No fear, no mercy. It is all those people need. They will understand that help is now here."

"Yes, I know but it was different than Toll. I was scared."

The old man softly spoke again as he comforted the young man. The Huntress stroked Ian's hair. "The Giants know their place now and they also know the task before them. It will be a long and hard task. Let this new fear run through Edaun." The

Seer watched Hunter as he stormed toward them and he did his best to comfort Ian. "We must allow them to run their course."

Hunter drew reins in front of the trio. His big body was covered in drying blood. The sight of Hunter caused the Huntress to shiver. "It is done Seer." He dismounted in the dust cloud.

Pity had quickly replaced the hard anger in his eyes. He walked straight to Ian. "Ian it's ok to feel as you do. That is how much love is in your heart." He took Ian from the Seer's embrace and lifted Ian's chin to look in the young man's face. "Don't lose that. It is the mark of a true ruler. I realized today that we are not the seed. We are the avenging giants. You Ian, are the true seed to rule Edaun. We are the seed to destroy the vial people causing the trouble." Hunter shifted his look to the Seer. "Now I know and accept our duties to the people of Rhea!"

The Seer smiled. "True! After this day, Edaun will know the taste of fear! Alexar will know the giants truly have come."

Hunter looked at the Huntress. Seeing sorrow in her eyes, he smiled "My lady, I must look a mess. I think we will need a bath"

Hunter looked back toward the town. The remaining crew were coming to join them. The towns people were standing outside the city in front of the low wall. Hunter draws his sword and holds it in his right hand. Both of his massive arms went up as he sounds his war cry one last time. Ian grins and joins in.

The Seer somberly looks at The Huntress. "We must now be ready. It has begun." She gave a quick nod.

The returning raiders stopped in their place and raised their weapons to join in with their leader. Hunter changed his sword to the opposite hand and raised his fist with his thumb side to his heart. The people cheered. Tunk and Jinx stood in their stirrups and returned their brothers salute. The entire hill copied the salute toward Hunter.

After the war party was reunited, Ecott spoke to his comrades. "My brother and I wish to continue in this quest Master Hunter, but we need to find information about the rest of our family"

"You owe us nothing archer. You may stay here as I said." Hunter looked at each of brothers of Brant. "You both did well this day."

"My lord, we do wish to stay with you. If you order us, we will do what we can to defend Brant." Nuel looked to his brother then he lowers his head as he finishes. "We did leave our post. You told us to stand." Nuel choked.

Ecott finished fighting back tears. "One of the heads on the wall was our father's. That's why we charged in. We wanted to kill the ones that had done that!"

Tunk put a hand on each brothers' shoulder. "If you two are willing to ride with us. I myself welcome the proven skills of your bow."

Hunter looked to the Avandarian leader. "Huntress, these two wish to check on their family. They may remain in Brant." He looked at the young brothers. "I only ask that you allow them to return to us in the forest when they are done."

"I'll post an escort to bring them in, only if they are here well before darkness

The Huntress looks to Ecott and Nuel for an answer. Ecott grabs his brother by the arm and excitedly answers as they run. "Yes, we will my lady!" The brothers stopped to face the Huntress then bowed. Turning again they quickly jumped on their horses. Both raced down the slope. Their yells turned the townspeople.

You could see the look of relief on the people of Brant when they did not see that another attack was returning to them.

The Huntress raised her hands. "It is time. We will return to the forest! The avengers need bath, food and rest!" The Huntress assembled her warriors still standing at the tree line. She signaled for their return into the forest.

"Maleah! Post six archers!" She waved toward the town below. "Escort the brothers to the camp that was set up. We are finished here. Make haste!" Six women bow, then take to their hidden places to keep watch over Brant. Those pledging to the band looked at the Huntress with questioning eyes. She looked to each of them. "You are welcome to visit and take up refuge, but you all know what you must do when the party leaves." They each grin as they bowed.

The ride back seemed longer in the silence of the forest. The war party rode deep in thought again. These thoughts were different than earlier. These thoughts drifted back to the encounter of the morning's fight. The troop rode along the earlier path then turned south.

Not returning toward the area they had left earlier, the band looked from one to the other all keeping wary eyes on their quiet ushers. Each started thinking were these women angered by what they saw.

Hours passed and the stillness of the woods had a soothing effect yet unnerving effect. They stayed to the south trail and soon large willow trees began to crop up. The air started to become heavy and moist. A strong mint aroma filled the air. Low voices were heard humming a beautiful melody.

The Huntress turns her horse to stop in front of the weary party. "See to our guests. I have other needs to attend." She looks across the haggard faces. "My thanks go out to the war party. You all have done well. A great blow was dealt to Alexar this day, now dismount and enjoy the rest of the day. You can walk easily to the bath from here." Without another word she spun her mount to head east.

Attendants reached for the reins as each dismounted. The party walked down a short narrow path. The air held that strong mint smell. A heavy steam was slowly seeping onto the path. O'Cey and Jinx stopped to stare at the moss covering decorative rock work. A small waterfall stood off to the left of the pools. Further to the left stood another door.

O'Cey turned to his brother. "Look Mac! It be the same as the stone of our new home." Mac nodded. Dil grins as he remembers his last time with Mac at the stream.

Hunter looked at the portal and his mind went back to their last day of his normal life. "Hey guys how long does it seem now?"

Jinx stood quiet. Tunk spoke up. "Like another life Hunt."

Mac nodded. O'Cey grunted and Dil giggled.

Heavy steam vapors rose out of several small hot pools. The strong mint aroma flowed with the steam cloud adding a pleasant and relaxing mood to the area. The sound from the bubbling water added to the mood and everyone looked in wonder at the beautiful stone walls that were weaving around the pools. The pool's the beckoning waters seemed to ease everyone's moods.

The air was beginning to fill with several other sweet aromas such as ginger, and lilac mixed with cinnamon. They all watched as women dressed in gray poured buckets into the pools. The Seer waved his right hand. "You are the first of outsiders to see this. These are the public baths of the Avandarians and they are as refreshing as they smell and look. Just wait until you get in the wonderful waters."

The maidens began to strip of their soiled clothes as Dil stood with his mouth agape. Mac chuckled as he wiped his hand across his younger brother's face.

Jinx laughed. "Don't know how it feels yet but they sure smell good. What is that strange scent? Like a sweet mint." Everyone nodded and smiled at the wonders of the spa. Their exhaustion was trying to taking over each of them. Jinx spoke quietly to the ones close to him. "Damn, all good looking too."

Merveela walked up to stand by Jinx. Her big eyes smiled as she spoke. "It is called honey milk. If you press the flowers, the sweet juice aids in breathing problems. Boil them and the aroma speaks to you for itself. Oh and yes, all good looking." She giggled as she walked to a pool and stripped.

Jinx laughed. "It's like our eucalyptus or menthol." A puzzled look came from Merveela as she lowered her small body into the pool. "It's our name for a similar plant." She nodded, but the faraway look was still there as she was sitting. "Hot body little thing, huh Tunk?" Tunk grinned.

The guides lead them to the small waterfall and told them to wash the crust from their bodies then relax in the pools. Everyone dumped their clothes and walked into the small water fall to wash off the dried blood. Slowly the heat and the honey mint soaked their tension and pain away. The warm bubbling waters seemed to chase their problems to the back of their minds and all their troubles were subsided for a short while.

All the hate they saw inside Brant slowly drifted away during the time they soaked. There were no thoughts of what was ahead, only freedom from the new world and it's evilness.

The splashing of the nearby falls seemed to take them to a better place and time. Reality snapped back when a servant in white announced the meal had been prepared and will soon be ready for them to partake of it.

To their surprise clean togas now lay in place of their filthy clothes. They dressed in clean clothes provided by their hosts. No one spoke of the day's events as the entire party arrived to another council area. The tables were overflowing with a delicious spread. The brothers from Brant had returned and were seated at one of the eating tables.

"Ecott! Nuel! Glad to see you two again!" Hunter walked over to the brothers giving each one a hug. "Was all well back home?"

The brothers looked at each other. Ecott, the eldest softly spoke. "No. Our whole family is gone."

Nuel wiped his eyes and nodded. He drew a deep breath. "You are all the family we have now."

Jinx was standing behind Hunter and to the right of Mac. O'Cey was behind Nuel with Tunk. Dil stood beside the chair Ecott had been seated in. Before the others could speak, Dil spoke out with authority. "You will always be a part of this family. The Blood of Brothers will forever welcome lost and orphans as part of their family."

Mac look astonished. "Aye, me wee brother speaks for all." Each member patted the brothers on a shoulder. "But I say now it be time to eat! Now sit!"

The meal was eaten in the now too familiar silence. A silence they were all becoming awkwardly accustomed to. The little of what was left over from the meal was cleared away. The day's happening was now becoming conversation.

"I see you two found some soap too." Tunk laughed as he looked at Ecott.

"Yeah dried blood does have a terrible smell." Ecott looked to the empty table.

Nuel cleared his throat and looked at Hunter. "When we saw our father's head spiked on the wall, we just could not stand there my lord. They placed him there as decoration!" He slammed his fist on the heavy hard wood table. "I cannot describe the anger I felt at that moment!"

O'Cey growled. "It be alright laddy. I think you did better than I would have. I would be there soon as O'Cey saw it to be him."

"Aye!" Mac barked his remark. "I would flip too!"

O'Cey laughed. "Brother you be crazy always. Mac, you flip all the time!" The broken laughter did not change the growing mood. Sadness for the innocent who had died for no reason.

Tunk lowered his head in reverence. "All I saw was that poor woman. Tortured and hung naked as food for those nasty creatures!" Slamming his fist on the table this time. "They sliced her womanhood from her chest and Jinx you saw her death look. She was still alive when they done it. She was conscious and they done it! Just for the laugh! And all those innocent little kids."

Jinx nodded. "The horror was still on her dead face from the torture, I saw it too."

Dilman spoke out on what he saw. "How can anyone do that to the children hanging in the trees. This is the evil of the men of Alexar. Seer, I wish to do all that I can to remove him from these people and return them to a better life." The seer quietly nodded.

"I saw her and the children too. Ian, I know you had your doubts on what we did but it's the only language these ruthless people will understand." Hunter lowered his eyes from Tunk's stare. "I just hope and pray that it doesn't get to a point where we enjoy it." Looking up to face all the eyes around the table. "We need to stay to our path. Freedom for Rhea and as the blue wizard said, a better life for these people."

"I know this to be true now." Tunk looked at Ian. "It doesn't help what your people have endured already, but we will make it better now that we are here."

Ian wiped away a tear as it rolled down his cheek. "I saw it all my brothers." Standing so all could hear him. "I will not rest until Rhea is free! I will try to do what I must do, but . . . ." The Huntress had quietly joined the sitting warriors. She spoke softly as she interrupted Ian.

"I trust that all was to the liking of all of your needs, brave ones?"

Hunter stood to greet her. "Yes ma'am, it was what we needed and more than we expected."

She stood at the head of the table. "My watch to the east have informed me that two groups of riders are heading south. They ride hard as if looking for something or someone." She studied the warriors before her. "It would appear they may be heading for Brant. They will come near to where you camped before you entered these woods by the morrow." She studied each face again. "Your message carrier should be intercepted by their scouts at the high sun on the morrow well that is if the poor animal does not die. Reports say it has been running hard. I do know you will face many more battles before this evil is gone."

O'Cey scowled. "My lady, how long till they be in Brant?"

"From where they will camp, I say two sun rises and they will reach the eye. Your message may slow them for one more day maybe, but I say they will move faster when they meet with him."

Jinx strained to see the sun through the thick canopy. "And how much time do we have until sunset?"

The Seer took a seat by Dil. "In your time five hours. I also agree with the Huntress about battles. Alexar has control over most of Rhea. We will see many more deadly fights before we see any sort of peace. But I will say they will not rush in on you next time. Fear is now in their hearts"

Hunter stood and pushed his chair under the table. "Then we have a set schedule. If we wake at dusk, can we travel through these woods of yours to get a lead over them?"

The Seer cleared his throat. All gave him the attention he wanted. "I know timing is bad now but I must say the wizard needs to go to Nod." Eyes turned to Dil. "He will be facing a powerful wizard in Alexar. He needs this trip to be able to survive at that time. Training with my brothers will teach him control as well as more of his powers."

O'Cey nodded. "I know you be right Seer if you say he must go, I say Mac to go as his protector." Nate looked at Mac and nodded.

The seer also nodded at the order from O'Cey. "Yes, every user of the power needs a good sword hand for protection. Mac shall go."

O'Cey slapped the table. "As I say then and it be done!"

Mac slapped the table. "Hey Dil me boy, we ride!" Looking at the Seer, a wicked grin claims his face. "Seer even if you had said no, I go with the wee one anyhow!"

The seer grinned. "I cannot say no to a fine swordsman as you Mac, you are to go. But not now we need to rest it will be a long ride. The Huntress has secured a party to lead us north to the coast. There will be a boat from there to Nod. The rest of you will go south." Dil yawned and the Seer answered with one of his own. "I agree wizard, now we rest."

The Huntress nodded. "I take it this dusk is when the sun fades away." Hunter nods "Then we can be at the southern end of these woods by sunrise."

O'Cey barks his harsh laugh. "Good! We have time then to lay good traps!

The Seer rose from his seat. "Good!"

Each of the war party fades quietly into the silent darkness. Each searching for solitude to think and to reflect where they have been and what they may face on the morrow. All reach different areas of the dense forest for the much needed rest. Sleep came hard to all. Each of their minds raced but each one arrived to the same outcome in the long thought process. Everything is necessary however it may come. There is always death and it had to come to those among the war party or to their enemy each face. Show no mercy, kill or be killed. As each faded into their slumber, peace crept into each of their hearts and minds.

Rhea was to be freed and they were the war machine to make it happen.

Chapter 11

The Word

Standing in front of his pool of sight, Alexar stares as Brant is attacked. The efficiency of this new army amazed him. Their merciless slaying of the troops under the control of Edaun appalled him. His troops fell and they fell fast and hard. The ease of the victorious new threat weighed heavy on him. The hand reaches up for payment Alexar spits in the bony blue palm. "I shall not feed you until you give me the answers I seek. How do I deal with them?" He slaps the water as doubt clouded his mind. Can his real troops of Edaun hold against this growing army this well led army of deadly killers. The unknown boy wizard looked strong and deadly in his own right.

"I need to know how to deal with them!" The pool boils then goes smooth. "Do you not hear my words! Now show me then I will let you truly die!" Alexar moves across the floor to a rear chamber. The chamber door opens with a slam then after the wizard walks through, it closes just as hard. The torches fade in the room of the pool.

"Light!" The dark chamber lights up. Alexar stops in front of a large wooden table. Rustling through vials double lined in racks, he grabs a green bottle. Thinking for a few seconds, he grabs a red one. He cackles as he turns to a cauldron in the center of the room. A black bubbling brew was already fiercely boiling. The wizard raised both vials, one in each hand. "If the pool will not show then this will show me the weakness of the giants that dare to strike at me." His bony wrists bend. The vials are turned over releasing the colors into the boiling cauldron. A gray mist rises and suddenly shapes appear. Each shape began to form faces. Ian's face appears. "Who is this boy? Mist, who is he?"

The mist churns. Another face was revealed. "What does the Huntress have to do with him?"

The mist turned in on itself again. The Emerald then the Crimson Knights appear. "I grow angry with you Mist, show me the weakness of the Giants! I have not seen these two facing my minions or the worthless soldiers."

The mist churns and rolls one last face appears. "The Wanderer!" Alexar rubbed both hands under the hood. He pushes the heavy hood from his head and rubs his bony chin. "If I catch the Wanderer, will I find the answers?" The almost skeletal face looked deep into the boiling caldron.

"So, am I to get the boy, the Avandarian witch and the wandering Seer. Who are the warriors in clothes of metal?" He shook his head and the few long sprout of hair danced from his ancient head. "The armored warriors, who are they?" Alexar throws a small fit.

The mist folds again on itself. A last face forms. A larger face grows and takes on a deadly look. Finally, Hunter stands before the wizard. Sword drawn challenging the old man. Alexar slaps his hands in the mist but the image stands firm. The image towers at it's full height over the wizard. Quickly Alexar spins and storms out the room.

Alexar is laughing as he approaches the pool. When he reaches the edge of the rock wall, both hands are in the air. Suddenly two fish appear.

"Pool of sight!" Alexar growls as he twirled the fish in the water. The blue hand flashed grabbing both of the fish then quickly disappeared.

Alexar slams a fist into the water. "I grow angry with you too Seer! Show me what I seek!" He splashes the water again, but no sign came from the water. Alexar goes into a frenzy. "I hold your life in my power, now show me what I seek!" The fish bones flew from the water. Striking Alexar in his narrow chest. In disgust Alexar spits in the pool and storms from the room again. He enters the corridor as he snatches his hood in place. "Gauvin! Gauvin!"

A voice outside the door spoke. "He and some men have gone to the Outlands, my Lord."

Spinning to face the guard. "Where's the battle witch? Rodona! Where is she?"

"She assembled several of her men to followed, sire."

"Who are you!"

"Barune, My Lord."

"Captain Barune, assemble your men!"

"I have none sire. I am but a guard my lord, not a captain."

"No more Barune, you are now a Captain. Assemble your men and ride to Brant!"

"Sire. Everyone knows I'm a guard, how do I?"

Before he is finished, Alexar lays a hard right hand to Barune's face. The ensign of his ring leaves a bloody mark on the young man's cheek. "You now wear my mark for your insolence! Now go retrieve a command for yourself and do my bidding! If they need proof show them my mark!"

"Yes my Lord."

"I shall meet you in the courtyard for your assignment!" The soldier salutes then runs to do his duty.

* * *

Hunter is awaken and looks around him. The Seer stands quietly watching the large warlord. "Lord Hunter, whom did you see in your sleep?"

"Oh Seer, I didn't know you were standing there."

The Seer nods as he walks closer. "Sorry to appear to be checking on you my son. I heard you speaking harsh to someone in your dream world. May I ask whom you saw?"

"It's ok sir. I think it was this wizard you called Alexar."

The Seer nodded again. "I thought as much. His face woke me as well. He then knows who we are. Did he speak to you?"

Hunter laughed. "No he was trying to fight me with his feeble hands. He is a very old man."

"Yes but he is dangerous. Let us get the others and prepare to leave these woodlands." Hunter nodded as he was rising from his make shift bedding.

The party was awakened as the sun died in the western sky. The heavy shadows of the forest kept the vision of the sun from its inhabitants. The Huntress dressed in her battle clothes, was standing in the center of the ring. The entire troop was assembling there. "I bid the champions of Rhea good dusk."

Hunter grinned. Everyone said their salutations in return.

She looked to the Avandarians assembled in their seat of the stands. "I have decided to accompany this war party. In my stead, Urlanda, the mistress of the bow, will lead the protectors of these forest." The band looked shocked. "It is better this way. I also have set my honor guard to be at her call. I expect each of you to obey her as you have me. The Seer has been prepared to depart with the wizard and his champion. Ian will also go on that journey with them. Two of your longbow men also asked to accompany them for added protection Lord Hunter." Hunter nods. "But I think they all need to hurry and wish their farewells now. Edaun stirs. Evil has seen the faces of this freedom revolution. The Avandarian counsel wish for all here a long life."

Hunter walked toward the ring but the honor guard who encircled the outer ring, blocked his progress. "You are right on their leaving soon, but if you leave can you return?"

The Huntress displayed a weak smile. "I would like to say yes but I cannot. Once a defender of the forest leaves they shall not return. Yes for visits but no longer to live."

"But you are pledged to defend this forest. Why would you give that up?"

"I feel I can give my services to the greater of Rhea and its people."

"Is that what you truly wish?"

"If not I would not have decided to abandon my sworn duty here. Besides if we cannot stop the darkness from taking over, then these trees will not have a chance to survive at a later time. I am sworn to protect this wonderful place but I am also sworn to the rightful master of Edaun. Alexar is not the true ruler. That ruler is among us now."

"You are welcomed to ride with us and give aid as you see fit, Huntress."

After their short debate she ended the talk. "It is settled then. Now in my stead I wish all here peace and well being." She looked at the women seated in the stands. "I say to all who defend the Forest of the Whispering Pines, in my heart, I still serve with you." She stepped down from the speaker box and took the reins of her sorrel. With much grace she leads it out of the circle. She swung in the saddle and watched the surprised warriors as they found their mounts ready and waiting. "If all is ready, we have some ground to cover by first light." Their clothes lay clean and folded on their saddles. The crew discovered the wagons loaded and each member climbed quickly into their places.

The Huntress turned to face the war party as they climbed on their mounts. She smiled when noticing they still wore the sleeping togas. "We travel an obscure path so stay close to your lead. We will stop at day break, then all sleep a short while." She smiles. "After you awaken, you may then dress." Her laugh made each of them look at their clothes.

Jinx laughed. "I guess we look silly in these, right?" The Huntress spurred her mount. "I do believe I am comfy. How 'bout you Tunk?"

Merveela giggled as she nodded from her pony before following the Huntress.

The warriors fell in single file. Grumbling as they rode. Tunk looked down as his toga. "Yeah I like it. At least O'Cey is the one that looks like a refrigerator with a head and not me."

* * *

Agent Johnson stood by a stone pillar. "Smith it does looks like the other one."

The younger agent nodded, "Yes sir. They found two more that I know of. One is on a piece of property just purchased by the

McNure brothers. They are in that same sword fighting bunch as the three diggers we are looking for."

"Have you questioned them yet?"

"No sir, they can't be found either."

"What?"

"Yes sir. I say they seemed to have vanished too, sir. Funny thing is, their foot prints end at their pillar sir."

"What's going on here Smith? Agent Brown, come here!"

Another young agent ran to stand with them. "Yes sir?"

"What do the labs say of these pillars?"

"They don't have a clue as to what it's made of, sir. No one knows what they are for either."

"So we now have three strange stone pillars that we know of. Made of something we don't have any idea of. People have vanished as if they have walked into these things. A creature no one can explain what it was and all this started by a simple jewelry robbery. I need answers. Someone give me the right words to explain all this." He looked to each of the other agents. "Well can somebody say something."

Smith cleared his throat. "Humor me for a minute. sir. What if these things are doors and everyone we've looked for has entered it."

Johnson laughed. "You know how that sounds? Strange, but if that is possible then that could be the answer."

Agent Brown laughed. "He sure took that better than I thought he would have." Johnson snapped his head to look at him. "Yeah, we had talked about it and what else could explain what happened. All the tracks at each of these things lead into it and no one can be found. What else can it be?"

Johnson shook his head. "I won't argue with you. I've seen some of the same things you two have." Johnson scratched his chin then added. "But can you explain that to the top brass and not me?"

*   *   *

As the sun's first rays cut the blackened sky, the Huntress led the Blood of Brothers out of the southern end of the forest. "We will make camp here. Maidens have scouted to the east and they are camped there to ensure we will not be surprised in our sleep."

Everyone was tired from the long night's journey and as soon as the horses were taken care of, all of them were ready to find another place to sleep. O'Cey walked over to talk with the Huntress. "Lassie? How much time afore they arrive?

"On the morrow by noon meal."

O'Cey nodded his big woolly head. "Good, we need to scout a good place to defend." O'Cey stared to the west. The high bluffs looked like a giant wave breaking on the coast. He pointed. "What be that way?"

The Huntress turned to look in the direction he pointed. "Leads to Brant." A smirk came on her face. "You must enter a gorge to reach Brant. You have a good eye blade master."

O'Cey smiled, a gleam shone in his eyes. "Do you know the number that ride on Brant?"

215

"The eyes said around forty. Maybe the same in Nimenoles and Pumoarans coming from the south."

"We will be ready my dear!" O'Cey growled. He turned to retrieve his bed roll.

O'Cey walked to the spot where Hunter and Jinx were sprawled on the ground. "Hunter, O'Cey sees the place we need to be." Hunter split one eye at the burly man. O'Cey grunted as he unrolled his bed. "We'll talk later."

*　*　*

"Seer, I miss O'Cey already." Dil stared down the trail they had traveled. He looked back to the front past the women escorts. "What is Nod like?"

"You are a curious one. It was best you left as you did. I was thinking O'Cey may have changed his mind. He does appear to be hard of head at times." Mac roared a laugh and the Seer smiled. "No offense, it is good to be that way at times. As for Nod, you will see soon enough."

Mac gathered his sweet composure. "How long fore we be there?"

It was the Seer's turn to laugh. "You have the same bull head as your eldest brother." Dil made a funny squeal then snapped his head to show a big grin to Mac. Mac grunted. "You three are good people. Mac, stay as you are." Mac beamed his smile back to Dil and the Seer laughed again. "Brothers do show love in funny ways, right Nate?" It was Nate's turn to grunt. "Anyways, we can be in Nod within seven days if all goes well."

"Good! Sooner we get there, the better. Dil gets schooling, then we get back to helping the others." Mac tried to hurry the riders in the lead. They kept their pace. Mac grunted again as he fell back in his place behind the wizard.

Mac rode with his eyes searching the forest for hidden Avandarians. He smiled and waved each time he spotted one.

Chapter 12

Blood of Brothers

The crew was up before the others and they prepared a quick noon meal. Each of the ten men took turns watching the outlining area as the others worked. As they stood watch, they saw the Avandarians standing guard at the woods edge.

After the Avandarian guards were satisfied, they waved to each of the men. One by one they faded back into the heavy shadows of the forest.

The rest of the party slowly awoke to a good cold meal waiting for them.

O'Cey stood as he ate, studying the way into Brant. Every so often he would pace their camp, stop and look toward the large rock outcrop on the horizon. The others ate and watched O'Cey. "Hunter!" Hunter was giving his plate to one of the crew.

"Yeah O'Cey."

O'Cey pointed in the direction he had been studying. "Look!" Hunter scanned the horizon as he walked to stand by O'Cey. "I say we lay and wait in there." Hunter nodded.

The Huntress was at Hunter's side. "Brant had a garrison in there. You must travel through a gorge, then through the Needle's Eye to reach Brant. That is why Brant was sought; its easy to defend."

Hunter looked in her large hazel eyes. "You sure you want to ride with us?" She didn't have to nod, her big smile answered him. "Ok, let's go see what we can see."

A rustle from the tree line turn the whole army. Two camouflaged battle maidens stood as statues. The Huntress and Merveela walked to meet with them. The conversation was brief and the Huntress nods before turning to leave them. The maidens stood unmoving as their counterparts returned to the war party.

Hunter called the brothers. "Ecott do you and Nuel know the entrance to this eye?"

Ecott spoke first. "Yes we both do."

"Good then you lead and scout ahead. Don't wander off. Stay on a straight line to the opening.

Nuel spoke next. "Yes my lord." Hunter shook his head before turning to leave.

The Huntress returned from her briefing. Speaking in a loud and clear voice, "The messenger has been intercepted by scouts from Gauvin's men. He will be with Gauvin on the morrow's high sun. Gauvin leads twenty five men wearing his colors and twenty wearing Rodona's colors. They say Rodona leads another fifteen behind Gauvin and she will join him at the end of this day."

"Sixty warriors with two captains, oh well. How long until they arrive here?" Jinx's tone spoke his thoughts. "These will be better trained men, right?"

"I would say, yes. They will camp here or near here two days from now." She grabbed the reins of her horse. "They will not risk entering the way to Brant in the dark."

"We may just set watch there anyway." Hunter mounted Sequoia. "Get the wagons to the pass. Keep the movement close.

Do what you can to leave no trail! One man on the wagon with the driver to keep watch, everyone else stay behind the heavy wagons and cover the tracks! Maidens hide our camp and do what you can do to cover our movement! All bow women stay with the wagons and help with the cover up and watch as you can!" Moving his huge stallion in a circle. "Tunk! Jinx! Make us disappear!"

Jinx and Tunk looked at each other and Tunk laughed. "Just like old times huh, bro!"

Jinx nodded. "Gotcha Hunt! We're history!" The people of Rhea searched each other for answers of the strange words passed between the giants.

Hunter moved his huge stallion to the lead stopping by Thunder. "O'Cey ride ahead with the brothers and the Huntress. Find scrubbers to run behind the wagons when we hit the pass." O'Cey nodded. Hunter turned to Merveela as she was set ready by the Huntress' side.

"Little one, will you ride with," pointing at Jinx and Tunk, those two and keep them out of trouble please?" She giggled as she spurred her small shaggy mare toward the rear.

The caravan slowly moved to the large bluffs to the west. Men walked behind the heavy wagons pushing the rutted sod to cover some of the signs of travel. The archers followed them fixing what was left. Each man and woman took turns scanning the horizons around the slow moving troop.

Jinx and Tunk perfected the job the others started of hiding the tracks. Merveela added her touch, using woodland elf songs and waving her hands over the ground to heal the damaged foliage of the sod. The day was long and tedious. Everyone slowly reunited in the mouth of the gorge except the three finishing the repair work. O'Cey watched as the brush he found was tied behind the wagon wheels, the slow march continued. Slowly the wagons were out of sight moving deep inside the pass. The sky began to grow dark as clouds overtook the setting sun. Lightening arched across the blackening ceiling.

Hunter remained standing in front between three large, flat bundles of cut evergreens. Each large bush was tied behind the last of the horses. Hunter looked out from the pass as the last three arrive. "I see no trace of our travel from here."

Merveela dismounted. "The other giants hid the travel well."

Tunk laughed. "You helped too, with your, exaggerating waves of his hands over the ground, elf magic." She joined in with his laughter.

She looked at Hunter. "It was easy, everyone did a good job. That made mine easier." Looking up at the cloud cover, "the coming storm will help too."

Hunter mounted again. "The others didn't stop long, they were fast hooking the drag lines behind the wagons and kept moving. They're still covering their trail from here to where we'll be going deeper inside. Check behind 'em, lil' one." Merveela nodded. "Let's try to get way inside before total darkness comes." He turned his mount and one of the brushes came to life dragging behind him. The small elf grinned as she shook her head as she watched his tracks get wiped away.

Jinx and Tunk were back in their saddles. Their brushes were set. Jinx looked at Merveela. "Can you help with dirt, too?"

She shook her head. "There is nothing to heal and the rain will help with those bushes."

Tunk stopped several times studying the steep walls of the gorge. The sun's last rays of light fought the choking clouds and shone on a small opening ahead. Rain drummed slowly on the canyon floor. "That must be the eye thing the Huntress spoke of." Merveela nodded.

Jinx dismounted at the opening. He stepped off the width then stepped under the opening. "Man, barely eight feet across and maybe seven feet tall. I don't see Sequoia or Thunder out here, so they must have ducked to go in." Looking at Tunk, he laughed. "I hope these two crazy ones will too."

Slowly they pulled their horses heads down to clear the low ceiling, lightening crackled behind them. They softly coached the hyper war horses through the low ceiling opening. Jinx and Ghost appeared on the other side. Merveela rode out behind him.

Tunk blew a quiet breath as he let Nightmare straighten. "You did good boy." The rain barely fell on their side of the pass.

They walked up to the small camp fire, still dragging the trees. Hunter met them. "I was fixin' to come look for ya'll." He looked at the ground and pointed at the tied trees. "Let's drop those at the opposite gap. O'Cey made good plans for them."

After they dropped the brushes, they walked to the hidden picket line. Jinx started pulling the saddle from Ghost. "I think at first light we need to check the base of the eye. We may need to fix it." He winked at Hunter.

Hunter nodded. "Cool, there's food waiting. We'll turn in so we can get an early start." He lifted the saddle for Merveela. The small elf shot a frown at him.

Hunter laughed. "Get use to it sweetheart." She slapped her thighs as she stomped toward the camp fire.

Tunk was brushing Nightmare. "How far is Brant from here?"

"They say another day up this gorge, from here."

"Man, this thing is awesome." Tunk straightened his saddle and tack over a large rock, looking at the basin they were bedding in.

Hunter finished brushing Merveela's mare. "You two finished yet? Let's eat."

Tunk looked at Hunter. "You groomed a midget horse and can't wait for us. Ok, I see how you gonna be."

Jinx laughed.

The camp was silent as four archers sat guarding the eye. Hunter broke the quietness with a low whisper. "You think we need to have someone ride into Brant?"

Jinx lay still for a few seconds. "I've been thinking of that all day. I don't see how there could be enough men left there to help us right now."

"They are sitting ducks." Hunter rolled over on his side. "What I've been thinking is maybe a show of numbers?"

Tunk blew a silent whistle. "We'll just do what we can do. Can we protect what may come from Brant if the enemy sees them? I don't know. You know it could backfire."

"You may be right." Hunter sighed. "We may be in for a hard fight, brothers."

Jinx rubbed his face. "We sure could use Mac's sword and Dil's gift when it comes." The storm had passed and stars filled the little sky that they could see.

Sleep did not come easy for the warriors. The first watch rested on the sisters from Brant. The young women listened to the tossing around their bedded companions made as they wrestled for sleep. The night slowly stretched on. The foursome decided to stay up longer to let the replacing guards have a little more sleep. As slow as the night crept on so did the rounds. Each pass of encircling the camp looked the same, each time they hugged the walls of the gorge as close as they could.

The moon rode high and the light was brightly shining off its full face. Keeping in pairs, the four guards circled the camp again in opposite directions. They finally made plans for the last round. Meet near the eye then wake their relief on the return.

The full moon casts long shadows across the ground. Arrie was circling the Brant end of the large bath tub shaped camp site. She looked up to the rim of the gorge above as she laid a hand on the shoulder of her youngest sister Kari. "Look up, someone's there." She whispered. Instantly they both melted to the ground while scanning the top of the massive walls above them.

"Where? I did not see anyone." Her low whisper froze in Arrie's ear frantically she scanned the area. Gone. The minutes dragged by and the long minutes made her doubt her own eyes. Sleep was pulling her eye lids down. She shrugged it off and decided to rise, stopping for one last search. "There! By that dark blue shape jutting out to our left, almost straight over us." The whisper barely reached Kari's ears.

"Do we sound the alarm now?" Kari didn't take her eyes from the slow moving figure.

Arrie looked across the camp for the others. "Kari. I do not see Bari or Canari. It might seem that our sisters have seen them too." Arrie didn't see Kari's nod, she was still looking for the other two sisters.

* * *

Bari and Canari lay in the shadows across the camp from the other two. "Bari, who do you think that is up there?"

"I do not know right now. I do not care." Bari softly spoke as she studied the other side of the camp. "Right now we need to reach the others?"

"Do we wake the camp?" Canari stroked the notched arrow.

"No, I think we need to wake Ecott and Nuel first."

"I saw Arrie and Kari hide across there. I say they are looking straight up at whoever is up there too." Canari looked to the needle's eye. "I say one of us should crawl to wake the others." The shadow retreated from its hiding spot.

* * *

"Let's both go Kari. We need to rouse the others." Arrie and Kari started their crawl.

* * *

"I'll go first. You keep close eye on the rim. The brothers are the closest." Slowly Bari lay flat facing the sleeping forms.

"Ok, go slow, I'll watch." Finding a marker, "See the dip near the long shadow?" Bari nodded her answer. "Good, reach that, then stop and I will follow. Whenever you feel it is clear, continue on. I will be behind you."

Bari slid across the ground, heading toward Ecott.

*   *   *

Arrie stopped before making her crawl and looked toward the needle's eye. She smiled when she saw a figure sliding from the shadows. "Kari, it looks as if our sisters have seen them also." Kari strained to see the slithering form on the basin.

"Moves like Bari." Kari studied the passages into the camp.

Arrie looked back to the catlike form hardly seeing it's movements. "Looks like she is heading to wake the brothers. Watch the rim, I will watch the eye." Kari studied the dark sky circling the entire rim. "Canari will follow so we will need to watch everything."

*   *   *

Time froze as the two moved on each of the brother's side. Bari, whispered to Ecott. "We are being watched, lay still." Canari did the same to Nuel. The brothers woke quietly.

Canari spoke to both. "Lay still until you are fully awake. Someone is watching us from the rim west of the pass to Brant."

Ecott slowly turned and studied the top in silence.

Nuel spoke first. "Who could it be? If it were from Alexar, they would have attacked us already."

Bari looked to the eye. "Maybe not, they may not have seen where our guards are yet."

Ecott broke his silence. "Maybe, but I doubt that."

"Are you saying we are no concern to anyone?" Bari hissed.

"No, I say you would have a slit throat if the right ones are there and wished to attack us. If we were the watch we could also be dead from a silent blade of one of Rodona's color guard." Ecott looked from the ridge to the eye. "I say it is just someone curious to who may be down here."

Nuel disagreed. "Maybe, I say no. I also say someone make way to Hunter and the others." Slowly they split each heading to one of the giants.

* * *

"Captain Gauvin, Rodona and her men have arrived."

"Good, bring that winch to me." The battle scarred soldier bowed as he left his commander's presence. Gauvin turned to look at Conn still tied to the horse. The dried scalps caught the light of the fire as the tired nervous horse swayed.

"Please Master, release me." Conn's dried throat moaned. "Take these things off me. Please, sir." Tears rolled down the lieutenant's dirt crusted face. His pleading brought only laughter from Gauvin.

Gauvin watched the light of the full moon bounce off Rodona's breast plate. He watched her graceful body movement as she came toward him. "You are a well built woman. I can see why Alexar longs to bed you."

His twisted smile told her he blamed her for someone's blunder. She looked at the blood caked man strapped to the horse. "What are you doing with him!

"I do nothing." he laughed. "I think he was sent to us from Brant. Looks like a message to me."

The female mercenary stalked over to the restrained man. She held his shamed head up by the hair. Conn screamed as he tried to pull away. She studied the tuffs of hair and blood dried meat tied to him. "Who did this to you Conn?"

"They stormed into Brant in the middle of the night." Gauvin laughed. Conn dropped his reddened eyes to look at the ground. He mumbled on. "There was a host of them." Gauvin snorted and Conn's eyes flashed at him. "And the Giants are here!"

Gauvin stormed over to the helpless man. "You say they came in the cover of darkness!" Conn's head nodded in spasms. "And you say they are the giants of lore!"

Rodona grabbed the hilt of her sword. "Gauvin! Enough!"

Gauvin grabbed his sword, spun to his left to face the battle maiden. "Woman! You have spineless warriors in your command!" Gauvin glared in her eyes. "I say they were drunk and the wretched old people of Brant did this!"

Rodona laughed. "You are a fool, Gauvin!" She pushed him away from Conn, pulling her knife, she quickly slashed the binders. Her eyes never left Gauvin. "As far as spineless, pull that sword if you dare to be that big of a fool!"

Gauvin breathed slowly through clamped teeth as he glared at her. He walked toward her. "I fear no one! No man, and never a woman!"

Rodona laughed. "I do not wish any one to fear me. I want them to face me and not run. Fear ruins a good battle."

Gauvin realize he was trembling and tried to cover it with a laugh. "I will see that you are delivered to Alexar personally. I may even watch the dried up man have his way with you!"

She stepped forward to get a closer look at him. She stared directly into his eyes. "My sword is pledged to the ruler of Edaun. Alexar just happens to be in that position. If I find out another is the true ruler you will get your wish." The smirk on her lovely face could have frozen a bonfire. "And your wish will then be the taste of my blade! I will not kill you until I let you watch Alexar die first to my blade."

She snatched Conn from the horse. "Clean yourself and be ready to face your night thieves!" Rodona backed away, keeping her eyes on Gauvin. "I fear no man Gauvin and I do not want any man to fear me. Be the man you claim you are and face me with your sword any time!"

Gauvin laughed. "I surely do not fear you, woman!"

Rodona laughed. "Good, when I do face you then I can count on you not pissing your pants and running away as if you are a little girl." Still laughing she spun around and gracefully walked away.

Gauvin stared in the darkness where she vanished. He drew his sword. When her footsteps went silent, Gauvin spun. His sword found it's mark; Conn's throat. As the defenseless man fell, Gauvin yells, "Bartog! Remove this dung heap!" The scarred soldier reappeared and he set out on the task without a word. Gauvin stopped Bartog. "If she asks, he ran at his first chance."

"Yes my lord." Gauvin disappeared in the darkness.

*   *   *

Hunter and O'Cey were the first awakened by the guards. Hunter stopped the archers from waking the others. He studied the moving shadows. "If they wished us harm they would make those large rock rain down on us. What do you say O'Cey?"

"Aye they could have stormed us." He looked to the eye. "I say they be recon or maybe someone wishing to join?"

Hunter lowered his eyes from the rim to look at the sisters. "Right now I say the sisters need to get some sleep, you all did good. Did ya'll stay up longer than you were supposed to?" The four nodded as one. "You did a good job. Make sure you sleep close to the others." He looked to Ecott and Nuel. "Brothers, wake four of the crew to watch with you. I'll stay up a while." He looked at O'Cey. "I'll wake Jinx in a few hours. He can help with the next watch."

O'Cey grunted. "Me eyes be no good?"

Hunter laughed. "No, they will be better in the morning when I sleep in." O'Cey grunted again, as he retook to his bed roll.

Hunter pulled his six guards together. "I need you to make yourselves be seen, we are being watched. If you take rounds stay as concealed as possible, the two in the open keep a close eye on the ones patrolling. But don't look directly at the ones moving we don't need those on the hill to watch our patrols whereabouts."

The sun rose to see no trouble had come to the camp. Jinx woke Tunk and told him of the night's sighting. They both woke O'Cey.

Jinx studied the top of the gorge surrounding them. "O'Cey what say we take a few of the crew up there. I think we can scale

230

these walls. Anyways, we may be able to scout what we can up there."

O'Cey yawned as he nodded. "I say aye, so let's be on the way."

Jinx nodded.

Tunk was set to the preparations of their defense. "Looks like a long day ahead of us."

Everyone worked on hiding more of the signs left by them in their travel.

The search party fought the steep walls and all made it safely to the top. Tunk and the Huntress worked with Hunter setting up the defense of the bowl shape camp ground.

The archers were scouting crags in the wall for good positions. Hunter called all the remaining archers and assembled them. "Everyone set?" The nods told him all he needed. "Each of you need to be ready as if you have no retreat. We need to defend these grounds with our lives if need be." Looking up to the men studying the rim of their bowl, "I need the lookouts to get in their places, we need to be ready in a seconds notice. We have blackened Alexar's eye and we will do it again on the morrow, now look alive!"

Two hours past noon, the search party came back with the others. The searchers ate while Jinx called the others to discuss their findings. "The few tracks we saw looked like moccasins. The crew say they don't recognize them."

The Huntress looked to the top. "The lost tribes are to the west. I have never seen them. What if they heard the giants have come into the light? They may be looking for you."

Hunter gave a suspicious nod. "Maybe." He got to his feet as he studied the small army. "We have all come far and we cannot falter now. Watch out for each other, cover everyone's back. Everyone has shown we are willing to die for each other. We have all proven to be as close as family, as blood brothers."

Hunter paused to looked to the rim then continued. "Again, we will depend on you archers to do the impossible. We will face around sixty men and maybe thirty trolls with Pumoarans. I thank all of you now and I pray I can thank each of you again. We have figured we could see our enemy by noon tomorrow." Hunter looked to the ground then he walked away.

Leister nudged Jinx. "Is he ok my lord?"

Jinx nodded. "Hunter always has concern for his troops, bro. He is the leader and he feels he is responsible for all of us."

The crew leader nodded. "We will do our best not to let him down then."

Tunk put a big hand on Leister's shoulder. "I know you won't let him down Leister. Rhea depends on all of us not to fail."

The twenty one archers raised their empty bows toward Hunter. The five maidens of the blade raised their swords. All the women warriors bow their heads in respect to their new warlord. Tunk, Jinx and O'Cey added theirs to the air all looking to Hunter. The Huntress and Merveela raised the bows in one hand and their blades in the other. Hunter stopped his walk feeling the eyes on him and turned. When he saw the display he smiled. He pulled his sword and raised it high in his left hand, his right fist went to lay thumb side to his heart.

Chapter 13

United

The next night came and passed in silence. Their visitors were not seen looking down on the sleeping war party. No fire was lit, no hot food cooked. Everyone woke to a cold meal before sunrise; hard tack biscuits and salted beef.

Everyone fixed more of the meal as a snack for later. Water was stored in all battle positions and the battle stations were readied. Blockades built the day before were disguised. The battle field was set with death pits and the deep holes with spiked poles lined their bottoms. Trip wires stretched the outer ring; each wire would throw it's victim into more hidden spikes.

The archers took their spots and paired off, spaced twenty feet apart. The Huntress and Merveela bows on standby. The two accompanied another archer stationed to the left of the gorge leading to Brant.

The lookouts were in place on the other side of the eye. Listening for sounds of any advancing enemy. The noon sun was beaming from its peak. Leister and Conal watched from the darkness of the eye as their mounts stirred nervously. Leister wiped his eyes. "What's that smell?"

"Run! Nimenoles!" Conal turned his long legged bay. They both burst out of the eye waving frantically.

"The trolls lead coming in fast!" The two raced through the designated path. Both jumped to the right side of the trail many paces across from the Huntress.

A small company of Nimenole Trolls stormed through the eye. The swift sure feet of the Pumoarans flowed onto the new battle ground. The lead trolls turned a sharp left and another group entered the eye as their screams echoed from the heavy walled tunnel.

Hunter, Jinx, O'Cey and Tunk were standing with bows in hand in the middle of the field. Each had their arrows notched and pulled to their cheeks. The battle maidens knelt one to each side of the giant warriors with swords ready in hand.

"Stop'em! Now!!" Hunter sounded for the barrage to begin. Arrows rained on the charging trolls. Pumoarans died, falling from under its surprised rider. Some of the trolls died and the others turned to run for the ten humans blocking the path in the middle on their trail. They would not see another battle as a second wave of arrows stopped them. More mounted trolls split the eye and some tried to round the right side. Empty Pumoarans ran down the center and the few lone trolls were spread out running on foot coming straight onto the field jumping over their dead companions. More arrows filled the air and more claws carried trolls through the eye. The second group was no opposition to the well placed arrows.

More Nimenoles rode toward the battle. Their gruesome snarls blended with the war whoops from the swordsmen. The quick Pumoarans and their riders began to flow deeper toward the defenders. The traps came into play as the Pumoarans tripped into the deadly pit. Other trip wires took out other Pumoarans trying to circle the war party. The wires removed legs and sent their riders into the secured spikes angled behind the wires.

No one from the band was hurt. The trolls and Pumoarans never saw the center of the battle field. Some of the trip wires were broken by the armored hide of the Pumoarans. Their death screams overtook the war cries. The trolls flipped to safety and continued on foot toward Hunter and the other swords.

"Ready with swords!" Hunter raised his blade and the maidens were already in their battle stances as eight trolls raced in. The others welcomed the fight.

The last troll fell as sounds of horses racing toward the eye filled the gorge. Hunter turned as the others readied to face the incoming threat. Hunter smiled, his thoughts were clear. Old battles didn't clog his thinking and the rest of the bands capabilities reassured his earlier doubts. His eyes narrowed his sinister smile broadened. Would they be confident in the ability of the trolls and their mounts? Could they know the ability of their new foe? Proud warriors know only one thing, they are invincible.

Hunter knew men and he knew the soldiers. He knows the men would think the trolls did most of their dirty work and they would ride in as heroes not expecting anyone to oppose them. He knew his archers would remove a third of the riders before they realized they were wrong.

The men looked like a fast moving parade as they exited out of the eye. Arrows took flight to welcome the proud men. Arrows filled the air as a black cloud of death. Dead men fell from their mounts. The others realized the plan didn't go as planned. Gauvin tried to weasel his way to the rear. A stray arrow took out his mount. The quick thinking leader grabbed hold to a soldier on his left. The man helped his captain to the horse's back only to be thrown from his own mount. Gauvin moved to ride at Rodona's side.

Unlike the trolls, the men rode in tight formation and the survivors raced over the dead. They saw the group of swordsmen on the field. Twenty four men turned as one behind Rodona. Gauvin still at her side studying the situation. She was leading them to face those men. Slowly her eyes widened with the sight of the Avandarians. Her mouth went dry at the size of the giant men standing with the women of her race.

The patient archers waited as the last of the trolls had fell to the blades of the swordsmen. More than half of the new attackers were on the killing field. The basin filled with the battle cries of the giants. Maidens joined in with their own vocals.

The force of Alexar was pushing into the wake of death. Troll and Pumoarans bodies littered the ground. Arrows sticking out of thirty of their own men in the wake of the charge. Horses died as arrows rained in on the enemy. Rodona watched as footed swordsmen encountered the four giants controlling the center of the field. Five women fought at the command of the large warriors. Her people sworn to the Forrest of the Whispering Pines.

She watched in amazement of the swordsmanship. They dominated the attacking soldiers. Again an arrow removed the horse from Gauvin. He hit the ground hard. Rodona slowed to help him. Gauvin grabbed the woman throwing her from her horse. She cursed as he jumped in her place turning her mount to flee the death awaiting him. Ecott saw the coward and took aim. His arrow took flight only to strike another soldier riding up to the retreating man. Gauvin escaped.

Rodona drew her weapon and turned to face the deadly swords butchering the soldiers of Edaun. Only nine warriors stood between her and the unmarked swordsmen in front of her. The battle now belonged to the warriors. The archers stood guard.

The giant swordsmen battled the men of Edaun the battle maidens fought at the giants side. The enemy fell easily. Archers covered their comrades and none of their enemies passed the center of the bowl.

As Alexar's men were butchered, spectators slowly gathered along the western rim of the gorge. Nuel pointed when the first arrived and the archers watched the newcomers as closely as they watched the battle field.

Rodona was near the center of the death field and only a few men remained to fight for her. The last of her warriors fell and the giants moved to circle her. Hunter signaled for the end of the battle. Slowly, Hunter approached the lone woman. She squared off to face him.

"Do you wish to continue or do you wish to lay down your weapon?" Jinx within her striking distance. She spun toward him screaming as she lashed out at the man towered over her. He easily countered her advance. Rodona spun right and Tunk was there. She worked her sword to face him. He was quick to disarmed her.

The woman turned to see O'Cey put away his sword. She launched a hand to hand fight on the huge man standing as big as her horse. Every one of her swings were batted away by this huge man. Spinning with nowhere to go she dives into Hunter's rock hard stomach. Hunter catches her in mid air as she tries to squirm from his iron grip. She stops her futile fight as the Huntress now stood before her.

"Rodona! Do you still fight for Alexar or do you fight for the one you are truly pledged to!" The Huntress stood firm in front of the Battle Maiden of Edaun.

The archers signal to their champions of the onlookers. The giants watch as a few were descending from their height. The archers were and poised ready to strike.

Rodona had stopped her struggle so Hunter put her on the ground. He watched her as if she were a deadly viper.

"Cael you know I have vowed to protect Edaun!" Rodona looks at the Huntress she smiles. "If they are truly the rulers of Edaun, am I then pledged to them?" Looking at each of the giants, "Show me and I will do as I must. If not then you must slay me now for I will try to rise against you on the morrow!"

Hunter bent to help her to her feet. "How can I show you?" Rodona stared at the tattoo on the strange men's arm. "Is it right to kill the good people of Rhea and be the true ruler? I will not slay you unless you threaten me or my friends."

O'Cey roars a harsh laugh. "No need to fear him lassie, you try to hurt me friends, then you best fear O'Cey. 'Cause O'Cey will break your lovely neck!" She stared as he flexed his tree trunk sized arms as he finished.

"You speak very brave to an unarmed warrior, big man."

Again he laughs. "Then be me guest and arm yourself."

"O'Cey enough!" Hunter slaps his own broad chest. "Now are you or not as the other Avandarians? Have you pledged to protect Rhea or destroy it?" Rodona glared at Hunter as he continued. "Alexar tries to destroy these people not protect them as a good leader should. So do you follow him or will you give aid to the people?"

"I have slain no innocent nor have I commanded it to be done." She studied all of the giants. The archers were moving on the field each watching the movement of the newcomers arrows notched. Rodona looked as the host of archers were moving in. "I have been ordered to stop the uprising and I do as I have pledged!"

Hunter had grown tired of the argument. "Tie her! She will be charged when order has been returned to these lands." The Huntress started to object only to be silenced by the glares from Jinx and O'Cey. Ecott was in the midst of the group and tossed

Tunk a piece of rope he had retrieved from his pack. Tunk tied Rodona's arms behind her back.

Hunter looked at several men crossing the field of battle. "Jinx! Tunk look! Is that Bill? The one in the toga!" The whole entourage stared at the man. Hunter laughed. "Look, it is Bill! I told you that old fart knew something!"

End Book One

Epilogue

A giant shadow fills a small void in the endless twilight sky. Monstrous wings carry a mysterious creature over craggy spires looming into dark spaces far above the ground.

The winged beast lightly touches down on a high ledge. It gives a quick glance over its broad shoulders and frowns to the western world beyond his sight.

With a deep grunt, he turns and silently enters a hidden cave. A low rumbling voice came from the bottom of the lair. "What news have you brother?" As the nine foot three gargoyle entered the dim lit cavern.

"Lerden, it seems the seed have arrived. I also know the giants now roam the world."

The second voice steps noiselessly from the deep shadows. "You have seen proof of this?"

"Aye!" It is not hard, they leave proof laying all about in their wake."

"Then it is time for us to do that in which we are bound to do. When will these puny humans ever learn?" Lerden turns and walks silently back into the deep of the black cave the other follows. "Kemp is there more?" The giant mass stops their silent march to look at his comrade.

Kemp's deep graveled voice speaks again. "The written word does speak of these vengeful giants. I do believe they have aligned themselves with the seed." Lerden's hard stone face changed expression even though hidden in the darkness, Kemp saw it. After a brief time They continue their silent walk ending in a dimly lit cavern. Methodically they both started to don their weapons.

After a while, the two giant wing warriors leave their place of seclusion and take to the sky. Their large leathery wings are the only sound made as they quickly cross the dark sky.

*   *   *

A blazing fire burns. Alexar stirs the concoction in the caldron as it boils he chants. "Open your eyes my children and spread your monstrous wings. Awake my beast and take to the air. Come to my bidding and destroy at my will. Take command of the night control the day. Your master calls and you must obey." He turns a vial of amber colored liquid into to waters. As the liquid hits the bubbling brew, the wizard mixes the concoction and a blue smoke rises. Alexar laughs. "Now you three giants of Thorn fear my wrath. Fear this! Fear the wrath of Alexar!!!" Alexar waves both his bony hands wildly over his head and cackles. "Awake my prized beauties! Remove this new threat from your master. Alexar calls to you to arise!"

*   *   *

A cave just south of Nod emits a growl as two large yellow eyes flicker open to look into the darkness. The ground rumbles as something comes to life again. Boulders tremble and fall from the sealed door way in the earth. The smell of sulfur fills the air.

*   *   *

Soft sands of Neach tumble as a monstrous head rises to look at the fading sunlight. It's blue eyes search the skies. A long overdue yawn allows frost clouds to leave its large mouth. As the creature shakes off its slumber more sand shifts. It's long spinney back uncovers. Giant wings stretch. The beast takes flight.

The Master of Edaun

"Time of the Forgotten Past"